Lady's Man

Turn the page for more acclaim . . .

Lip
Service

Suzanne Simmons

St. Martin's Paperbacks

LIP SERVICE

Copyright © 2001 by Suzanne Simmons Guntrum.

All rights reserved. No part of this book may be used or reproduced in any manner whatsoever without written permission except in the case of brief quotations embodied in critical articles or reviews. For information address St. Martin's Press, 175 Fifth Avenue, New York, NY 10010.

ISBN: 0-312-97299-7

Printed in the United States of America

St. Martin's Paperbacks edition / February 2001

St. Martin's Paperbacks are published by St. Martin's Press, 175 Fifth Avenue, New York, NY 10010.

10 9 8 7 6 5 4 3 2 1

For Jan and Jim Simmons:
forever family; forever friends.
I love you both.

If you prick us, do we not bleed? if you tickle us
do we not laugh? if you poison us, do we not die?
and if you wrong us, shall we not revenge?

— WILLIAM SHAKESPEARE, *The Merchant of Venice*

Lip
Service

Chapter One

Skunk.

The stench was unmistakable.

Trace Ballinger swore softly under his breath. Rounding that last curve in the road, he was pretty sure he'd heard a thud against the front wheel of the Jeep.

"Stinks to high heaven, doesn't it, Buddy?" he said to the golden retriever sitting at attention on the passenger seat beside him. Buddy whined in response.

Headlights reflecting off wet pavement, Trace accelerated into the next turn.

The rain had started even before he'd left New York City. By the time he'd reached Poughkeepsie, light drizzle had become a downpour. Luckily he had waited until rush hour was over before leaving for Grantwood.

"Luck didn't have jackshit to do with it," Trace muttered under his breath.

He made his own luck. He always had. After all, it had been his decision to wait until evening, until bumper-to-bumper traffic along this stretch had thinned to an occasional car or semi.

He cranked up the volume on the radio. Trisha Yearwood was singing about how it was going to be a cold, hard night.

Trace agreed with the lady.

Depending on the traffic, the weather and his mood— Trace acknowledged the latter was often the decisive factor—the drive usually took him two hours door-to-door. His door was on East 89th Street; what had been Cora's was at the end of an impressive allée of chestnut trees on several hundred acres just north of Rhinebeck.

He still vividly recalled his first trip to Grantwood nearly eight years before. After graduating from law school and passing the Massachusetts *and* New York state bars with flying colors (he wasn't necessarily smarter than the rest of his class at Harvard Law, but he was older, tougher and more determined), Trace had been assigned to do grunt work at the firm.

Six months in a windowless cubicle and he'd been chomping at the bit. A year and he'd been stir-crazy. In fact, he had been on the verge of quitting Dutton, Dutton, McQuade & Martin when the summons came: Cora Grant had personally requested his presence at the monthly meeting with her attorneys.

Even Dutton, Dutton, McQuade & Martin couldn't afford to piss off a client like Cora Grant with her millions. So he had made the journey up Route 9 for the first time.

"Crazy" Cora had taken one look at him that afternoon—he'd been dressed in the typical "uniform" he still wore outside the courtroom: a pair of faded Levi's, a white dress shirt (usually *un*pressed), a well-worn leather jacket (he'd picked it up for ten bucks at Goodwill back in the lean, the very lean, years and he'd hated to part with it, so he never had) and a pair of scuffed boots—and, with a conviction that had never once wavered right up until her death a week ago, announced: "I like you, Trace Ballinger."

"I like you, Mrs. Grant," he had responded.

Trace had been surprised to discover that it was true. He did like the old woman. She was different. All right, she was downright peculiar. Cora Grant didn't march to a different drummer—something that was frequently said about him, sometimes behind his back, sometimes to his face—she marched to a whole different band. Yet Trace had never once thought she was crazy in the lock-her-up-and-throw-away-the-key sense.

Cora LeMasters Grant, eighty years old and eccentric, had made their relationship clear from the start. "I want you to call me Cora," she had insisted.

Trace had replied, "Okay."

She had leaned forward and asked, almost eagerly, "Do you suffer fools gladly?"

Trace knew his eyes had narrowed to two dark slits. "I don't know about gladly, but there are worse things in this world than being a fool."

He had apparently given the correct answer. Cora had nodded her head and said, "I agree." The next question popped out. "Do you have any gray hair?"

"Yes."

She had almost smiled. "So do I." Then she had inquired, "How old are you?"

"Thirty-one."

"You look older."

People frequently thought he was.

"You're not a kid," she had observed, studying him intently.

"I'm not a kid," he had assured her.

Hell, he hadn't been a kid since he had attended elementary school in a working-class neighborhood of Pittsburgh; a neighborhood with railroad tracks running along one side and factory smokestacks on the other. Even then he'd known things a kid shouldn't know.

"Do you smoke?"

"I quit."

"When?"

It was God's truth: "Twenty years ago."

Cora blinked several times in rapid succession. "You quit smoking when you were eleven?"

"Yup." Trace added, "I wasn't your typical eleven-year-old."

"I can see that." Cora went on. "Do you drink?"

"The occasional beer." It was all he could afford, but he hadn't told her that.

She had ignored the cadre of high-powered attorneys in the room and continued to quiz Trace. "Do you curse?"

"Sometimes," had seemed like a judicious reply.

Sitting back in her chair, the elderly woman had charged, "Tell me something about your childhood."

Trace had hesitated. He didn't like talking about himself, but if there was ever a time and place, something told him it was here and now. "According to my mother, I was a handful from the moment I was born. Apparently I didn't understand the word *no* until it was more or less beaten into me. I was also a classic underachiever in school."

"Why?" Cora had interjected.

"I was bored."

"Go on."

Trace had been grilled before about his past, usually by an officer wearing a badge and a uniform. "I was a rebel and all-around hellraiser by the time I was ten or eleven," he admitted to the elderly woman. "I got in trouble with the law at thirteen. I dropped out of school at fourteen."

Cora Grant had been openly curious. "Didn't they come looking for you?"

"They?"

She'd shaken her head in puzzlement. "Public school officials. Truant officers. Social workers."

Trace knew Cora Grant had never set foot inside a public school in her entire life. As a matter of fact, she was a product of the finest *private* school education money could buy.

He'd given her the sanitized version of the story. "They looked for me. They didn't find me."

She had not pursued that line of questioning. "What did you do next?"

Trace had paused and then decided to condense nearly a year of traumatic events into one sentence. "I went to work in the steel mills alongside my dad."

"What about child labor laws?"

He'd cocked a brow. "What about them?"

Cora had appeared taken aback. "How did a fourteen-year-old get a job in the steel mills?"

He had been frank with her. "I lied. Said I was eighteen." He'd shrugged his shoulders; shoulders that still looked like a steelworker's. "I was big for my age. And my father vouched for me. That was good enough for the foreman." Trace had laughed; it had not been from amusement. "That and the small wad of twenty-dollar bills that exchanged hands under the table."

A soft expletive had been blurted out by one of the younger partners in Dutton, Dutton, McQuade & Martin who was sitting in the library at Grantwood at the time.

Cora Grant had ignored the outburst. Trace had followed her lead and done likewise.

"What happened next?"

Trace's mouth had thinned. He didn't have to tell her everything about his private life. That's why it was called private. He'd moved his head. "I decided to get out."

"You left the steel mills?"

He'd nodded.

Cora had arched a gray eyebrow in his direction. "And you eventually ended up at Harvard Law School."

In a nutshell, "Yes."

"One day I'd like to hear the rest of your story," she had said, curious but polite.

"Maybe one day I'll tell it to you," he'd responded, making no promises.

At that point in their conversation Cora LeMasters Grant, gnarled, arthritic hands folded on her lap, had leaned forward in a chair that was even older than she was—Trace figured the ornate piece of furniture was museum quality and probably from the period of a French Louis—and said, "I've heard you're brilliant."

No guts, no glory. "You heard correctly."

She hadn't been in the least put off by his arrogance. "I want you to be my attorney."

That had raised every head in the room.

He'd mulled it over for a second or two. "I accept."

"It won't be easy," she'd warned him.

"Anything worthwhile rarely is," had been his response.

Cora had finally smiled at him. "I do believe we will get along splendidly, Trace Ballinger."

"So do I, Cora Grant."

And they had.

Looking back, Trace could see that afternoon had been the turning point in his career and in his life.

"Your career *is* your life, Ballinger," he muttered to himself as he took the next turn at sixty.

He was driving too fast. Hell, he always drove too fast. He worked too hard. And he played too little. On the way to becoming a highly successful lawyer he had gone from being the classic underachiever to the classic overachiever.

The truth was he routinely worked eighteen-, even twenty-hour days. His only form of recreation was running in the park with Buddy. His idea of the perfect evening out was a Knicks game . . . when he could get tickets.

On the radio a sultry female voice was singing, "I promise you won't ever be lonely."

He wasn't lonely.

He was alone.

There was a difference.

Without taking his eyes off the road, Trace reached over and rubbed Buddy's neck. The golden retriever was another outcast from society. Trace had found the stray collarless, tagless, half frozen and bone-thin when he'd been running in Central Park one morning the winter before last. Buddy had followed him home, and they had been together ever since.

"Need to take a stretch, pal?"

Buddy whimpered and raised his head.

"Better be sure," Trace warned him. " 'Cause it's raining cats and dogs tonight. We're both going to get soaked if we stop and get out of the Jeep."

Buddy whimpered again.

Trace let his speed drop below sixty as he looked for a place to pull off the highway.

He wasn't sure what gave him a split second of warning. Maybe it was the sound of the tire blowing or maybe it was the steering wheel vibrating in his hands, but suddenly it was all he could do to keep the Jeep under control.

"Son of a bitch." Trace gritted his teeth and concentrated on preventing the vehicle from careening into the thicket of trees along the side of the road.

Time was suspended.

The rain was a sluice of unrelenting gray.

There was nothing but pitch-black above and below and to either side.

Luckily—there was that word again—the speedometer quickly plummeted from fifty to forty to thirty and eventually all the way down to zero.

Trace pushed the brake to the floor. The Jeep came to a dead stop. He shifted into park and turned to check on Buddy. The retriever stood up on the passenger seat and barked once, twice, three times, and wagged his tail wildly back and forth.

"I couldn't have said it better myself," Trace agreed, blowing his breath out in relief and ruffing the dog's neck. "Let's take care of the call of nature first, then I have a tire to change." He peered out the window at the cold, dark, wet night. "Looks like we're going to get soaked to the skin, Buddy."

Chapter Two

She'd never believed that Cora was crazy.

Eccentric? Yes. Obsessed? Definitely. Fragile? Yes and no. Lonely? Wasn't loneliness the fate of most people? Reclusive? Increasingly so as she'd gotten older.

Her great-aunt had always been a bit peculiar, but she had not been insane.

"At least no more or less than the rest of the human race," Schuyler Grant thought out loud as she steered the Jaguar through the rain-enshrouded night.

How long had it been since she'd visited Grantwood, since she had last seen Cora?

Too long.

Years.

Nine years.

Schuyler's chest tightened. It had been the spring she was twenty. She'd been studying art history at the Sorbonne (just as her mother and her older sister, Katherine—Kit to those who knew her well—had done before Schuyler) when the devastating news of the accident reached her. Two boats had collided, then capsized, off the coast of Mexico: one was a high-powered speedboat suspected of being used for drug smuggling; the other was her family's yacht. All souls aboard were lost. She had immediately flown back to the States for the funeral of her parents and her sister and Kit's fiancé, and then she had left again within a few days, unwilling to stay, unable to stay.

Schuyler took a deep breath and concentrated on the dark ribbon of road in front of her.

It had been nearly a decade since she'd seen her great-aunt, and now it was Cora's funeral—well, Cora's memorial service—and the unusual stipulations in her will that were finally bringing Schuyler home.

According to family stories (which had been legion), Cora LeMasters Grant had been the perfect product of her time and social class—a dutiful daughter, a popular debutante, a genteel and a gentle woman, a wife and mother, an accomplished hostess, a pillar of society and a doyenne of refined tastes—until tragedy struck.

Schuyler had been headed down an entirely different path when life *and* death intervened.

In spite of the sixty-year difference in their ages, in spite of the lengthy separations and despite the fact that they seemed to have little in common, she and Cora had shared one bond: They had both lost everyone dear to them.

She wasn't going to think about that now, Schuyler told herself as she reached up to straighten the black silk Hermès scarf wrapped around her head *à la française*. She was going to concentrate on the task at hand: getting herself from JFK to Grantwood.

The night was dark and rainy. The air had a definite chill to it for late April. She was tired—exhausted—after the long flight from Paris and she wasn't as familiar with Route 9, she realized, as she had once been.

She had no one to blame but herself for the situation she was in. It had been her choice. Cora's lawyer had arranged for a limousine and a driver to meet her at the airport. On her arrival in New York, she'd decided to rent a car instead. So she had tipped the uniformed chauffeur and sent him on his way.

She'd wanted to be alone, and she was alone. So what if it was dark? So what if it was raining? She was a good driver. A darned good driver. An excellent driver. She managed to get around in Paris traffic, didn't she?

Still, for the past few miles she had been using the distant taillights of the vehicle in front of her as a guide.

Schuyler took in another deep breath and held it for a count of three. Then she slowly exhaled and willed her shoulders to relax. The voice of the inimitable Charles Aznavour, singing in his native French, came from the Jaguar's stereo system. She softly hummed along. The *chanson* was very French and very *triste*: It was all about love found and love lost and the loneliness that inevitably followed.

She wasn't in or out of love, and she certainly wasn't lonely. She had dozens—hundreds—of friends on both sides of the Atlantic. In fact, all over the world.

Schuyler reached over and turned off the music. "So why depress yourself?"

She took in another deep breath and became aware of a familiar, pungent odor.

Skunk.

She wrinkled up her nose with distaste.

Then, all of a sudden, the headlights of another vehicle were directly behind her, gaining on her fast, momentarily blinding her in the rearview mirror.

"You're too bloody close," she groused aloud.

Pressing her foot down on the accelerator—she suddenly wished she'd traded her stiletto-heeled Ferragamos for a pair of sensible flats before starting out—Schuyler watched as the speedometer edged up five, then ten and finally fifteen miles an hour.

The vehicle behind her increased its speed as well.

She decided to try the opposite tactic and deliberately slowed down, hoping the tailgater would grow impatient going forty, then thirty-five, and pass her.

The vehicle slowed and maintained its position directly behind her, bright lights burning into her retinas.

Schuyler muttered under her breath in French. If there had been a fast-food restaurant or a gas station or any public facility along this stretch of Route 9, she would have turned off and sought safety in numbers. Anything to get the creep off her tail. Unfortunately, there was nothing but black road, black sky and black rain.

She speeded up.

The tailgater did the same.

She slowed down.

The car behind her followed suit.

It wasn't that she was afraid, Schuyler told herself—she had lost her fear of many things, *most* things, nine years ago—but she was annoyed.

Car lights inched closer, then seemed to disappear for a moment. Then there was a definite thud as the rear bumper of the Jaguar was hit from behind.

Schuyler licked her lips nervously and pressed down on the accelerator.

There was another thud and the Jaguar lurched forward as it was hit again.

Now she was frightened. This was no longer just a nuisance or even someone's idea of a bad joke. It was serious. Someone was trying to run her off the road.

She'd read about carjacking, of course, about accidents deliberately being caused, of purses being snatched and women abducted . . . and worse.

Schuyler's mouth suddenly went dry. She couldn't seem to swallow; there was a lump wedged in her throat. Her heart was in her stomach; her stomach plummeted to the floor of the rental car. She gripped the leather steering wheel and hung on for dear life.

Bright lights approached again. There was a curve just

ahead. She accelerated. Then, there in the distance, she spotted the taillights of a vehicle parked by the side of the road.

She had to take a chance. Better the devil she didn't know than the one she did.

Schuyler began to slow down. In a split second she saw the scene before her: a Jeep with the rear end jacked up and a man bent over changing what she assumed was a flat tire. There was also a large dog, sitting and watching him. Both man and dog appeared to be soaked to the skin.

Too close.

Schuyler realized she was too close to the disabled Jeep when the lunatic hit her rear bumper for the third time, sending the Jaguar spinning off the road. The mystery vehicle flew past her at a high rate of speed and disappeared into the night.

Slow motion.

As if in slow motion, the man looked up and then straightened. For a moment he was caught in her headlights like a startled deer. Schuyler Grant turned the steering wheel hard to the right and prayed that she wouldn't hit him.

Chapter Three

It was a close call.

A damned close call.

One minute Trace had been intent on getting the flat tire changed so he and Buddy could be on their way; the next he'd watched his life flash before his eyes as he was caught in the blinding glare of headlights barreling straight toward him.

At the last possible moment the car veered sharply and spun on its rear wheels, sending out a spray of rainwater and pellets of wet gravel that showered him from head to toe.

Not that he wasn't already drenched.

Whoever was driving the Jaguar—the distinctive hood ornament and the sleek shape of the automobile's body made identification easy enough even in the dark— slammed on the brakes and then appeared to collapse over the steering wheel.

For an eternity or two the only sounds were the rhythmic *swish-swish* of the windshield wipers arcing back and forth across the Jag's front window, and the rain.

"Stay!" Trace gave the command to Buddy before he approached the sports car. He tapped on the driver's window with his knuckles. "You okay?"

There was no response.

He tapped louder and rephrased the question. "Hey, are you all right?"

A head was gradually raised; a face was slowly turned

toward him. Trace caught a glimpse of ghostly white skin against a contrasting black background.

Without a sound the window was lowered and a woman's voice answered. "I don't know."

He'd give it one more try. He carefully enunciated each word. "Are you hurt?"

The question was taken under consideration. "No," she told him at last.

Trace stood there, rain dripping from every part of him that it was possible to drip from. "You almost ran over me," he pointed out unnecessarily.

There was sudden concern on the part of the sports car's driver. "Are you all right?"

Trace realized he'd lost his sense of humor sometime in the past quarter of an hour, probably about the time the tire on the Jeep had blown. There was no mistaking the sarcasm that laced his voice. "Good of you to ask."

"Is your dog okay?"

"Buddy is fine."

"And your Jeep?"

"It still has a flat tire, but it's no worse off than it was before you almost plowed into it."

"I'm sorry."

"So am I."

Trace couldn't see the woman's face clearly—she had some kind of scarf wrapped around her head—but he noticed that her words were slightly slurred and there was a definite tremor in her voice.

"It wasn't my fault," she insisted.

Really?

He had to ask. "Whose was it?"

A hint of indignation surfaced in both her voice and manner. "Didn't you see the other vehicle?"

Trace stood there in the rain, feet planted shoulder-width, hands splayed across his hips gunslinger-style, thumbs hooked through the belt loops on his Levi's. "What other vehicle?"

"The one that ran me off the highway," she stated in her own defense.

Trace shook his head.

She raised a hand to adjust the head scarf. She moistened her lips with her tongue. "Someone deliberately bumped into the rear end of my car."

Innocent until proven guilty was for the courtroom. "I didn't see another vehicle."

"There was one." She immediately launched into an explanation. "The car came up fast behind me a few miles back. I speeded up. So did the other driver. I slowed down. He—"

Trace raised a hand and interrupted. "How do you know it was a he?"

That stopped her cold. She thought about it for ten, maybe fifteen seconds. "I don't know. I suppose it could have been a she. Anyway, whoever it was slowed down when I slowed down. Then he or she rammed into my bumper several times." The woman admitted to him, "Frankly, I was getting nervous. I spotted your Jeep and decided to pull over. That's when my car was hit again and I was sent flying off the road."

Trace didn't sugarcoat the incident. "That's when you almost ran over Buddy and me."

"Yes."

He wasn't sure he believed her.

"You think I'm lying, don't you?" she said.

He thought it was real likely that the lady was trying to cover her derriere. Not that he blamed her. Most people would do the same under the circumstances.

"I'm telling you the truth," she insisted.

Rain dripped into Trace's eyes. He slicked his hair—it wasn't long and it wasn't short—back from his face and suggested, "Maybe you just *thought* you saw another car."

She was quick to take offense. "Are you saying I imagined the whole thing?"

He didn't answer her question. Instead he asked another one. "Do you smoke?"

"No."

"Have you been drinking?"

"No, I haven't been drinking," came out in an adamant tone. She shot back. "Have you?"

Trace leaned over and put his face pretty much in hers. "I never drink and drive."

"Well, neither do I," the woman claimed, rubbing a hand across her eyes.

"Tired?"

"Yes."

"You wouldn't be the first person to fall asleep at the wheel," he suggested.

"I didn't fall asleep." The Jaguar's driver glanced at the clock on a dashboard filled with fancy gauges and dials. "But it is getting late."

"So it is."

"Listen, I really am sorry about all of this." She made a graceful gesture with her hand. "Can I help?"

"With what?"

She turned her head and looked at him squarely. "I could hold an umbrella over you while you fix your car."

Trace had to give her credit for trying. "I think it's a little late for an umbrella."

After a moment she volunteered, "I could supply a flashlight while you change that flat."

Trace made to leave, then stopped. It would make the

job a whole lot easier *and* faster if he could see what he was doing. "I might take you up on the offer."

An elegant eyebrow was arched in his direction. "Might?"

He felt it was only fair to warn the woman in fashionable black. "You'll get wet."

Was that a smile he detected on the full-lipped mouth? "I've been wet before," she said, her voice slightly husky and more than a little amused. "I won't melt."

Trace wasn't so sure about that.

He was even less sure when she opened the door on the driver's side, swung her legs around, reached back for an umbrella, pressed a button on the tortoiseshell handle that instantly inflated the contraption, grabbed a flashlight from the glove box and started to get out of the Jaguar.

Legs.

Hers were long and lean and lithe. They were the kind of legs that seemed to go on forever.

Trace didn't mean to stare, but the hem of her skirt was hiked up above her knees—hell, it was pushed all the way up to midthigh—either that or it was one of those really short styles popularized by a hit TV show several seasons ago. Short or long, her skirt shouted designer and looked expensive.

Luck.

It was just his luck to be run over—well, *almost* run over—by a fancy woman in fancy clothes driving a fancy automobile who wouldn't know one end of a tire iron from the other.

Better the devil she didn't know.

That's what Schuyler had told herself in the split second before the lunatic in the car behind her had run her off the highway. Now she had to wonder if she'd gotten herself out of one sticky situation only to land in another.

She wasn't certain what had possessed her to leave the relative safety of her vehicle and volunteer to help a total stranger change a flat tire . . . in the pouring rain . . . late at night . . . in the middle of nowhere.

Well, it wasn't exactly the middle of nowhere. But she had reached a deserted stretch of road where the Hudson River was on one side and a state park on the other.

Guilt.

That was the reason she had offered to hold a flashlight while the man finished changing the tire on his Jeep. After all, she had *nearly* run over him and his dog.

"Nice shoes," he commented, glancing down at her high heels. "Italian?"

"Yes."

Apparently he felt it was necessary to warn her. "They're going to get ruined."

"I don't care."

He shrugged his broad shoulders as if to say, *Hey, lady, I don't care if you don't care.*

They walked the last few feet to the disabled SUV. The man went down on his haunches in front of the flat tire. "Aim your flashlight right there."

Schuyler flipped the flashlight on and did as he instructed. It was still raining steadily. Clasping the umbrella in her other hand, she tried to hold it at an angle that would provide some protection for both man and beast.

She found herself feeling sorry for the poor bedraggled dog. The animal sat and waited patiently, his fur plastered to his body, only making the occasional whimper.

She finally broke the silence. "Why don't you let your dog stay in the Jeep?"

Dark eyes glanced up at her. "It's not my choice."

Schuyler didn't understand. "Not your choice?" Whose was it, then?

The bolts were removed one by one from the wheel. Then the man explained to her without really explaining. "Buddy won't stay inside if I'm out here."

She was curious. "Why not?"

His reply was terse. "Buddy goes where I go," he said, taking the flat tire off before putting the spare on.

Was that Buddy's choice or his owner's? Schuyler wondered.

"If Buddy had his way he'd never let me out of his sight," was added.

There was something to be said for the loyalty of man's—and woman's—best friend.

For the next few minutes the stranger concentrated on the task at hand. He'd obviously changed a flat tire before. He seemed to know exactly what to do, which was more than she could say for herself, Schuyler realized.

She kept the beam of light focused where the man had told her to. As a result, his face was partially illuminated. After a minute or two Schuyler found herself studying his features. His hair was dark brown, possibly even black, with a sprinkling of gray at the temples. There was a hint of curls along the back of his neck and below his ears, maybe due to the rain.

His eyebrows were definitely slashes of black. His eyes were intelligent, focused, perfectly spaced on either side of an emphatic nose. Between the rain and the yellowish tint of the flashlight, she couldn't tell what color his eyes were. They may have been hazel or green or even blue.

His face was interesting: angular, hard-edged, chiseled. He wasn't young and he wasn't old. Her best guess was mid-thirties. Possibly pushing forty. She was willing to bet that he'd earned every line on his face.

The stranger was tall, noticeably taller than her own five feet eight inches, plus stiletto heels, Schuyler recalled as she'd stood beside him after getting out of her car.

The impression the man gave was one of strength—physical and mental—of resourcefulness, of experience, of having lived life, of having survived.

At the moment Schuyler was only hoping to survive the rest of what had turned out to be a miserable evening.

She was wet through and chilled to the bone by the time the stranger stood up and said to her, "That should do it. Thanks for your help."

Her feet and hands were blocks of ice. Her teeth were chattering. "You're welcome."

The man escorted her back to the Jaguar. "The rain is finally letting up," he observed.

"So it is."

Schuyler opened the door on the driver's side, deposited the umbrella and the flashlight in the back and slipped behind the wheel. She turned on the ignition and pressed the button for the window. It slid down noiselessly.

The man in the wet clothes leaned over and remarked, "I hope you don't have far to go."

She was deliberately circumspect. "I don't."

He straightened and took a good look around, not that there was much to see in the dark. "It appears that whoever was harassing you is long gone."

Schuyler inclined her head slightly. "Is that what you think it was: harassment?"

"Maybe." He rocked back on the balls of his feet. "People can be peculiar."

"Yes, they can be."

He shook his head from side to side. "Sometimes even so-called normal people will do strange things."

There was something in his voice that made Schuyler

think he was speaking from experience. Anyway, she wasn't about to argue the point with him.

He dug around in the back pocket of his jeans and took out his wallet. "Here's my card."

She drew a momentary blank. "Your card?"

"My business card. Just in case you'd need to contact me." He shrugged. "The insurance company might decide to give you a hard time if there's any damage to your car."

Schuyler took the white, rather damp and slightly dog-eared card and slipped it into the handbag on the seat beside her. Then she pulled out a small leather case, scribbled her name on the back of another business card and offered it to him. "This is the name and telephone number of my attorney." She turned on the heater full blast. "Just in case you'd need to contact me."

Without bothering to look at it, the man slipped the card into his wallet.

"Safe trip," he finally said, thumping one hand lightly on the roof of the Jag.

"The same to you," she replied, pushing the button that closed the window.

Schuyler shifted the car into gear and pulled out onto the highway. A glance in the rearview mirror showed man and dog standing there side by side, watching as she drove away.

Mrs. Danvers supplied Trace with a stack of towels that had once been used by the Grants' chauffeur to polish the family's Silver Cloud. The Rolls was long gone. The chauffeur had died the year before last. The towels remained.

Trace made sure Buddy was dried off, fed and watered before he accepted the housekeeper's offer of sandwiches and a shot of medicinal whiskey. He sat at the kitchen table and ate in silence, letting Mrs. Danvers do the talking.

"She's here," the woman announced over the rim of her coffee cup.

Trace swallowed. *"She?"*

"Miss Grant."

He took another bite of ham and cheese—with a dollop of Dijon mustard—on rye. "Ah, Miss Grant."

"She arrived a few minutes before you did and went straight to her room without taking so much as a cup of tea or one of my homemade cookies." Mrs. Danvers's feelings had obviously been hurt. "In fact, she scarcely spoke a word to me."

Trace offered a logical explanation. "Perhaps she's suffering from jet lag."

Mrs. Danvers bit her lower lip. "Perhaps."

"It was undoubtedly a long flight from Paris," he said.

"Miss Grant did look a little the worse for wear."

"I don't look much better myself," Trace said with a self-deprecating laugh, driving a hand through the still-damp hair at the back of his neck.

"I thought it might be me," the woman confessed with a nervous laugh.

"You, Mrs. Danvers?"

She nodded her graying head. "It's the name, you see."

Trace didn't see. "I'm afraid I don't understand."

"Didn't you ever read the classic romance novel *Rebecca* by Daphne Du Maurier?"

He shook his head.

Elvira Danvers explained. "Well, most people—at least most women—have. Anyway, there's a housekeeper in the book who goes quite mad by the end of the story and burns her master's house to the ground." There was another nervous laugh from the housekeeper/cook. "*That* Mrs. Danvers goes out in a blaze of glory, if you'll pardon the pun."

"Surely people don't mix you up with a fictional character," Trace said, astonished by what he was hearing.

Mrs. Danvers straightened her shoulders. "You'd be surprised what people will say and do."

He was an attorney. He lived in New York City. Very
little about anyone or anything surprised him anymore.

The housekeeper confided in him, "In fact, I was once
fired from a position for burning the toast at breakfast."

"You're kidding."

"I'm not kidding. My employer was convinced I intended to incinerate not only the kitchen and myself, but
an entire three-story brownstone." She gave a sigh. "I've
never burned anything since."

"I'm sure Miss Grant's behavior is no reflection on you,
Mrs. Danvers. She was probably just tired."

"You're no doubt right, Mr. Ballinger. You usually are.
Please don't trouble yourself on my account." Elivra Danvers changed the subject. "Would you like to have another
sandwich?" she inquired, nudging the plate of thinly sliced
baked Virginia ham, imported Swiss cheese and deli rye
toward him.

Over the past few years he'd learned how to get along
with Cora's housekeeper-cum-cook. "Nobody makes a better sandwich than you do, Mrs. Danvers."

"It's a pleasure to cook for someone who enjoys food
as much as you do, Mr. Ballinger." Elvira Danvers shook
her head—her hair was neat and tidy, as was her general
appearance, despite the unusually late hour—and clicked
her tongue against the back of her front teeth. "Poor Mrs.
Grant had so little appetite toward the end, you know."

He knew. Poor Cora.

"A cookie?"

The housekeeper had baked his favorite kind: Peanut

butter with chocolate chips. Trace thanked her and helped himself to several.

Mrs. Danvers pushed her chair back, rose to her feet and began to clear away the dirty dishes. She kept an immaculate kitchen. "Now that you've had something to eat, it's time you got out of those wet clothes before you catch your death."

Trace apprised her of his plans. "I'm headed upstairs right now for a shower."

"Just leave your things over the side of the tub," the housekeeper instructed as he left the kitchen several minutes later. "I'll see to them tomorrow."

Trace stripped and stepped into the shower. The whiskey was beginning to warm him nicely from the inside out; the hot water would do the rest. He spread his legs, leaned forward and let the pulsing spray beat down on his neck and shoulders.

He almost felt human again by the time he wrapped an oversize bath towel around his hips—there was a discreet white-on-white G embroidered on one corner—and wandered back into the adjoining guest room that had become his home away from home.

Buddy was sprawled at the foot of the bed, softly snoring. The retriever didn't even bother to raise his head.

Trace poured himself a second glass of whiskey—Mrs. Danvers had thoughtfully supplied a tray with a crystal decanter and a matching crystal glass—and went to stand at the window.

He took a sip of the expensive alcohol and felt the welcome warmth all the way down to his stomach.

He gazed out at the landscape. The view from this wing of the house was usually unparalleled, but tonight he couldn't see a thing: not the chestnut trees swaying in nearby Grant's Wood, not the stars in the sky overhead, not even the lights along the Hudson River. There was nothing but fog and a fine mist.

Since that fateful trip to Grantwood nearly eight years ago, he had stood at this window on more than one occasion and pondered the meaning—or at least the irony—of life.

Funny thing, irony.

He had spent his first thirty years hating the Grants and everything they stood for. He'd cursed their name. Sworn his revenge. Now he was one of them.

Well, *almost* one of them.

"It's time for bed, Ballinger," he finally said aloud as he glanced at the clock on the mantel.

Trace turned off the lights and crawled between fine sateen sheets. He punched his pillow a couple of times and then propped one arm up behind his head. He stared into the darkness.

So Miss Grant had arrived from Paris.

His appointment with Cora's great-niece and heir to the Grants' fortune was scheduled for ten o'clock tomorrow morning in the library. He wasn't looking forward to their first meeting.

Trace closed his eyes. A face appeared: It was the young woman in black with the ghostly white skin. The young woman who had nearly run over him on the road. The young woman with the voice like silk over satin and legs that went on forever.

Who was she?

Then he remembered the business card she'd given him before driving off into the night. He had stuffed it into his wallet without even looking at it. The lady had said he could contact her through her attorney if there were any problems.

Trace threw back the covers, sat up on the edge of the mattress, got to his feet and made his way to the dresser where he'd dumped his wallet and keys.

He grabbed his wallet—it still had that damp leather smell to it—and returned to bed. He flipped on the lamp, dug around, came up with the business card and held it to the light.

Trace glanced at the name printed on the front, then put his head back and laughed, really laughed, for the first time in a long time. The golden retriever at the foot of the bed opened his eyes and raised his head. "If there's any trouble, Buddy, it looks like I'll be contacting myself."

The lettering on the business card clearly read: TRACE BALLINGER, ATTORNEY AT LAW.

It was no surprise when Trace turned the card over and saw the signature scrawled on the reverse side. He absently rubbed his hand back and forth across his bare abdomen. "It seems we will meet again, Miss Grant."

Chapter Four

The next morning Schuyler walked out of her bedroom, the same bedroom she had slept in as a child when her family visited Grantwood, turned left and took the back stairs, the "servants' " stairs, down to the kitchen.

But she didn't end up in the kitchen as she'd expected to. Instead, she found herself standing in front of a pair of French doors that opened up into a two-story conservatory filled with exotic plants and tropical palm trees.

She retraced her steps. This time she turned to the right. Several minutes later she tried a door at the end of a hallway (the door and the hallway appeared to be identical to a dozen others in this wing of the house) and ran straight into a brick wall.

Schuyler groaned.

Cora had been at it again.

Her great-aunt's compulsion to build—most people labeled it an obsession—had started long before Schuyler was born. While no one seemed to know the reason behind Cora's "projects," there had been plenty of speculation over the years.

Some said the old woman had too much time on her hands and too much money in the bank.

Some said she was lonely.

Some maintained she was simply eccentric.

Some whispered she was crazy.

Sometimes Cora's building ventures were legitimate: like the conservatory that had been added since Schuyler's last visit to Grantwood. More often the renovations ap-

peared to be change for the sake of change—or for heaven
knew what reason—and took the form of a hidden chamber, a secret passageway, a spiraling staircase, a castle turret, a window without a room, a room without windows or
even a door.

It had not always been like that, of course.

Grantwood had originally been constructed in the middle
of the nineteenth century by Schuyler's great-great-
grandfather, William T. Grant, as a wedding gift for his
bride, Lucy.

Said to be brilliant, bold and utterly ruthless, William
Tiberius Grant had also been the founder of the family for-
tune and one of the so-called robber barons of his era. His
name was often mentioned in the history books along with
John Jacob Astor, Jay Gould, "Commodore" Vanderbilt,
J. P. Morgan and John D. Rockefeller.

During his lifetime William T. Grant had acquired, with
equal enthusiasm, everything from railroads to factories,
from steel mills to coal mines, from oil wells to banks, from
cratefuls of European antiques to priceless Old Masters.

In the days before income tax, government regulations,
public opinion polls or charitable, patriotic or moral con-
cerns (it was Vanderbilt who had so famously said, "The
public be damned"), William T. could easily afford to
spend several million dollars building his dream house on
idyllic acreage along the Hudson River, and several times
that amount, it was rumored, on furnishings.

Cora was the widow of William T.'s eldest grandson
and eventual heir. She had come to Grantwood as a bride
of twenty. The year had been 1931. Since she had become
mistress of all she surveyed, the house had become less of
a family home—well, a family mansion—and more of an
elaborate and bizarre "folly."

Schuyler's childhood visits to the strange old woman

and the stranger house had been a little like Alice tumbling down the rabbit hole into Wonderland. Nothing was what it seemed to be. No one was who they appeared to be.

As an adult, Schuyler realized that living at Grantwood would be unsettling. The house was perpetually in the process of being torn down, added on to, changed or remodeled. In fact, Cora had kept an architect and a construction crew on retainer. There was no beginning and there was no end.

Well, there would be an end to it now, of course, with Cora's death, Schuyler reflected. She sighed and closed the door on the brick wall.

She gave up trying to find her way to the kitchen and returned to her bedroom. She picked up the in-house telephone and rang the number for the housekeeper. "Good morning, Mrs. Danvers."

There was a definite hesitation in the responding voice. "Good morning, Miss Grant."

Schuyler knew she had been abrupt with Elvira Danvers the previous evening when she'd refused the woman's offer of tea, cookies and conversation. Frankly, at the time, she had been too wet and too tired to care.

An apology, in the guise of an explanation, was given. "I was so exhausted on my arrival last night that I'm afraid. I wasn't paying attention when you escorted me to my bedroom."

"You can't find your way downstairs," deduced the woman on the other end of the line.

There was no sense in pretending otherwise. "So far I've run into the conservatory and a brick wall." Schuyler placed one hand on the waist of her Armani suit. "Could you please give me directions to the kitchen?"

She detected a certain relief in Mrs. Danvers's tone as the housekeeper said, "You'll want to go to the center hallway. It's easily recognized because the wallpaper is a blue floral pattern of forget-me-nots. The staircase you're looking for is behind the third door on the right."

"Thank you, Mrs. Danvers."

"You're welcome, Miss Grant."

"Your coffee is delicious," Schuyler was saying to the housekeeper some fifteen or twenty minutes later, having successfully found her way downstairs.

"Would you like another cup?" inquired Mrs. Danvers as she moved about the large kitchen with a long-standing familiarity and an easy efficiency.

"Yes. I would." Schuyler held out her mug. "Thank you."

"A breakfast roll?"

She accepted and took a bite of the warm sconelike bread. It practically melted in her mouth. "I thought the baguettes in France were wonderful, but we don't have anything like this." She took another bite. "You're a marvelous cook, Mrs. Danvers."

A faint hint of color crept up the housekeeper's neck and onto her cheeks. "Thank you, Miss Grant."

Schuyler polished off several of the breakfast rolls. She realized her last meal—she hadn't had much appetite and had mostly pushed the chicken cordon bleu around on her plate—had been on the airplane earlier the previous evening.

Content and satiated, she sat back in the comfortable chair and sipped her coffee. "I hope you don't mind that I've invaded your kitchen this morning."

"Oh, I don't mind," Mrs. Danvers replied.

Schuyler gazed around the one room in all of Grantwood that might be described as homey. The kitchen was decorated in shades of yellow, delft blue and white. One entire wall was glass with a row of paned windows overlooking green lawns that stretched all the way to the Hudson River.

There was a collection of antique cookie jars—Schuyler's personal favorite was the Humpty-Dumpty—and copper pots in abundance. The pots hung from the ceiling above the center island, dangled from ornamental hooks and were stacked in glass-fronted cabinets.

"I've always preferred eating in the kitchen to one of the dining rooms," she confided to the older woman over her second cup of excellent coffee.

"So did Mrs. Grant." The housekeeper sat down across from her. "As a matter of fact, I don't think the formal dining room has been used in the seven years I've been in service here."

"I suppose the formal rooms were utilized more in the family's social heyday," Schuyler ventured. Then she paused and remarked, "Strange, but I didn't notice the informal dining room on my way downstairs." One fingernail was tapped against her lower lip. "I could have sworn it was next to the kitchen."

"It was."

She frowned. "Was?"

She was informed by the housekeeper-cum-cook. "Mrs. Grant had that room completely remodeled about five years ago. It's a wine cellar now."

"Cora didn't drink alcohol."

"No, she didn't."

Schuyler bit her tongue. It was past time—long past time—for criticism of poor Cora. "I want to thank you for taking such good care of my great-aunt. I know she considered you her friend as well as her housekeeper."

Elvira Danvers dabbed at the corners of her eyes with a plain, white, old-fashioned handkerchief. "Mrs. Grant never complained, of course. Not even to me. But I suspected something was wrong when she was off her food. I tried to entice her to eat by making her favorite dishes, but she just didn't have any appetite."

"I'm sure she appreciated your efforts, anyway."

There was a sniff and another dab of the handkerchief. "It's a comfort to think so."

Schuyler carefully broached a delicate subject. "Just as I appreciate your continued help until it's decided what the future of Grantwood will be."

The handkerchief disappeared into a pocket. Hardworking hands were clenched together on the table in front of the older woman. Worry lines appeared at the corners of her eyes and mouth. "Going to sell up, are you?"

"I don't know what I'm going to do." This wasn't the time or place to discuss her plans with Mrs. Danvers.

Besides, first things first. And first on the list was tomorrow's memorial service for Cora.

"Mr. Ballinger thought it would be appropriate to serve a buffet luncheon after the memorial service," the housekeeper stated, back to business as usual.

"I quite agree."

A list was placed on the kitchen table in front of Schuyler. "I have the menu ready for your approval," she was told.

Schuyler finished her coffee. "I have complete confidence in you, Mrs. Danvers. May I leave the arrangements for the luncheon in your capable hands?"

Elvira Danvers seemed pleased by the request. "You may."

Schuyler needed fresh air. "Thank you again for the delicious coffee and rolls. I believe I'd like to take a walk before my meeting with Mr. Ballinger."

"It's a lovely morning for an outing after the rain we had last night," the housekeeper commented.

*   *   *

Trace was soaked to the skin—this time with sweat—when he made the turn at the end of the drive and started running back toward the house, Buddy at his heels.

He sprinted past a group of dilapidated outbuildings that had been the kennels, the carriage house and a blacksmith's house; then along a series of ornate trellises that had once led into what was said to be the finest English rose garden outside England itself.

Good outdoor help had been hard to come by, according to Cora. Consequently, the roses were long gone. The trellises were in sad disrepair. The prized garden was an indiscriminate mass of dense and overgrown vegetation.

Trace spotted a woman walking in the direction of the river and what was known as Lucy's Lookout. He couldn't see her features clearly from this distance, but her stride was measured, confident, long-legged, familiar.

He'd know those legs anywhere.

Her hair, sans scarf, was down around her shoulders this morning. He hadn't realized it last night in the dark and the rain, but her hair really was the most extraordinary color: a kind of fiery red with golden highlights.

She was tall, but not too tall. She was slender, but not too slender. She had a nice figure, a damned nice figure. She was, of course, dressed to the nines.

Yup, Miss Grant had arrived from Paris.

Trace reached up and ran his hand along the line of his jaw. His beard was like sandpaper.

He needed a shave.

He glanced down at the sweat-stained T-shirt with NYU emblazoned across the chest.

He needed a shower.

His gaze dropped farther. His running shoes and gray sweatpants (he'd taken a pair of scissors to the legs when

the elastic had worn out; as a result they hit him somewhat
incongruously between knee and ankle) were splattered
with mud.

He needed a shave, a shower *and* a change of clothes.

"I don't think we should introduce ourselves to the Miss
Grant until we've cleaned up. What do you say, Buddy?"

The golden retriever turned his head and gave a soft
acknowledging bark.

Besides, something had been niggling at Trace since the
previous evening and this was the perfect opportunity to
check it out.

He skirted the ten-car garage—it had originally served
as Grantwood's stables and measured only slightly less than
the length of a modern-day football field—and entered by
one of the back doors. Buddy trotted along at his side.

There, in a stall on the opposite end of the garage from
where he'd parked his Jeep, was the vehicle in question.
No wonder he hadn't spotted the sports car before.

Last night Schuyler Grant had maintained that someone
had rammed into the back of her automobile several times
and then deliberately run her off the road. The truth hadn't
particularly mattered to him when the woman in black had
been a stranger.

Now it did.

Trace went down on his haunches until he was eye level
with the rear of the Jaguar. He ran his hand along the surface of the bumper. There was no mistaking the dents and
scratches that were consistent with what his client had
claimed.

"Damned if she wasn't telling the truth," Trace muttered
under his breath.

Chapter Five

His eyes were blue.

Not a pale, anemic, washed-out shade of blue, but the wild, savage blue that warriors once painted across their faces before charging into battle.

He was tall—at least several inches over the six-foot mark—broad-shouldered, muscular and mature: all the things Schuyler had glimpsed by flashlight the previous evening.

What she hadn't noticed the night before, Schuyler realized as she stood in the doorway of the library, was the man's compelling presence. He possessed a kind of cool self-assurance, an almost in-your-face arrogance and plain old male sex appeal.

Not that there was anything plain *or* old about him.

The stranger—who wasn't quite a stranger, she supposed, after their close encounter on the road—dominated the library at Grantwood, and this crucial first meeting.

That gave him the upper hand.

That made him, in her opinion, dangerous.

Schuyler quickly composed herself, which consisted chiefly of putting on her "game face" and finding something to do with her hands. In the end, she chose to leave one hand down at her side and slip the other into the pocket of her jacket.

For a moment or two she simply stared at the man standing on the other side of the neoclassical Italian library table of bronze and inlaid marble. She moistened her lips before saying, "It's you."

There was a short, brittle pause. "It's me," he agreed in a resonant baritone.

That's when it dawned on Schuyler. He knew who she was. "You're not surprised to see me."

"I'm not surprised."

She advanced into the room—her heels were silent on the Louis XVI Savonnerie rug—and stopped short of the library table, which, judging from the official-looking papers spread across its surface, was being used as a desk. "How do you know who I am?"

It wasn't exactly a smile and it wasn't exactly a frown that Schuyler detected on the man's features. "I dug out the business card you gave me last night."

"I'd forgotten we exchanged business cards," she admitted. His was still in her handbag.

He did everything to convey an air of nonchalance but shrug his shoulders. "I didn't forget."

"They're both imprinted with your name," she concluded belatedly, uncertain if she was amused or annoyed by the situation.

"Why don't we make the introductions official?" the man suggested, stepping around the library table and coming toward her. "Trace Ballinger."

She extended her right hand. Her voice and demeanor were businesslike. "Schuyler Grant."

His handshake was appropriately firm. "I see you made it last night."

"As did you," she observed.

"A little worse for wear, but yes, I made it." Trace Ballinger regarded her with an air of puzzlement. "By the way, what happened to the car and driver I hired to meet you at JFK?"

"I dismissed them . . . him."

He gave her a hard blue stare. "Why?"

After last night's incident, her reason was going to sound fairly lame. "I prefer to drive myself."

"Do you?" It was a rhetorical question.

Schuyler removed her hand from the pocket of her suit jacket. "I drive myself all the time in Paris."

His disapproval was thinly disguised as impatience. "New York isn't Paris."

She knew that.

"You were damned lucky last night."

She knew that, too.

The next thing out of his mouth wasn't a suggestion; it was an order. "Next time leave the driving to the limo service."

If there was a next time—which Schuyler highly doubted—she would do exactly as she pleased. And if he didn't like it, Trace Ballinger could go straight to the dogs!

Collecting herself, and looking around the library, she inquired, "By the way, how is Buddy?"

"Dry, warm and well fed. He's napping on a king-size bed at this very moment."

"Lucky dog."

"Very lucky dog."

Something occurred to Schuyler. Something that was said last night. "I thought Buddy never left your side."

"He usually doesn't. But he wasn't invited to our business meeting."

There was a discreet knock on the library door. Trace spoke up. "Enter."

It was Mrs. Danvers with a tray of coffee things and a plate of cookies. "As you requested, Mr. Ballinger," she said, wheeling in the serving cart.

He smiled at the housekeeper. "Punctual as always. Thank you, Mrs. Danvers."

"You're welcome, sir. I'll see that you and Miss Grant

aren't disturbed," she guaranteed as she backed out of the room.

Trace Ballinger smiled again as the woman closed the library door behind her.

"We might as well be comfortable," he suggested to Schuyler, indicating the chair opposite the one he'd apparently been occupying. "Would you like a cup of coffee?"

"Yes. Thank you." She took a seat while he poured.

Cora's attorney played the gracious host surprisingly well. "Cream? Sugar?"

"Neither." She always took her coffee in the European fashion: very strong and very black.

"Cookie?"

"What kind are they?" she inquired.

"Peanut butter with chocolate chips."

"No. Thank you."

Several minutes later, over the rim of her coffee cup, Schuyler began. "I understand you've been my great-aunt's attorney for eight years, Mr. Ballinger."

Trace Ballinger sat down, casually crossed one leg over the other, finished off the cookie in his hand, brushed the crumbs from the lapel of his leather jacket, plucked a non-existent speck of lint off his jeans and answered, "That's correct."

She watched him closely. "You're a partner with Dutton, Dutton, McQuade & Martin?"

"I am."

Schuyler continued with her cross-examination. "Did you come to Grantwood for the monthly meetings with my great-aunt?"

He was a man of relatively few words. "In the beginning."

"And later?"

He appeared to be completely at ease. "Cora asked me to come more often."

Schuyler was curious. "Why?"

He rubbed his hand back and forth along his jaw. "I think because she was lonely."

Without a word Schuyler rose from her chair and stood, coffee cup in hand, her back to Trace Ballinger, studying the eclectic collection of paintings, hung floor-to-ceiling in the nineteenth-century tradition and encompassing portraiture, landscape, trompe l'oeil, still lifes, a large Brazilian canvas and a depiction of the Tower of Babel.

Once she was certain she'd regained her composure, Schuyler turned to the man and, lowering her voice half an octave, agreed, "I'm sure she was lonely."

Trace Ballinger was the first to look away. He cleared his throat. "Shall we get down to business?"

"Yes. Let's." Schuyler placed her cup of now-cold coffee on the serving cart and resumed her seat.

"Your great-aunt made several stipulations concerning the reading of her will. The first is that you physically return to Grantwood for the occasion. The second is that initially I present the document to you alone."

"Is that customary?"

"I don't know about customary, but it's not the first time I've run into it, either."

"Please continue."

"There is a copy of Cora LeMasters Grant's last will and testament in front of you. We'll cover the significant points this morning and then you can take your time reading the document over during the next few days and ask me any questions that might arise."

So far it seemed cut-and-dried.

"Cora made provision for a number of institutions, including her favorite charities, her alma mater, several art museums and the like during her lifetime. The beneficiaries now named—besides yourself, of course—are listed beginning on page thirty-four."

Schuyler rifled through the hefty sheaf of papers until she reached the appropriate page.

Trace elaborated. "The primary bequests will go to Cora's neighbors, Adam Coffin and the Frick sisters, Ida and Ellamae; your cousin, Jonathan Tiberius Grant; and the housekeeper, Elvira Danvers. There is provision made for several other longtime employees, including the head gardener, although Cora had already outlived most of her household staff at the time of her death."

Schuyler's head came up. On her walk this morning she couldn't help but notice how ill-kept the grounds were. "Does Grantwood have a head gardener?"

"I believe Mr. Barker is essentially retired."

"Essentially?"

"The gentleman is nearly ninety."

"I see."

"He mainly digs around in a small vegetable patch outside his cottage."

"Who sees to the grounds?"

"The landscaping and maintenance is done by a local company: Ground Zero."

"Well, from what I saw this morning, Ground Zero missed a spot or two the last time they were here."

Trace almost smiled at her. "Or even an acre or two." He shook his head from side to side. "I tried to convince Cora to use another company, but . . ."

"Cora could be stubborn."

His mouth curved. "She preferred to think of herself as strong-willed."

Schuyler sighed. The same had frequently been said of her. "I'm afraid it's a family trait."

He stroked his jawline. "Is that your way of telling me 'forewarned is forearmed'?"

"I suppose it is."

Trace returned to the business at hand. "On page thirty-six you will see that there are smaller monetary gifts designated for everyone from the butcher to the mailman, from the local girls who came in to read aloud to Cora to the seamstress who altered her clothing."

Schuyler quickly scanned the long list. "I'm vaguely familiar with some of the names."

Trace inclined his head slightly. "I'm sure most of them will be present tomorrow for the memorial service."

Schuyler hated the very thought of meeting and greeting dozens of unfamiliar people; men and women all dressed in black and wearing an appropriately somber expression on their faces.

They would come out of curiosity, of course.

And for the money.

In the end, it was always about the money.

"They aren't coming merely to find out what you look like after all these years, Miss Grant, or to hear whether or not they've inherited a little something from Cora," Trace said as if he'd read her mind.

She was stung. "Aren't they?"

"Not all of them. Some of those attending will genuinely want to pay their last respects to your great-aunt."

She wasn't sure what made her say it, but the words were out of Schuyler's mouth before she could think better of them. "I half expected to see your name on the list of beneficiaries."

Trace Ballinger stiffened. "It would not only be inappropriate, but highly unethical."

She tossed out, "Besides, you must be getting a hefty fee as executor."

He was suddenly angry with her. Schuyler could feel the raw emotion across the small space separating them. It was almost a tangible force.

Wearily, she rubbed a hand across her eyes. "I'm sorry. That was unforgivably rude of me."

"Yes. It was."

She was going to have to eat her words and swallow them along with her pride. "I can only plead exhaustion and a momentary lapse in good manners. Please accept my apology."

It was a full thirty seconds, maybe more, before the man said, "I accept."

"Please go on."

"As Cora's attorney my job was twofold: to preserve her wealth and then, at her death, disperse it according to her wishes. I won't go into all the details this morning, but several trusts were established in your name. Control of one of those trusts, currently in the amount of twenty million dollars, will pass to you on your thirtieth birthday"—he glanced down at a date scribbled on a pad of paper in front of him—"at the end of the summer."

Schuyler listened with a growing sense of dread. "Didn't Cora tell you?"

Trace Ballinger slowly raised his eyes to hers. "Tell me what?"

She took in her breath and counted to ten. Then she slowly exhaled. "I don't want—I have never wanted— Grantwood or the Grants' money."

"Cora told me." The man shoved the legal papers to one side and looked at her across the library table. "Your great-aunt said you could do whatever you wish to with the house and the money. Give it all away if you don't want it." The lawyer levered himself to his feet. "Now comes the important part."

"The important part?" Schuyler repeated, puzzled.

The man in the faded blue jeans and the beat-up leather jacket—she wondered if they were the same clothes he'd been wearing the night before—paced back and forth between the library table and the nearest wall of bookcases. "While Cora may not have had any right to ask a favor of you—those were her words, by the way, not mine—that is precisely what she has done."

Schuyler couldn't imagine what he meant. "What are you talking about?"

"The real reason Cora asked me to meet with you alone this morning," he stated.

"I don't understand."

"You will."

At least Trace hoped like hell she'd understand.

He paced back and forth, then stopped in his tracks, planted both hands on the edge of the library table and leaned toward the elegant woman on the other side. "Strictly speaking, the favor your great-aunt is asking of you isn't part of any legal document. You can honor her request or you can simply ignore it. It's up to you. Whatever you decide, it won't change the conditions of her will."

Cora's great-niece sat there in her chair and waited, without moving, without speaking, without any change in the expression on her patrician features.

Miss Grant played her cards close to her chest, Trace decided. He bent over and reached into the leather briefcase at his feet. He took out an envelope, came around the table and held it out to his client.

It was obvious she didn't want to take the envelope from him. She simply stared at it.

He decided to try a different approach with her, one that had occasionally worked on a wary client in the past, although the present situation was unique, he had to admit.

Trace lowered his voice and suggested in an understanding tone, "It won't bite."

Still, she hesitated.

Trace noticed that her eyes appeared to have changed color along with her emotions. He could have sworn that her irises were brown when she'd first entered the library. Now they were some shade between green and gold.

It made him think of the mood rings that had been popular when he was a boy. At the age of nine he'd wanted one more than anything else in the world.

Or so he'd thought.

He hadn't had the money to buy the coveted ring from the five and dime on the corner, so he had stolen one from the counter while Mr. Franks wasn't looking. After that he'd felt guilty as hell every time he saw the old man.

Stealing the mood ring had taught Trace a valuable lesson. There was no joy if you took something that wasn't honestly and rightfully yours. And in the end, after carefully wiping off his fingerprints, he'd thrown the ring away.

As far as he could remember, the damned thing had never changed color, anyway.

Schuyler Grant's eyes, on the other hand, had.

For some reason he suddenly wanted to make this easier for her. "Cora asked me to reassure you. You don't have to read the note inside the envelope if you don't want to."

She raised her eyes to his. "Do you know what the note says?"

"More or less."

Her voice altered. "Do you think I'm a terrible coward for not wanting to read it?"

His free hand found the back of his neck. He rubbed the skin there and tried to think of a diplomatic answer. There wasn't one. He opened his mouth.

Schuyler waved aside whatever he had been about to say. The movement sent her silky hair into motion. "I withdraw the question. You're my lawyer, not my confessor."

She took the envelope from his hand and, using a ceremonial dagger from the library table as a letter opener, slit the envelope neatly along the crease. She removed the single sheet of stationery inside—stationery he immediately recognized as Cora's—smoothed out the fold and read to herself.

Trace thought she paled slightly, but he wasn't certain. Her skin was fair—like very fine porcelain—with just the slightest sprinkling of freckles, anyway.

She held the piece of paper out to him. "Cora says you'll explain if it's necessary." Her eyebrows rose a fraction of an inch. "Well, it is necessary."

The note was written in the shaky handwriting that had been typical of Cora's penmanship the last few years of her life. With the disease that had plagued her joints and created disfiguring knobs on her fingers, even on good days it had been difficult and painful for her to write. The note was short, no doubt from necessity.

Cora had used a fountain pen. Every now and then there was a faint smudge of ink on the paper. For some reason that made Trace pause and swallow hard.

He read the note.

My dear Schuyler,
I have one final request of you. Lay the ghosts to rest. For my sake. For everyone's sake. And especially for your own sake.
It was never you, dear girl.
It was always me.

Cora

P.S. If necessary, Trace will explain.

Trace read the cryptic note twice before looking up. "Cora wants me to explain."

An expectant, "Yes."

He took a deep breath and unceremoniously blew it out. "I'm not sure I can."

Hell, he was going to sound like the crazy one if he blurted out everything to her.

"Try."

First he'd attempt a diplomatic approach. "Your great-aunt was different."

A determined chin was raised an inch or two in the air. "People referred to her as Crazy Cora."

So Schuyler Grant was aware of the nickname. "Cora wasn't crazy," he stated in the woman's defense. "Although as she got older she became a bit more peculiar."

"We agree that my great-aunt marched to a very different drummer." His newest client took in a deep breath. "You still haven't explained."

"Cora also suffered from osteoarthritis."

"I'm aware of that."

Trace was taking his time getting to the point, but he needed to lay the groundwork. After all, Miss Grant hadn't seen her great-aunt in a number of years.

"Cora frequently mentioned not sleeping well at night, possibly the result of arthritis pain, possibly the normal sleep disruptions that can come with age."

Schuyler made an appropriate remark. "You seem to know a lot about older people."

"I represent a number of elderly clients," Trace explained. "Anyway, Cora's hearing and eyesight weren't what they once were. I suppose most of us can expect to suffer some decline in our faculties by the late eighties."

"I suppose we can," she agreed.

He might as well dive right in. "Sometimes Cora thought she saw and heard odd things."

"Odd things?"

Trace made a gesture in the general direction of the lawn that stretched all the way to the river's edge. "Lights flickering in the gazebo. Noises in the dead of night."

She sat forward. "What kind of noises?"

"Moaning, for one."

"Moaning?"

"Like some kind of wounded animal, according to Cora."

"And for another?"

"It was described to me as the sound of a pickaxe hitting metal," Trace related.

"Did anyone else ever see or hear anything?"

"No." Trace took a deep, sustaining breath before adding, "Cora also claimed to have seen Lucy."

"Lucy?"

"Your great-great-grandmother."

Fine nostrils flared. "Where?"

Where else? "Lucy's Lookout."

Schuyler Grant sat back and regarded him for a long time. "Was she senile?"

"I doubt it," he replied. "Lucy died at the relatively young age of forty-three."

"I meant Great-Aunt Cora."

Trace honestly believed the answer to that question was, "No."

"Was she delusionary?"

"I don't think she was. But she did retreat more and more often into the past."

Her sigh was a little sad, a little wistful. "Which isn't unusual for an elderly person."

"Not unusual at all."

" 'Lay the ghosts to rest.' " Schuyler Grant fell silent. Then she looked up at him. "May I ask you a question?"

"Of course."

She opened her mouth and then closed it again. Finally she blurted out, "Did Cora believe that Grantwood was haunted?"

Trace wasn't going to lie to her. "Yes," he said.

Chapter Six

So he did own a suit.

Schuyler had wondered what Trace—sometime in the past twenty-four hours she had stopped thinking of him as Mr. Ballinger—would be wearing today.

The memorial service for Cora had been crowded: standing room only. Schuyler had been seated in the front row of the chapel, and she hadn't gotten a good look at Trace until after they had returned to Grantwood for the buffet luncheon prepared by Mrs. Danvers.

At the moment her lawyer was on the other side of the Salon Louis XIII with its silk-covered walls and mingling of Dutch and Italian influences. He was standing beside a fireplace modeled after that of a sixteenth-century Venetian palazzo, with his back to her, talking to the minister and several of the other local residents.

He looked right at home.

One glance told Schuyler that Trace's suit had *not* been bought off the rack. The material was expensive and beautifully cut, and the jacket was precisely fitted to his broad shoulders, long, muscular arms and narrow waist.

Until this afternoon Trace Ballinger had appeared, at least sartorially, to be a cross between a cowboy and a Hell's Angel. Schuyler was amazed by how well the man cleaned up.

"Do you think the sandwiches are tuna fish?" came a quavery voice from directly behind her.

Schuyler turned.

"I'm allergic to tuna fish. One bite and I break out in

hives. Swell up like a balloon. Can't breathe. Probably drop dead. Otherwise I wouldn't care, you see."

She only hesitated briefly before speculating, "It's Mr. Barker, isn't it?"

Myopic eyes regarded her with less curiosity than the plate of suspect sandwiches. "Yip. I'm Geoffrey Barker. And who might you be, missy?"

She hadn't recognized the old gardener and obviously he hadn't recognized her, either. They had both changed a great deal since the days when her family had visited Grantwood.

Schuyler stood a little straighter, not that she had ever been one to slouch. "I'm Schuyler Grant, Cora's greatniece."

Using his cane for balance, the elderly man leaned precariously toward her. "You don't look anything like her."

Schuyler couldn't think of a response to this statement, so she answered his question instead. "The sandwiches you asked about are chicken salad. The ones at the other end of the buffet are salmon and cucumber and lobster salad."

"I'm not allergic to chicken or salmon or lobster," the retired gardener announced.

Schuyler wondered how he could manage the buffet table when he was already leaning heavily on his cane for support. "May I fix a plate of food for you, Mr. Barker?"

"Yip, you may," he replied with a perfunctory nod of his snowy-white head.

"What would you like to drink?"

"I'll have a whiskey. Straight. No ice." He wagged a gnarled finger at her. "Take my word for it, missy. That's the key to living to a ripe old age: avoid tuna fish and drink a shot of whiskey every day." With those words of wisdom, the elderly man made his way to an empty chair and plunked himself down.

Schuyler filled a plate with what she hoped Mr. Barker would regard as acceptable foods, poured a generous shot of whiskey into a crystal tumbler and delivered lunch to the octogenarian.

He tucked the linen napkin into the front of his tweed three-piece suit, stabbed a forkful of lobster salad and took a bite. Then he downed a good swig of his drink before declaring, "Mrs. Grant always did know how to throw a first-class shindig."

There wasn't much Schuyler could say to that. Naturally she'd never been to one of Cora's famed parties. That had been long before her time. Even before her parents' time. But not, apparently, before Geoffrey Barker's.

"I was never a guest at one of Mr. and Mrs. Grant's fancy affairs, mind you," he clarified, as if *not* to do so would be misrepresenting himself. "But I did set up the outside party tents, arrange the tables and chairs, string lights around the gazebo and along the garden pathways, even fetch and carry from the kitchen whenever we were a little short of help. Then at the end of the evening the staff was allowed to watch the fireworks from the south lawn." The old man thrust his head forward suddenly. "The fireworks were always my favorite part of the festivities," he said.

"How long have you been here at Grantwood, Mr. Barker?" Schuyler asked politely.

He considered his answer before speaking. "Going on seventy years. I was a lad of seventeen and low man on the totem pole back when I first hired on as a laborer." He muttered to himself, took another bite of lobster salad and another healthy swig of his whiskey. "In those days it required at least thirty of us to keep up with the grounds. Of course, we didn't have all the fancy equipment they use around here today. We did everything by hand. It was back-breaking work, I'll tell you."

Ground Zero had much to answer for, Schuyler decided.

After the last drop of whiskey had disappeared, Geoffrey Barker handed over his plate and empty glass, and proudly struggled to his feet, declining her offer of assistance. He balanced on his cane, looked around the roomful of chattering people and said bemusedly, "Don't suppose this is the time or the place to discuss plans for her private garden with Mrs. Grant."

Schuyler stared straight into the old man's eyes. His gaze seemed fixed on some distant horizon she couldn't see. "Great-Aunt Cora's private garden?"

He smacked his lips together. "That's the one. We've got to get started if she wants the garden ready for the summer season." Then the retired head gardener lowered his voice. "Can you keep a secret, young lady?"

"Yes."

He moved his snowy head up and down several times. "You look like the kind who can. You're not all fluttery and flighty like so many of these modern young females."

"Thank you."

He dropped his voice to a confidential level. "Mr. Grant has created a special surprise for his wife's birthday. Only a few of us know anything about it and we're sworn to secrecy."

Schuyler waited and she listened.

Eighty-seven-year-old Geoffrey Barker seemed pleased with himself as he went on with his story. "After all, it isn't every day the mistress of Grantwood turns thirty."

Schuyler gave a small sigh and agreed with him. "No. It isn't every day."

He chuckled and poked her with a bony elbow. "Her wish is about to come true, if you get my drift?"

"I'm afraid I don't get your drift," she confessed, setting his plate and glass down on the nearest available surface, which happened to be a rare eighteenth-century Italian commode.

Her companion was practically whispering. "The lady has always wanted a wishing well."

Schuyler knew her expression was one of puzzlement. "A wishing well?"

Geoffrey Barker raised a shaky finger to his pencil-thin lips. "Shush, missy. It's a secret."

"I won't tell anyone," she promised.

His distress was visible. "Be sure you don't or it will mean my job," he warned her.

"Rest assured, your secret is safe with me, Mr. Barker," Schuyler told him.

Geoffrey Barker gave a satisfied nod of his head. "The master has had a wishing well built in the middle of the mistress's private garden. It's been quite a challenge, I'll tell you. The work had to be done without her knowledge." Then he stated matter-of-factly, "Well, I'd better be on my way home. I walk a little slower than I used to."

"Thank you for coming, Mr. Barker."

"Give my best regards to Mrs. Grant." The old gardener paused and rubbed a hand along the side of his ruddy cheek. "But she's dead, isn't she?"

"Yes. She is."

"Then my best regards to you, Miss Grant," he said with another respectful nod.

Schuyler saw him to the door, where his nephew was waiting, before returning to her other guests.

"Did you choose the Edna St. Vincent Millay poem, Ms. Grant?" inquired one of the Frick sisters as Schuyler made her way around the group still socializing in the salon.

"No. I didn't."

Schuyler's denial was ignored. "You obviously feel the same way about Millay's poetry as I do," declared the tall and painfully thin Miss Frick.

Schuyler inquired with a carefully straight face, "How do you feel about her poetry?"

"I adore it," Ellamae Frick enthused. "It makes me feel sad and a little melancholy. What better way to feel than sad and melancholy when one is attending a funeral?"

"A memorial service," Schuyler amended.

" 'The soul can split the sky in two,' " Ellamae Frick quoted with a definite flair for the dramatic. She went on with apparent delight, "Yes, indeed, Cora would have approved of your choice of poems for her funeral service, Ms. Grant."

"Thank you," she said, recognizing defeat when it stared her in the face.

Another creature appeared between them. The newcomer was as soft and round as Miss Ellamae Frick was hard and angular. She was also a good six or seven inches shorter than her sibling. "Have you asked Ms. Grant to tea, sister?"

"We were discussing Edna St. Vincent Millay's poetry, my dear Ida, not refreshments."

"The refreshments are delectable," twittered the shorter Frick. "Don't miss the lobster salad at the far end of the buffet table. Delicious. Absolutely delicious." Ida Frick peered at Schuyler over the rim of her bifocals. "Is it your own recipe, my dear?"

"No. It isn't."

"I must have the recipe. That is, if you don't mind giving it to me. You're not one of those cooks who insists on secrecy and keeps all your wonderful recipes to yourself, are you? You do share them with other like-minded gourmands?"

Schuyler was defeated twice in as many minutes. "I

would be happy to give you my recipe for lobster salad, Miss Frick."

"Did you hear that, sister?" The rather round woman dressed in layers of funereal black was positively quivering with excitement. "Ms. Grant is going to share her recipe with me." Fleshy pink hands were clasped together in front of a more than ample bosom. "How generous. How magnanimous. How simply marvelous." Miss Ida Frick suddenly paused and frowned. "Oh, dear, what was I saying before I was interrupted?"

"You were saying that we must invite Ms. Grant to tea," prompted Ellamae.

"And that handsome Mr. Ballinger Cora was always so partial to. He must come, as well." Apparently Ida Frick had the habit of changing the subject without giving the slightest warning. "Are you related, my dear?"

Schuyler was confused. "To whom?"

The woman's eyes blinked rapidly behind her bifocals. "To Mr. Ballinger, of course."

"No. I'm not."

There was no stopping this Miss Frick, either. "Since the man's surname is Ballinger and not Grant, he must be a cousin from the other side."

Schuyler opened her mouth and then shut it again. If she couldn't fight them, she may as well join them.

"Speaking of which," began Ida Frick, gazing up at her young hostess expectantly, "I wonder when Cora will contact us."

"Contact us?"

"From the other side."

Schuyler was more than confused; she was confounded. "The other side of what?" she asked.

"Why, this earthly plane, of course."

Ellamae felt it was necessary to point out, "Perhaps Ms. Grant isn't a believer, sister."

"Perhaps not yet," came Ida's reply. "Shall we say a week from Thursday at four o'clock, then?"

"A week from Thursday?"

"For tea?"

Schuyler was nonplussed. "I'll check with Mr. Ballinger and give you a ring, shall I?"

"That would be most kind." Miss Ida Frick hovered nervously. "You won't forget the recipe for lobster salad."

"I won't forget," she reassured the woman.

Schuyler breathed a genuine sigh of relief as the Frick sisters headed toward the buffet table. What she really wanted about now, she realized, was a large, stiff drink. Perhaps Mr. Barker was right about the shot of whiskey.

"My God, it can't be," came a smooth, cultured male voice from somewhere above her left shoulder.

She turned.

"It is you," he declared.

She frowned.

"You're all grown up, cousin."

Schuyler stood and stared at the gorgeous man in front of her. He was tall and tanned, blond-haired and brown-eyed, beautifully groomed and beautifully dressed. How could she have forgotten how beautiful he was?

"Johnny!" she exclaimed.

He smiled at her. "Who else?"

"Johnny," she repeated, breaking into a smile herself.

"How long has it been, Schuyler?"

She couldn't take her eyes off him. "Nine years."

A slight frown momentarily marred the otherwise flawless features. "That long?"

"That long." Schuyler knew exactly. It had been at the memorial service for her parents and Kit.

Johnny stepped back and made a production of looking her over. Almost as if he were waving a wand, he gestured with his hand. "Living in Paris agrees with you."

"It does."

Johnny Grant's admiration was very appreciative and very male. "You're very French," he stated as if he would know. "Very soignée. Very chic."

She was dressed in a simple black dress with simple black pumps on her feet, and carrying a simple black handbag. The dress was Gucci couturier. The shoes and handbag were Prada. The price tag on the outfit was nearly as much as the simple black Jaguar still parked in the garage outside.

"As are you," she said, wanting to laugh for the first time in a long time. She moved closer to her distant cousin and lowered her voice to a whisper. "Johnny, are you normal?"

His expression was priceless. One elegant eyebrow arched. "Is anyone?"

"You know what I mean," she mouthed.

Understanding dawned. "Ah, I see you've met the inimitable Frick sisters."

"Yes."

He gave a little private laugh and suggested, "A bit eccentric, aren't they?"

"Hmm."

"One might even say otherworldly."

"One might."

"Have they invited you to tea yet?" he inquired, his dark brown eyes shining with humor.

Her answer was a wary, "Yes."

Johnny knew something she didn't. Schuyler could see it in his expression.

"Then you'll be plied with delectable cakes and confectioneries, have your ear talked off and perhaps take part in a séance. You may get even get to meet the Fricks' brother, Theodore. Teddy for short," he informed her, one hand at the waist of his expensive and impeccably tailored suit.

Schuyler had no choice but to press the point. "What does Teddy do?"

Her cousin was enjoying himself. "As far as I know, he collects things."

"Things?"

"Funguses. Or is it fungi?" Jonathan Grant ruminated. Apparently her handsome cousin decided he had teased her long enough. "Actually Teddy Frick is some kind of botanist. Well respected in local academic circles, from what I gather."

Schuyler breathed a sigh of relief. "Oh."

Apparently Johnny was going to make amends for needling her. "I know what you need right now."

"What?"

There was that irresistible smile again. "A reassuring hug, a cousinly kiss and a promise to fetch you a drink."

"You're not normal, Johnny," Schuyler declared, slipping her arm through his. "You're perfect."

Chapter Seven

Okay, so maybe he should have warned her about the Frick sisters, Trace realized belatedly.

But it wasn't as if the word *eccentric* were new to Schuyler's vocabulary. Besides, she was a big girl now. A woman, to be absolutely accurate and politically correct. A woman who had been on her own since the age of twenty. She could take care of herself.

If she couldn't, the golden-haired Adonis taking her into his arms seemed perfectly willing to help.

Trace watched as the strikingly handsome man smiled down into Schuyler's eyes and said something that made her smile in return. Then he planted a kiss on her cheek, missing her mouth by less than a fraction of an inch.

It didn't take a Philadelphia lawyer (and it sure as hell wouldn't take a New York lawyer) to figure out whose face was behind the Rolex smile: Jonathan Tiberius Grant.

Cousin Johnny.

Trace realized he was scowling. He settled a neutral expression on his face and reminded himself it was none of his business.

Not true.

Everything about Schuyler Grant was his business.

Cora had made it his business.

He had made it his business.

"You don't appear to be a happy man, Mr. Ballinger," someone said very close by.

Trace recognized Grantwood's next-door neighbor. "This isn't exactly a happy occasion, Mr. Coffin."

"Cora would disagree with you." Adam Coffin, gaunt of face and physique—more than one observer had remarked that he was appropriately named—came up and stood beside Trace. For a minute, perhaps longer, the two men observed the gathering of friends and neighbors. "Cora liked nothing better than a party."

Trace refused to alter his opinion. "I wouldn't exactly call this a party."

The sixty-something gentleman took a drink from what appeared to be a glass of tomato juice. "I suppose the occasion is missing a few key ingredients."

A few?

"Cora never hosted a single party, not even a dinner party, in the eight years I knew her," Trace stated. "In fact, she preferred to eat in the kitchen."

Adam Coffin gave his nearly bald head a shake. "That's because she was old and alone by the time you met her, Mr. Ballinger. I remember the gala affairs Cora and her husband used to throw here at Grantwood in the estate's heyday. I was just a boy, of course, so I wasn't invited. But my parents were always on the guest list." He chuckled; it came out sounding like a snort. "Still, I was a resourceful little bugger. Where there's a will there's a way."

"A way of what?" Trace asked, taking a sip of plain club soda with a twist of lime and keeping one eye on Schuyler and Johnny Grant even as Adam Coffin reminisced.

"Crashing a party."

Trace looked sideways at him. "You were a party crasher?"

"Yes," came the rather proud reply.

"How old were you?"

"Seven or eight." The man polished off his juice and

then proceeded to roll the glass back and forth between his palms. "I don't suppose you believe me."

Considering what he'd been up to at the age of seven or eight, Trace figured crashing an adult party was pure kid's stuff. "As a matter of fact, I do believe you."

It was another minute before Adam Coffin commented, "Cora was always partial to men in general and him in particular."

"Who in particular?"

A gesture was made in the general direction of the re-uniting cousins. "Johnny."

She'd never said anything personal to Trace about her distant relation. "Really?"

"Cora often mentioned how charming and how witty Johnny was, what good company he could be." Adam stared down into his empty glass as if he weren't sure how it had gotten that way. "At least when he was younger."

"I take it he hasn't been around much lately."

"Now and then. From all accounts, Jonathan Grant is pretty much wrapped up in his business ventures."

Trace could hardly find fault with that. "Exactly what are his business ventures?"

"The usual. Investments. Banking. Real Estate." Adam Coffin shrugged his thin shoulders. "Whatever the rich do to become even richer." They both studied the nattily attired man across the room. "Johnny appears to be doing well for himself."

"Clothes don't necessarily make the man," Trace observed.

"True," Adam said in response. Then he gingerly put one hand into the pocket of his jacket. "I wonder if Johnny's still in her will," he speculated, thinking out loud.

Trace didn't react.

His companion reddened in the face. "Sorry, Ballinger.

'I wasn't fishing for information. I simply forgot for a moment that you were Cora's lawyer."

"No problem."

He still didn't take the hint and drop the subject. "I suppose we'll know soon enough."

Trace was noncommittal. "I suppose we will."

"After all, Johnny likes expensive clothes and fast cars and beautiful women," was the other man's frank appraisal.

Most men did.

"Or at least he used to. I wonder if Cora had any plans for the two of them," speculated the older man.

Trace was interested. "The two of them?"

"Johnny and Schuyler. He's still single. She's back from France. The rich tend to marry the rich. And there's nothing to stand in their way."

Trace didn't move a muscle. "They're cousins."

Adam Coffin moved his head from side to side. "Distant cousins. Removed at least three or four times, according to what Cora told me." Then the man sighed and brushed at something on his cheek. "I'm going to miss Cora. She was the only friend I had after my parents passed away. Except for Moose, of course."

"Moose?"

"My dog."

"I have a dog."

Adam's first question was: "What breed?"

Trace set his glass down and unbuttoned his coat. The Salon Louis XIII was getting a bit warm and stuffy for his preference—or maybe it was the damned suit. "Buddy is half golden retriever. I'm not altogether sure what the other half is."

"Buddy was a stray?"

"Yup."

"So was Moose, in a manner of speaking." Grantwood's

neighbor launched into his story. "I'd gone into town for groceries. On the drive back I happened to spot a brown paper bag lying discarded along the side of the road. I still don't know why I decided to stop my car, let alone open the sack and look inside. But there was Moose. He was just a puppy. A puppy somebody had thrown away like a piece of unwanted trash." Adam's voice was filled with disbelief. "I took him home with me. Stayed up with him all night the first night. Wasn't sure he was going to make it, but he did. That was five years ago and we've been together ever since."

Trace was only half joking when he suggested, "You should bring Moose over sometime to meet Buddy. We run a couple of miles every morning."

Adam Coffin got the strangest expression on his face. "Moose is right here."

Trace's mouth twisted into a wry smile. "Right where?"

Adam moved his hand, the hand he'd gingerly inserted into the pocket of his suit jacket. A moment later a tiny, nearly hairless and definitely gaunt head emerged.

The old saying about dogs and their owners looking alike popped into Trace's head. After clearing his throat several times, he ventured, "Moose is a . . ."

"Chihuahua."

Chapter Eight

Schuyler rolled over, opened her eyes and stared at the clock on the bedside table.

Three A.M.

It was in the wee, small hours of the night and she was wide awake.

She reminded herself that if she were still in Paris she'd already be up and on her way to her office at the museum, stopping just around the corner from the Louvre at a small café that served hot coffee and mouthwatering *pain d'épices*.

But she wasn't in Paris. She was in New York—in the New York countryside, to be precise—and in New York it was the middle of the night.

Unfortunately, Schuyler recognized the signs that indicated she wouldn't be falling back to sleep anytime soon.

She pushed herself up straight in the four-poster bed and fussed with the pile of pillows at her back. Once she had made herself as comfortable as possible, she gave a small sigh and stared into the moonlit room.

She'd always felt safe and happy in the Yellow Room; named, at least in part, for the yellow silk covering the walls and the black and yellow patterned antique French carpet on the floor.

The rest of the decor was set off with a suite of extraordinarily detailed French Empire furniture, originally a gift from Napoleon I to Maréchal Soult. There was an equestrian painting by Alfred Dedreux, in the English manner, hanging above an ornate commode, and a double portrait by Hesse above the bed. The Hesse depicted two sisters and had always been one of Schuyler's favorite paintings in the family's art collection.

On sunny days the Yellow Room was especially bright and cheerful. There was a row of floor-to-ceiling, south-fronting windows opposite the bed, and a splendid view of the gardens and the expanse of green lawn all the way to the river.

By moonlight, however, the room took on an entirely different atmosphere.

Darker, denser.

Moodier.

More sensual.

Suddenly restless, Schuyler tossed the covers aside, slipped out of bed and padded barefoot across to one of the oversize windows. She hadn't bothered closing the drapes. Now she pushed back the diaphanous undercurtains as well.

The night was clear. The moon was full. A midnight-blue sky was filled with stars.

From this vantage point she had an unobstructed view of the formal garden with the gazebo at its center, and beyond to the Hudson River and the rocky outcropping known as Lucy's Lookout.

Cora claimed she had seen Lucy.

Schuyler didn't believe that her great-aunt had suffered from dementia at the end of her life, and neither did Trace Ballinger. But the mind could play tricks on the young and the old alike. Sometimes you saw and heard what you wanted—what you *needed*—to see and hear.

Brushing a stray wisp of hair back from her face, Schuyler leaned forward and pressed her cheek against the windowpane. Her reflection stared back at her, eyes huge and dark, pale skin appearing even paler in the wash of moonlight.

She and Cora had seldom, if ever, seen eye to eye. Perhaps that was the reason her great-aunt had always kept her at arm's length. It was Cora who had encouraged Schuyler to return to Paris after the tragic boat accident. In fact, it was Cora who had insisted that she remain in France.

Yet, when it was all said and done, Schuyler discovered, family was family.

"I give you my word, Cora," she whispered. "I will stay until the ghosts are laid to rest."

Not that she believed in ghosts.

It was at that precise moment Schuyler thought she heard something. She cocked her head to one side and listened. There it was again.

Maybe it was simply the wind in the trees. Maybe it was a branch rubbing against the house, or a small nocturnal animal in the nearby thicket known as Grant's Wood.

It was an eerie sound.

A kind of *un*human sound.

Then Schuyler saw a strange flash of light. It came from the direction of the gazebo.

There was another flash of light.

And another.

What the blue blazes was going on?

Cora had claimed to see and hear unusual things. Now, after being back at Grantwood for less than seventy-two hours, so was she. Was it a coincidence? Schuyler wasn't certain she believed in coincidences. It was almost as if somebody were playing games.

She detested games.

Dropping the curtains back into place, she crossed the Yellow Room, reached for her bathrobe, slid her feet into a pair of slippers she'd left beside the bed, grabbed her umbrella (it was the closest thing to a weapon readily at hand) and made her way out of the bedroom and along the center hallway.

There was the distinctive blue floral wallpaper and the now-familiar third door on the right. In less than ten minutes Schuyler was downstairs, had the alarm system disarmed and the deadbolt unlocked on the kitchen door.

When she had lost everyone of importance to her on that catastrophic day nine years ago, Schuyler had become a different person.

These were the painful truths she had learned. The past could not be changed. The future—the very next moment, even the very next breath—was promised to no one. The present was all anyone had, and the present was only *this* moment and *this* breath. That knowledge had given her a certain fatalism about life, Schuyler supposed, and a certain fearlessness.

She wasn't afraid as she set out to investigate the strange noises and the odd flashes of light. She walked briskly in the direction of the garden. She watched the treetops swaying in the moonlight. She took a deep breath and filled her lungs with cool night air. She gazed up at the stars in wonder.

She watched and she listened. A light flickered briefly near the gazebo and then suddenly went out. The strange sound came again, farther away this time.

"Silly, childish games," Schuyler declared aloud.

She reached down and opened her umbrella, settled it on her shoulder and twirled the tortoiseshell handle around and around in her hands.

Trace wasn't sure what had awakened him. One minute he had been sound asleep, the next he was wide awake.

"What the . . . ?" he grumbled as he pushed himself up on his elbows.

Buddy opened one eye, stared at him for a second and then went back to sleep.

The bedsheets were wound tightly around Trace's thighs, practically cutting off his circulation. He worked himself free, threw the covers off and stood up.

His reflection stared back at him from the full-length mirror on the bathroom door. In the moonlight he could see a naked man, skin glistening with sweat, dark hair matted to his chest and an erection rising from a thatch of thick dark hair between his thighs.

"You need to get a life, Ballinger," he muttered to himself. "Any kind of life."

Especially a sex life.

He padded across to the bathroom, grabbed a towel off the antique brass rack beside the shower and vigorously rubbed himself down until he was dry.

Driving his fingers through the hair at his nape, Trace exhaled on a curse. "Christ, how long has it been, anyway?"

Too long.

Ridiculously long.

Depressingly long.

During the past twenty-odd years there had been a few women in his life. (Fewer and fewer as he had gotten older and wiser.) He'd even been engaged once for a few months after accepting the job offer from Dutton, Dutton, McQuade & Martin. But Miranda had soon discovered that he was dead serious when he'd told her that his career came first, second and third, and a meaningful relationship with any woman, including her, a distant fourth. Eventually Miranda had given up on him and moved on to another up-and-coming young attorney at the firm.

Not that Trace blamed her.

His basic philosophy about the opposite sex was a simple and straightforward one: When it came to a woman—

any woman—a man was damned if he did and he was
damned if he didn't. It was a no-win situation.

Trace draped the towel around his neck, stalked across
the bedroom and stood in front of the window. He planted
his feet and gazed out at the moonlit night, absently rubbing
one hand back and forth along his jawline.

Funny, but he couldn't seem to remember what Miranda
looked like anymore.

Reaching for the carafe of water on a nearby table, Trace
poured himself a glass—half of the water spilled onto his
chest—raised it to his lips and drank thirstily. He took in
a deep breath and then slowly released it.

It was at that moment something in his peripheral vision
caught his attention. He froze with the glass in his hand.
Someone—or something—was making his or her way
across the lawn toward the gazebo. For an instant his heart
stopped beating.

Lucy.

Then he realized it was a flesh-and-blood woman. She
was dressed in a bathrobe with her hair flowing down her
back and she was twirling an umbrella.

It was Schuyler.

Trace craned his neck for a better view. He watched as
she strolled across the expanse of lush green lawn and under the natural arbor of topiary yews that led into the garden.

"What the hell is she up to?" he muttered under his
breath, finishing off the glass of water.

It could be a million different things. All right, half a
dozen. Maybe she was an insomniac. Or maybe she'd simply felt like some fresh air. Or maybe she had an illicit
midnight rendezvous.

Okay, so it was closer to three-thirty, but she could be
on her way to meet a man, a man like slick Johnny.

That didn't make any sense, of course. Schuyler didn't have to sneak around in the wee hours to have a liaison with Jonathan Tiberius Grant. She could get together with her cousin at any hour of the day or night.

So what was she doing?

It was none of his beeswax, Trace reminded himself as he climbed back into bed, turned over, gave his pillow a good punch or two and shut his eyes.

Five minutes passed.

Then another five.

Shit.

Trace threw back the covers and sat up on the edge of the mattress. He wasn't going to be able to fall asleep knowing that Schuyler was out there wandering around the estate on her own in the middle of the night.

Reaching for the pair of blue jeans and the shirt he'd tossed over a nearby chair earlier that evening, he quickly dressed. He thrust his bare feet into his running shoes; he didn't bother doing up the laces.

That quickly Buddy was awake. The golden retriever jumped down from the bed, trotted to the door and sat down to await his running partner, his tail thumping on the floor.

"This isn't fun and games time, Buddy," Trace warned his faithful canine companion.

But Buddy's tail only thumped faster.

Chapter Nine

There wasn't anyone in or around the gazebo. There was no sign of footprints on the garden path; no incriminating evidence lying about on the ground; no fingerprints visible on the white wooden railing encircling the structure.

Whoever had been here had come and gone.

Pressing the button at the base of the tortoiseshell handle, Schuyler neatly compressed her umbrella to one-third its opened size. Then she walked up the short flight of stairs and entered the gazebo.

The gazebo was constructed before the turn of the century—in those days there had been a small army of servants to fetch and carry from the main house—and the Grant women had entertained guests here nearly every summer afternoon.

Dressed in white muslin dresses and wearing straw hats with pastel ribbons floating down the back, they had sipped tea from wafer-thin porcelain cups, nibbled on delicacies served on the finest imported china and sat on heirloom furniture shipped to the Americas from historic castles along the Thames, the Rhine and the Seine.

It was called the Gilded Age: a time of conspicuous and unapologetic consumption, of competitive ostentation, a time to make and more importantly *spend* great fortunes.

The gazebo was empty now except for a few wooden benches added at a later date. Schuyler sat down on a bench, kicked off her damp slippers and tucked her feet up under her.

Someone entered the garden.

She knew instantly it was Trace. He came toward her through the night and her heart began to beat in double time. She couldn't seem to catch her breath. Every nerve ending in her body was on alert. A trickle of perspiration slid down her back and into the hollow at the base of her spine.

"Quelle bêtise!" Schuyler muttered under her breath.

This was ridiculous. She wasn't some young, impressionable girl. She was a mature woman. And Trace was a man just like any other man, although she had to admit she couldn't recall ever having this reaction to a man before.

What was it about Trace Ballinger that set him apart?

On some instinctive level she knew what it was. He was intelligent, even brilliant, yet he was also as tough as nails and deep down inside a little uncivilized. Maybe more than a little. Schuyler had a hunch that when Trace saw what he wanted, he went after it with a vengeance and with single-minded intensity.

He'd apparently left the house in something of a hurry tonight. His shirt was unbuttoned. His shoelaces were untied. His hair was uncombed and his face unshaven.

And he wasn't smiling.

Without preamble he said, "Do you have any idea what time it is?"

Schuyler glanced at her wrist. "I'm not wearing a watch, but I suppose it's around three-thirty."

He wasn't amused.

As Buddy romped in the dewy grass, Trace took an uncompromising stance at the bottom of the steps and positioned his arms across his chest. "Would you care to explain?"

Schuyler raised one shoulder in a dismissive gesture. "Explain what?"

He looked right at her. "What you're doing out here at this ungodly hour?"

Her response was terse. "No, as a matter of fact, I wouldn't care to explain."

Without warning he changed the subject. It was no doubt a tactic he'd learned in the courtroom to catch an unsuspecting witness off guard. "You're carrying an umbrella."

"I am."

Trace raised his face to the sky and held out his hand, palm up. "It isn't raining."

"Unlike the first time we met," she recounted, moistening her lips with her tongue.

His gaze fixed on her. "You were telling the truth."

"About what?"

Taking the steps two at a time, he joined her in the gazebo. "There was another vehicle."

Schuyler tried not to be smug about it. "I told you someone rear-ended my car."

His lips disappeared. "I know." He didn't mince words. "I believe you. I also believe it was deliberate."

She made a sound that signaled her agitation. "Well, of course it was deliberate. Nobody rams into the back of another automobile three times by accident. Maybe it was a carjacker after the Jaguar," she speculated in a husky voice, a tiny frog having suddenly lodged itself in her throat.

"Maybe." His eyes were dark, dark blue. "Or maybe you were the intended target."

She cleared her throat. "Are you suggesting that someone followed me from the airport all the way to Rhinebeck in order to force my car off the road?"

Trace paced back and forth. She noticed that his long legs carried him the length of the gazebo in five easy strides. He stopped and turned. "It's possible."

She was curious. "Possible, but scarcely probable. Besides, who would want to do a thing like that?"

"I don't know," he admitted, propping first one foot and then the other on the edge of the wooden bench, and leaning over to tie his shoelaces.

Schuyler went on. "If you're trying to frighten me, you aren't succeeding."

Trace straightened. "Too bad."

"Too bad?"

"I was hoping next time you'd think twice before summarily dismissing the hired car and driver." He changed the subject again. "So what are you doing out here in the middle of the night?"

She almost didn't tell him, but in the end she confessed, "I thought I saw something."

Masculine brows shot up. "Something?"

She gnawed on her bottom lip. "A flicker of light."

He frowned. "Where?"

Schuyler fidgeted with the tie on her bathrobe, intensely aware of Trace, of the imposing figure he made, standing tall in the light velvet blackness of the night. "Here."

"Let me get this straight. You spot a light in the gazebo at three o'clock in the morning. It's of unknown origin. As a matter of fact, it could be just about anyone or anything. And your first response is to run outside to investigate."

He was wrong. She corrected him. "I didn't run outside. I walked."

In a superior, and thoroughly masculine, tone of voice, he said to her, "Either way, doesn't that strike you as a bit foolish?"

"I don't like games," she stated.

"You think someone is playing games."

"I do."

Trace paused and considered what she'd said, then

shook his head slowly. "In that case, hasn't it occurred to you that they could be dangerous games?"

Trace didn't know if he wanted to throttle Schuyler or kiss her to within an inch of her life.

She was intelligent, yet she took unnecessary risks. She was naive for all her fancy-schmancy education and supposed European sophistication. She had a certain fearlessness that made him afraid for her. He liked to think of himself as a patient man, but she tried his patience to the limit. In fact, she was a damned aggravating woman.

She was also irresistible.

Yup, before it was all said and done, he'd either throttle her or kiss her.

"Not one of your better ideas, Ballinger," he muttered under his breath.

Schuyler spoke up. "I beg your pardon?"

"I said, coming out here in the middle of the night wasn't one of your better ideas."

"You can go back inside the house anytime," she pointed out. "No one is stopping you."

"Sure they are."

Schuyler's nose was raised in the air. She sniffed. "I can take care of myself. I have for a long time now."

He cast her a sidelong glance and showed his teeth. "Actually, I was thinking of Buddy."

She laughed.

Trace relaxed his stance and his shoulders. "So you do have a sense of humor."

"Doesn't everyone?" she said on a note of unsuppressed amusement.

"Nope."

Schuyler leaned forward and unself-consciously wrapped her arms around her legs: legs that had caught his attention right from the start, legs that he could see even with his damned eyes closed, legs that he suspected he'd fantasize about for a long time to come.

"Give me a for-instance of someone without a sense of humor," she said, challenging him.

Right off the top of his head Trace had an example for her. "Miss Frick."

She knitted her brows. "Which Miss Frick?"

"Either one."

Schuyler laughed again. He realized he liked the sound of her laughter. It was spontaneous and uninhibited and utterly feminine, like the woman herself.

"You're right," she acknowledged, tucking the hem of her bathrobe around her bare toes.

Trace plunked down on the bench beside her. "It's nice to hear a woman admit she's wrong."

Apparently she wasn't going to concede defeat that easily. "The fact that you're right doesn't necessarily make me wrong," she insisted. It was a subtle distinction, but a distinction nonetheless. "You should have warned me, you know."

He played dumb. "About what?"

She turned her head and rested her chin on bent knees. "Not about what. About whom."

"Okay, about whom?"

"Miss Frick."

"Which Miss Frick?"

"Both of them."

This time Trace laughed out loud. "You're right. I should have warned you."

She apprised him of the situation. "They've invited us to tea a week from Thursday."

"The Miss Fricks?"

She nodded.

Trace made a face. "Do we have to go?"

Schuyler huddled down into her cashmere bathrobe. "Under the circumstances, I don't see how we can refuse."

His surrender was swift and unconditional. "I suppose you're right."

She gave him an appraising look. "The Frick sisters seem to think we're related."

"You mean like you and"—Trace caught himself before he said the word *slick* in front of her cousin's name— "Johnny?"

"They didn't say, actually."

Then she shivered.

Trace noticed. "Cold?"

"Yes," she admitted.

He stood up, pulled off his shirt, reached over and draped it around her shoulders.

Schuyler moved her head, dislodging a wisp of hair, and protested. "You'll get cold."

"No, I won't."

Trace knew his shirt was still warm from his body heat. He watched as she snuggled down into the soft material and murmured, "Hm, it's smells just like you."

He heard himself asking, "What do I smell like?"

To his surprise, Schuyler began to tell him. "Kind of woodsy, kind of outdoorsy. I suppose it's the aftershave you use." She took another sniff. "Good, clean, old-fashioned soap smell, a hint of something I can't quite place and maybe a trace of Buddy." That quickly the golden retriever came lumbering up into the gazebo and poked his head under her hand.

Trace watched his dog practically swoon at Schuyler's feet when she reached over and began to scratch behind his ears. "You're a pushover for a beautiful woman, aren't you, Buddy?" he commented.

He could tell Schuyler was pleased by the compliment.

"How long have you and Buddy been together?" she inquired, patting the dog.

Trace attempted to keep his answer casual and failed. "Longer than most marriages I know of."

Her voice was suddenly softer. "How long is that?"

"A couple of years," he said with a small stoic laugh.

It was logical and natural for her to ask, "Have you ever been married?"

He stared in the direction of the river, picturing the ripples of moonlight on its silvery surface. "Nope." His gaze came back and found hers waiting for him. "How about you?"

Her reply was succinct. "No."

As long as they were on the subject of relationships, "Ever been engaged?"

"I nearly was once or twice, but no, I've never been officially engaged." She crooked an eyebrow.

"Once," he answered, knowing full well that was the information she was seeking from him.

She was curious. "What happened?"

He decided to satisfy her curiosity. "Miranda wanted to be number one in my life."

"And Miranda wasn't?"

"In those days I was busting my butt at the firm, trying to work my way out of the rock-bottom ranks at Dutton, Dutton, McQuade & Martin. What do you think?"

"I think you've worked very hard to get where you are," Schuyler said simply. "Any regrets?"

"None."

"Then you obviously made the right decision."

Trace threw caution to the wind. "Anyone special waiting for you back in Paris?"

Schuyler shook her head and then confirmed her single

status by saying, "No one special." Her statement was quickly rescinded. "No one human, that is. My two cats would be devastated to hear me say they aren't special. The French love their pets, you know. Especially their dogs." A knowing smile appeared on her face. "Which is why you must always look *down* when you're walking in Paris."

Trace chuckled. "I'll have to remember that if I ever get to Paris. Did you know Adam Coffin was carrying his dog around in his coat pocket at the luncheon this afternoon?"

"It must be a small dog."

"Moose is a Chihuahua." Trace went on, "Adam told me that he found him in a paper sack dumped along the side of the road."

"Moose is one of the lucky ones, then." She scratched Buddy under his chin. "Where did you find Buddy?"

"Buddy found me."

"Where did he find you?"

"Central Park. He followed me home. I let him stay. The rest, as they say, is history."

Schuyler turned a beautifully innocent gaze on him. "You have a good heart, Trace Ballinger."

He wanted to warn her: *Lady, I don't have a heart at all*. But he kept his mouth shut and ran a hand back and forth across his bare abdomen, maybe more from habit than anything else.

She was obviously trying to keep the quiver out of her voice. "I wish you'd take your shirt back."

"They say be careful what you wish for; you just might get it," Trace reminded her.

She shivered again.

"Still cold?"

"Yes."

"Do you want to return to the house?"

She sunk her teeth into her bottom lip and shook her head. "No. Do you?"

"I'm not the one who's half frozen," he observed.

A man was damned if he did and he was damned if he didn't.

Trace heard himself urging her, "You can move over next to me if you want. My body heat will keep you warm."

Schuyler hesitated, but not for more than a heartbeat or two. Then she scooted across the wooden bench and snuggled up beside him. He casually looped his arm around her.

"Hm, you are toasty warm," she murmured appreciatively, nestling closer.

He reached up to unsnag a strand of fine auburn hair that had caught on his beard stubble. "Told you so."

A muffled, "Why?"

"Why am I always so warm?"

Her head moved.

"Runner's metabolism," was his conjecture.

He inhaled a deep breath of night air and Schuyler's scent came with it. She smelled faintly of the wine they'd had at dinner. She smelled of something seductive, exotic and vaguely floral; no doubt some absurdly expensive French perfume. And she smelled of the April night and the April moonlight.

Maybe this wasn't his best idea. But then again, it wasn't his worst idea, either.

There was the old adage about fools rushing in where angels feared to tread. Trace acknowledged that he had been many things in his thirty-eight—almost thirty-nine—years, and an angel sure as hell wasn't one of them. But, at least up until now, he hadn't made a fool of himself too often. He had a feeling that was about to change.

He slowly turned Schuyler around in his arms and gazed down into eyes that went from a warm brown color to brilliant green to hot molten gold.

Then he kissed her.

Chapter Ten

Here was the real danger.

Not the mysterious flicker of light in the gazebo. Not the strange noise coming from the nearby woods. Not even the crazed driver who had run her off the road two nights ago.

But this man.

The moment Trace's lips touched hers, Schuyler realized she was in over her head. She had always been the one in control when it came to her relationships with men. Well, she wasn't in control now. In fact, she suddenly existed in a universe that was spiraling out of control. She felt as if she were free-falling without a parachute, as though she were balancing on a high wire and there was no safety net beneath her.

It was Trace's warmth keeping her from the cold. It was his smell filling her nostrils. It was his touch causing the tiny hairs at the back of her neck to stand straight on end, making her aware of the slightest change in the pressure of his hand, sending shivers down her spine and raising goose bumps on her flesh.

It was his taste on her lips, his taste on her tongue, his taste invading every particle of her brain.

She had no brain.

She couldn't think.

She could only feel.

Schuyler had never cared for games. She quickly recognized that this wasn't a game. This was very real. She had never been kissed so single-mindedly, so thoroughly, so completely, in her entire twenty-nine years.

Trace Ballinger was a man like no other man she had ever met. His kiss was like no other kiss she had ever experienced.

His mouth was perfect.

His lips were perfect.

His kiss was perfect.

Schuyler didn't make a habit of kissing strangers, or even men she knew well. Not like this. Not with her lips parted. Not as if she were starved and his mouth offered the only sustenance. Not as though she required his breath in her lungs in order to breathe. Not with her breasts straining against the front of her bathrobe even as they were flattened against his body.

She was warm. She was hot. She was burning up. The flames of desire licked at her flesh, teasing her, tantalizing her, consuming her, driving her to distraction.

She wasn't herself.

Who was she, then?

Who was this woman kissing this man back with every ounce of her energy and being?

Schuyler wasn't certain if she wanted to laugh or cry, object to Trace's kisses or beg him for more, push the man away or pull him closer. Maybe insanity ran in her family, after all.

"Trace?" Until he raised his head, Schuyler wondered if she'd said his name silently or spoken it aloud.

His eyes were the intense blue color of a summer sky just before dawn. "God, you taste good," he said.

"So do you."

His eyes darkened. "I could eat you alive."

Schuyler believed him. She shivered from excitement and from some elemental and primitive fear: a vulnerable female at the mercy of a larger and stronger male of the species.

"Still cold?" he asked.

"No," she answered with an ironic laugh. "If anything, I'm hot."

"You are that, lady."

She felt a flush of color spread across her cheeks. "That's not what I usually hear."

"What do you usually hear?"

She was honest with him. "That I'm ice-cold. That I epitomize the phrase 'cool, calm and collected.' That I'm aloof. Unapproachable. Hands off." She sighed. "Definitely hands off."

All the while she was talking, Schuyler was aware of her nipples poking through the layers of her clothing and rubbing up against Trace's bare chest. Her hands were splayed across that same bare chest. She could detect bone and muscle and a smattering of dark, crisp hair that encircled small, nut-brown male nipples, then arrowed down his flat abdomen and finally disappeared into the waistline of his jeans. She brushed her fingertips along the surface of his skin and he shuddered.

"Don't believe a word of it," Trace muttered, his lips leaving a trail of fiery kisses along the sensitive flesh just below her ear. "You may appear to be an ice princess on the outside, but you're all red-hot molten lava on the inside."

Schuyler wished she could climb inside Trace and look out, see what he was seeing, feel what he was feeling, comprehend the intensity of his arousal as well as her own.

What was it like to be a man aroused by a woman?

Trace was aroused. His erection was pressing against her thigh. The sensual heat poured from his flesh. He kissed her over and over again as if he couldn't get enough of her. As if he would never get enough of her.

Schuyler devoured him in return, greedy for the touch of his mouth, for the thrill of his tongue, for the taste of him, the smell of him, the feel of him.

This was passion, then.

Not the lukewarm, milquetoast imitations she had experienced in the past, but this desperate wanting, this insatiable hunger, this overpowering desire, this frightening need.

She had never felt like this before, and that scared Schuyler, too. This was the real danger.

Trace was the real danger.

It registered somewhere in the back of her mind that he was wearing his standard uniform of faded, threadbare blue jeans and nothing else. The stubble on his chin and along his jawline was like fine sandpaper. The sensation of his beard scraping her skin was incredibly erotic. She opened her eyes and studied the arch of his eyebrows, the suggestion of a noble, even emphatic nose, and well-shaped ears tucked close to his head.

"You are delicious," she murmured, leaning her head back and gazing up at him.

He laughed huskily. She could feel the movement in his chest, even in the taut muscles of his stomach. "I'll bet you say that to all the boys," he teased.

Schuyler wet her lips with her tongue and drew in a deep breath. "What were you like as a boy?"

"Wild."

"And . . . ?"

"Unruly." She was surprised when Trace went on without any further urging from her. "Unmanageable. Undisciplined. All piss and vinegar." He laughed again, not entirely from amusement, and shook his head. "Thought I was real tough. Thought I had all the answers. Thought I didn't need anybody."

"Maybe you were just afraid."

"I was that, too." He searched her face. "What were you like as a girl?"

"Tall."

He chuckled. "And . . . ?"

"A bit of a dreamer."

"What did you dream about?"

Schuyler was suddenly self-conscious. She heard herself hemming and hawing. "All kinds of things."

Trace seemed to sense her discomfort and let it pass. "When I was a boy with nothing—hell, with less than nothing—I used to dream about a girl with everything, about a girl exactly like you." He was dead serious. "Are you real, Schuyler Grant, or are you merely a figment of my imagination?"

"I'm not a figment of your imagination," she assured him. "I'm real. I'm flesh and blood."

Trace could vouch for the fact she was flesh and blood. He could feel the swell of her breasts and the tips of her nipples right through her nightclothes.

He was itching to touch her, to cup her breasts in his hands, to feel her nipples poking and prodding his palms. But he'd learned a long time ago that just because a man was tempted didn't mean he should give in to the temptation.

Trace wanted Schuyler Grant. He couldn't hide the truth from her even if he wanted to. His body was literally shouting the fact. After all, a man couldn't conceal his arousal. It was right out front for anyone *and* everyone to see.

And feel.

He wasn't going to apologize for his erection. Considering what they'd been up to, it was a simple and natural consequence of their actions.

It might be natural, Trace thought with a sardonic smirk, but it wasn't simple. Nothing would ever be simple when the woman was Schuyler Grant.

A man was damned if he did and damned if he didn't.

Schuyler might not be a figment of his imagination, but that didn't prevent his imagination from running wild. He could see himself untying the belt of her bathrobe and slowly spreading the cashmere lapels to each side. He could envision the front of her nightgown wet from his mouth, from his kisses, her breasts outlined beneath the fine material, her nipples clearly visible down to the smallest detail and readily accessible to his teeth, his lips, his tongue.

He could feel the texture of her skin against his tongue, taste her on his lips, smell her arousal.

He'd like nothing better than to strip the clothes from her body and make love to her on a bed of soft green grass, her skin covered with night dew and beads of perspiration.

He would brush bits of grass and leaves, even small twigs, from her breasts and watch her nipples respond to the unintentional caress. Well, perhaps not so unintentional, at that.

He wanted to see her body illuminated by moonlight and profiled against a backdrop of stars. He would settle her across his torso and persuade her to straddle his hips, wrap her long, lovely legs around his waist and lower herself onto his erection inch by excruciating inch. He would begin to fill her utterly and completely until she had taken everything he had to give.

The night air might be a little cool, but Trace figured they wouldn't even notice.

Then it would begin, but it would *not* begin slowly. It

would *not* start with feather-light kisses and gentle caresses
and an easy rocking motion.

Hell, no.

It would be hard and fast, and it would leave them both
gasping for air. First, it would be a thrust of her hips, then
his, then another thrust and another, stronger, deeper, driving them both right to the edge of that erotic precipice. And
when they climaxed, it would be mind-boggling, mind-
shattering, earth-moving.

Sweet Jesus, he could almost taste Schuyler, feel
Schuyler. He was in pain. He was about to burst. His penis
was throbbing. If he thought one more thought about her,
if he kissed her again, if he moved even a fraction against
her lovely body, he was going to come in his jeans.

"You sorry son of a bitch," Trace swore at himself out
of self-deprecation.

She blinked. "I beg your pardon."

He was supposed to be so bloody brilliant. Words were
supposed to be his stock in trade. Where were the right
words now when he desperately needed them?

"I . . . ah, said, I'm sorry," he stammered. "This isn't
professional behavior."

Schuyler tried to focus. "Professional behavior?"

Trace opened his mouth and out tumbled a mishmash of
words. "I am . . . I was . . . Cora's attorney and now, by ex-
tension, I'm your attorney."

It was lame.

Schuyler's sense of humor saved the day. She looked
around. "I don't see anyone from the ABA lurking in the
bushes."

Trace said the next thing that occurred to him. "We're
hot. We need to go back inside the house."

That shouldn't have made sense to either of them, but
somehow it did.

"Besides," he went on, "it must be very late."

Schuyler glanced down at her wrist. "I'm sure it is," she said, despite the absence of a watch.

Trace blew out his breath expressively. "I think we should call it a night."

She didn't argue with him.

They left the gazebo and retraced their steps along the garden path. Buddy trotted along at their side.

"Thank you for the loan of your shirt," Schuyler said politely as they reached the kitchen.

"You're welcome." Trace reset the alarm system and announced, "I'll walk you to your room."

"That's not necessary. I can find my way," she assured him.

"I know," he said.

There was no further exchange until they reached Schuyler's bedroom. She wrapped her hand around the doorknob, then paused and turned to him. "You haven't mentioned what wing of the house you're staying in."

"I guess I haven't." He might as well confess to her. She'd find out sooner or later. "I'm staying in this wing. I use the Blue Room when I'm at Grantwood."

Her eyes widened appreciably. "The Blue Room is only three doors down from mine."

Trace crossed his arms. "That's right."

She blinked several times in rapid succession. "You're practically next door."

"Practically," he agreed.

"Why didn't you say something before?"

Trace uncrossed his arms. "It didn't seem pertinent, somehow. But now you know where to find me if you need me."

On that note she said, "Good night, then."

"Good night."

She added, "Sleep well, Trace."

He wasn't so sure about that. He was coiled tighter than a spring inside.

Still, as he sauntered down the hallway toward his own bedroom, Buddy at his side, Trace managed to toss back over his shoulder, "Sweet dreams, Schuyler."

Chapter Eleven

Adam Coffin knew what people said about him. They said that he was something of an odd duck, that he looked like a cadaver, that he lived in a mausoleum.

Adam supposed he was and he did.

His ancestral home—his family had lived on the same acreage along the Hudson River for nearly three centuries, since the time of the Dutch patroons and the English land barons—was constructed of quarried gray marble. Four stories tall in some places, five stories in others, The Elms loomed large and somber and foreboding over the surrounding landscape.

Besides the existing house, which was built just after the Civil War, and an assortment of outbuildings, including a deserted gatekeeper's lodge and long-abandoned greenhouses, the estate boasted a magnificent grove of two-hundred-year-old elm trees and an unequaled view of the river.

In its prime The Elms had been considered the crown jewel of the stately homes and castles along the Hudson. Now it was room after dusty room that rarely saw the light of day and never heard the sound of human voices or childrens' laughter. In fact, there were rooms—even entire wings—of The Elms that no one had entered in a decade or two.

The winter after his parents had died, Adam Coffin had closed off most of the house. What had been the sense in heating twenty-odd bedrooms when he'd rarely slept, and when he had it had usually been stretched out on the sofa in front of the television set, or in a fireside chair with a brandy snifter in his hand?

Adam had liked his brandy in those days.

On more than one occasion he had awakened the following morning to discover another piece of his mother's prized crystal smashed to smithereens on the floor. After that he had begun to drink his brandy from ordinary—and cheap—water glasses he purchased by the dozen at K mart.

Adam had contemplated selling The Elms once or twice—there had been times, too many times, when the estate had felt like an albatross around his neck—but where would he have gone and what would he have done?

Then five years ago he had driven into town for another dozen drinking glasses and on the way home he'd found Moose in a plain brown paper grocery sack by the side of the road, and his life had been transformed.

The first thing to go was the brandy.

The second were his shoes when he was indoors. (Adam lived in fear of stepping on his tiny companion and doing him some irreparable harm.)

He and Moose lived simply in a handful of rooms, but those rooms were kept immaculate. Their day was structured around a healthy breakfast, a morning stroll (Moose usually rode in the pocket of his jacket), a good dose of poetry or literature (Adam often read Shakespeare and Milton and Donne aloud until he was hoarse), then lunch, an afternoon nap, a little housekeeping, a light supper, followed by an evening spent listening to classical music or perhaps watching one of a few select television programs on the Animal Planet.

Bedtime was ten o'clock sharp.

Adam Coffin had never been happier or more content in his entire sixty-seven years. Moose gave him a reason to get up in the morning, a reason to go to bed at night and a reason to go on living during the hours in between.

Cora had understood.

She'd always appreciated how it was with him even when he had been a boy, then a young man, then a not-so-young man, then a middle-aged man left all alone in a world that both mystified and frightened him.

For the first few months after he'd lost his mother and father, Cora had dinner sent over to him. Nothing fancy. A chicken casserole or a pot of vegetable soup. There had always been enough left over for lunch the next day.

For the first year she had telephoned him every evening just at twilight. She'd somehow known that twilight was the worst time to be alone.

And every holiday, including Christmas and New Year's, she had invited him to Grantwood to share a special luncheon in the big, bright, cheerful kitchen.

"Cora was a good friend to me . . . to us," Adam remarked to his diminutive companion as Moose settled down into his fleece-lined doggie bed for the night. "I thought it was a lovely memorial service yesterday afternoon and a delicious luncheon afterwards, didn't you?" Adam reached for a tissue and blew his nose. "We're going to miss her, aren't we?"

He turned down his bed and then straightened, thinking aloud. "Maybe I should have told her what we saw in Grant's Wood."

There weren't any fences or stone walls or boundary markers between The Elms and Grantwood, and Adam and Moose often found themselves wandering onto land that was officially part of the adjoining estate.

"At the time I didn't want to worry Cora when I knew she was in frail health. Now it's too late to tell her," Adam acknowledged with a sigh as he brushed off his clothes and neatly hung them up in the closet.

Moose rarely answered him. Indeed, on the infrequent occasions when the Chihuahua had attempted to make any sound at all he always ended up terrorizing himself back into silence, but that didn't stop Adam from carrying on with their conversations.

"I wonder if I should mention anything to Miss Grant since she's back in residence," Adam ruminated aloud as he prepared for bed. "Or perhaps to that young attorney. After all, Cora seemed to trust him implicitly."

He let that possibility rattle around in his brain while he went into the adjoining bathroom to wash his hands and face and brush his teeth.

"Of course, they'd probably think I was crazy. There were people around these parts who believed Cora was crazy, you know," he said, raising his voice so Moose could hear him in the other room. He stopped and gargled with antiseptic mouthwash. "Cora wasn't crazy. She just wasn't always sane."

That made perfect sense to Adam Coffin.

He understood because he had looked into the heart of darkness once or twice, himself.

" 'We live, as we dream—alone,' " he quoted, recalling what had been written on the subject by Joseph Conrad.

Turning off the bathroom light, Adam shuffled across to the bed and sat down to remove his slippers. It was only then that he remembered to tell Moose the wonderful news.

"I believe we may have inherited a little something from Cora. Maybe more than a little. We have an appointment with Mr. Ballinger tomorrow afternoon at four o'clock sharp here at The Elms." He climbed into bed and pulled the covers up to his chin. "We'll have to decide how we want to spend our windfall, Moose. I confess I've been giving it considerable thought, and I think we should start with a donation to the local animal shelter."

Adam switched off the lamp at his fingertips. He lay there in the darkness for a moment or two, then he said in a whisper, "God bless you, Cora."

"Goddamn you, Cora."

It wasn't fair. *She* had always had so much and he'd always had too little.

Far too little.

The very least the old biddy could have done was correct that oversight in her last will and testament. But she hadn't seen fit to leave him what anyone would consider his fair share.

As if that weren't bad enough, his own plans had been thwarted by Crazy Cora's death, too. If only he'd had more time. . . .

He swore under his breath and took another sip of the drink in his hand. He paced restlessly back and forth across the room. Then he paused by the window—it was some-one's else's frigging window, of course, since he was forced to live off the largesse of others—and watched as a man and woman strolled by.

Last night he'd been at Grantwood—he had spent more than one night there doing what had to be done—and he'd spotted a man and a woman in the gazebo.

For a minute or two, even longer, he'd wondered if Trace Ballinger was going to take her right then and there, out in the open and where anyone could see. His palms had begun to sweat; he'd had to wipe them off on his pant legs. He'd licked his lips in anticipation, speculating whether he could get close enough for a good look. But they'd sud-denly stopped and walked back to the house.

With the return of Schuyler Grant, the circumstances

under which he had to work had definitely grown more complicated. Still, he was clever; he managed to manipulate most situations to his advantage. Where there was a will, there was a way.

Then something occurred to him. Maybe, just maybe, Schuyler's return to Grantwood was a blessing in disguise. She could provide the distraction he needed.

After all, he knew what he had to do . . . if he dared.

And he did.

Chapter Twelve

Johnny glanced up from the *Wall Street Journal* lying open in his lap—he'd been reading for the past quarter of an hour—and smiled at Schuyler.

"You've done very well for yourself, haven't you, Johnny?" she concluded.

"Yes, I have."

Jonathan Tiberius Grant's name was mentioned in connection with any number of wheelings and dealings, IPOs and mergers. It seemed that her cousin had obtained his goal: He was a major player in the emerging financial markets.

She wasn't altogether serious when she said, "You not only run with the wolves, but it seems the bulls and the bears as well."

Johnny put the newspaper down on the bench, leaned back against the railing of the gazebo, stretched out his legs, interlaced his fingers behind his head and gave a contented sigh. "I may run with the wolves, but I don't think there is a more ideal place on a day like today than Grantwood."

Schuyler had to agree. It was one of those long, lazy afternoons poised between spring and early summer. The air was pleasantly warm. The birds were twittering in the treetops overhead. The scent of flowers hung heavily in the garden.

It was a lovely day, a perfect day, and yet she found she was restless, jittery, fidgety.

Crossing one leg over the other and smoothing the skirt

of her silk dress, she looked up at their ancestral home. "I seem to recall you always loved Grantwood."

Johnny took a pair of designer sunglasses from the pocket of his sports coat. "I did," he agreed, slipping on the dark glasses and reverting to his relaxed posture. "I still do. Although I haven't been back that often in the past few years."

"You're a busy man."

"Very busy. Besides, it wasn't as much fun visiting the old place when you weren't here," he claimed, raising his tanned face to the afternoon sun.

"Now you're flattering me."

"It's the truth," Johnny said, raising his right hand as if he were taking a solemn oath.

She was still skeptical. "You're just being kind because you know darn well I had a crush on you when I was thirteen and you were twenty-two."

Johnny smiled—it was all brilliant white teeth against golden brown skin—and appeared even more handsome, if that was possible. "You were a lovely young girl, Schuyler, but I don't think the family would have approved of me robbing the cradle. In fact, they'd have tossed me out of the house."

She smiled back at him. Then, after a moment, she confessed, "When I was younger I used to be afraid of this house."

He peered over the rim of his sunglasses. "Really?"

"Really."

"Why?"

"Sometimes it gave me the creeps," was all she was prepared to say.

Johnny made the logical leap. "Is that the reason you decided to live in Paris?"

"It was one of the reasons."

Her distant cousin persisted. "Are you going to sell?"

Schuyler frowned. "Sell?"

Johnny sat up and brushed an errant leaf from the sleeve of his jacket. During the past several days she had observed that his clothes were never wrinkled. His shoes were never scuffed; they were always buffed to a mirror sheen. There was never a strand of hair out of place on his head. In short, his appearance was immaculate.

"Sell Grantwood," he said at last.

"I don't know what I'm going to do about Grantwood. I have some business to see to first."

Johnny made a gesture in the general direction of the house. "Your lawyer seems to be hanging around. I would have thought country life was too quiet and too tame for Ballinger. It doesn't seem quite his cup of tea somehow."

Schuyler had had her own niggling doubts on that subject, but she wasn't about to discuss her misgivings concerning Trace Ballinger with anyone, and that included her cousin. "Trace has business to see to, as well."

The handsome man sitting beside her frowned. "No ulterior motive, then?"

"Ulterior motive?"

"You."

"Me?"

A frown returned to mar Jonathan Grant's perfectly proportioned features. "Personally and professionally you must represent a great deal of money to Trace Ballinger."

"I don't believe he's interested in money. At least not in the way you mean."

"Don't kid yourself. Every man has his price."

"Does he?"

Johnny expounded. "It may not always be financial gain, of course. For some people it's success, for others social position, for others a feeling of accomplishment."

"Then I suppose we all have our price, as you put it," Schuyler conceded.

There was an underlying intelligence in the man's voice when he theorized, "I wonder what your price is, my dear cousin. Could it be a sense of belonging?"

"Belonging?"

"Having a place to call home," Johnny said quietly as he gazed up at the great edifice.

Maybe there was more to her cousin than met the eye. Maybe he was more than just another pretty face, Schuyler mused as she studied the handsome man.

For that matter, she suspected there was more to Trace Ballinger and this business of Cora's than she'd originally thought.

In fact, it occurred to her, as she sat there basking in the afternoon sun, with the scent of spring flowers drenching the air, that at times nothing was quite what it seemed to be, that no one was who they had, at least at first, appeared to be.

Then again, perhaps she was being fanciful. Perhaps she was looking for mysteries and intrigues and things that went bump in the night where none existed.

Still, she was curious. "Why are you asking me about Trace Ballinger?"

"I'd like to know more about a man who has obviously captured your interest." A well-groomed eyebrow arched in an inverted V. "Someone you seem to find fascinating."

Schuyler's face grew warm. "There's nothing between Mr. Ballinger and myself but a professional association."

"That's good to hear." The man sitting beside her on the gazebo bench took off his sunglasses and looked straight at her. "You're going to be thirty at the end of the summer, aren't you?"

"Yes, I am."

"I'm closer to forty myself. It's time I settled down. Married. Had children." Johnny reached out and took her hand in his. He traced an imaginary line from the tip of her fingers to her forearm and back again. "I wouldn't be robbing the cradle now, would I?"

The breath caught in Schuyler's throat. "No, you wouldn't."

Johnny straightened his shoulders and took in a sustaining breath of air. The next thing Schuyler knew, his arms were around her waist and he was urging her toward him.

Then he kissed her.

She had dreamed about this moment since she was a young girl with a crush on an older and unattainable male. She supposed like most dreams it wasn't destined to come true.

Johnny's kiss was lovely, undemanding, even rather sweet. But there was no brass band. No pounding heart. No sweating palms. No sense of danger and no passion.

When he came up for air, her distant cousin murmured, "Promise that you'll think about it, Schuyler. That you'll think about us. It might give both of us what we want, what we need."

"I promise," she said.

"I see you have a rival, Mr. Ballinger," Adam Coffin remarked, glancing up from the chessboard.

Trace set his jaw and decided to plead ignorance in the matter. "A rival?"

His opponent made a movement with his head in the direction of the window, a window through which the couple in the garden beyond were visible. "For Miss Grant's affections."

Trace willed himself not to react. "I don't know what you're talking about."

Apparently his companion wasn't fooled for a moment. "I'm talking about your regard for the young lady."

Trace allowed his mouth to all but disappear. "My regard?"

The older man sat back in the comfortable leather chair opposite him. "Your interest, then."

"My interest?"

Adam Coffin cleared his throat. "I suppose I could be mistaken. I thought . . . well, never mind what I thought." He sighed. "I confess I understand very little about women."

Trace's hand hovered over a chess piece. "Don't feel bad, Mr. Coffin. There isn't a man alive who understands women."

The older man suggested, almost shyly, "Why don't you call me Adam?"

He nodded. "I'm Trace, then."

"Well, Trace, just between you and me, Jonathan Grant can charm the birds out of the trees."

"Schuyler isn't a bird."

"True."

"Well, hell!" Trace swore feelingly, realizing he'd made a strategic error the instant he moved his bishop.

"Your mind is somewhere else this afternoon," Adam Coffin pointed out. "This is the third time in less than an hour that you've made a miscalculation."

Trace knew what the next word out of his opponent's mouth would be.

Adam only hesitated briefly before saying, "Checkmate."

He conceded. "You've won."

Adam Coffin was a modest man. "It seems I have."

Trace refused to make excuses for himself. "You're the better player."

"I don't believe so," the older man said humbly. "But I enjoy our games nevertheless."

Their mutual interest in the game of chess had been discovered quite by accident the afternoon Trace had called on Adam Coffin at The Elms to discuss his inheritance.

Both men were content to maintain a companionable silence for a minute or two, one with his faithful dog in his pocket, the other with his sprawled at his feet.

Adam finally spoke up and said, "Miss Grant is an interesting young woman."

Trace refused to take the bait. "Hmm," he mumbled noncommittally.

It seemed that his companion wasn't finished. "She is also quite attractive."

Trace again responded with an ambiguous sound.

The winner of their match continued, "She seems to have a sharp mind and a quick wit." His shoulders were raised and then lowered. "She's different. Not surprising, I suppose. Cora was different, as well."

"She was," Trace agreed.

It was another minute or two before Adam Coffin proposed, "Johnny may be the perfect match for Miss Grant."

Trace scowled and declared, "Johnny Grant isn't the man for Schuyler."

"What makes you say that?"

"Gut instincts." Trace expounded, "He's rich. He's handsome. He's familiar. Too familiar. She'd be bored to tears within a year, two at the most."

"Perhaps." Adam seemed to take his opinion under consideration. "However, I understand that women don't always see men in the same light that other men do."

Trace had reached the same conclusion. "Even an intelligent woman has her blind spots."

A gray eyebrow was arched in a meaningful fashion. "So they say."

They both watched as the man in question took Schuyler into his arms and kissed her passionately on the mouth.

Trace came out of his seat.

Adam Coffin cleared his throat. "You wouldn't want to act foolishly at this point, I think."

The man was right.

Trace took in a calming breath, held it for a moment or two and then exhaled, allowing the sudden anger—hell, the full-blown jealousy—he was feeling to gradually dissipate.

He sat down again and turned to his companion with a self-deprecating smile. "Fools have a tendency to rush in where even angels fear to tread."

Chapter Thirteen

"Kind of makes you wonder how they managed before lawn mowers," Trace said, coming up beside her and gazing out at the vast expanse of green grass.

There was a crew from Ground Zero working on the estate this morning. Half a dozen men were mowing—the sound of revving engines and the smell of gasoline hung heavy in the air—while another half dozen were trimming and raking.

Nobody seemed to be in a hurry.

Schuyler was intensely aware of how close Trace was standing to her. Unsteadily her heart picked up speed. She moistened her lips before saying, "How did they manage before lawn mowers? I can answer you in a single word."

He seemed to find her claim vaguely amusing. "A single word, huh?"

She nodded. "Sheep."

"As in, 'Baa, baa, black sheep, have you any wool?' " he said, quoting the traditional nursery rhyme.

She nodded her head again. "Most of the historic houses along the Hudson River originally kept sheep. In fact, a man by the name of John Armstrong was sent a flock of Merino sheep as a wedding present by the Emperor Napoleon I."

Trace raised his eyebrows in well-simulated surprise. "Napoleon Bonaparte himself. I am impressed."

Schuyler wasn't certain if he was teasing her or not. She lifted the weight of her hair from her neck. It was unseasonably warm for the first of May. She wished she'd pulled it up into a ponytail as she used to do as a girl. "Did you know that some of the oldest Mayan ruins in existence are on an island in the Hudson?"

Apparently he didn't know.

"One of the wealthy landowners from this area had an entire ancient village excavated in the Yucatán, dismantled and shipped to his private island, where it was painstakingly reassembled. The ruins are still there," she said, smoothing the waistband of her designer slacks. "Naturally that kind of disregard for an archaeological site would be considered sacrilege today, but it wasn't uncommon one hundred and fifty years ago."

Trace ran a hand through his hair. "They looted. They pillaged. Then they partied."

Schuyler turned her head and raised her eyes to meet his. "Who did?"

"The industrialist robber barons who made their fortunes from railroads and Wall Street and all manner of shady dealings, and then built extravagant estates along the Hudson River with their ill-gotten gains."

"They were just men like other men," she reminded him, one hand going to her throat.

"Were they?" Broad shoulders were flexed. "In his day Jay Gould was determined to crush an uprising by his striking railway workers because they were demanding a lousy nine dollars per week in guaranteed pay. At the time Gould himself was making one hundred thousand dollars a week."

There was something in his voice, something Schuyler couldn't quite put her finger on. She passed her tongue over her lips and listened.

Trace continued. "While his employees lived in squalor, one robber baron thought nothing of squandering over half a million dollars on a stable with a glass-enclosed courtyard so his horses could exercise in comfort." He said, more to himself than to her, and almost as an afterthought, "It was reported that grown men wept with joy at the news of the so-called gentleman's death."

"How sad," she murmured.

He wasn't finished. "During his lifetime it was common knowledge that Cornelius 'Commodore' Vanderbilt, the granddaddy of rail barons, chased the housemaids, and anything else in skirts, until he was too damned old to do anything about it even if he did catch them. In fact, Mark Twain said that he'd never read anything about Commodore Vanderbilt that he shouldn't be ashamed of."

"Surely morality, or the lack of morality, doesn't know any class distinction," Schuyler argued.

"I'm not talking about class. I'm talking about wealth and pure, adulterated and incalculable greed," Trace said. "There's a hell of a difference."

Her skin prickled. "You talk as though you take their transgressions personally."

"I come from a long line of blue-collar workers and dirt-poor farmers," Trace stated. "What do you think?"

"I think all of those men are long dead and buried, as well as that way of life."

"Don't you believe it, sweetheart. The rich always have been—and always will be—different." Then he laughed, and it sent a chill down her spine.

Trace Ballinger would make a formidable enemy, Schuyler realized. Better to have him as a friend than as a foe. Still, she was determined to set the record straight. He wasn't the only student of American history in the room, after all.

"Did you know that Vanderbilt was the son of a poor farmer, as was Leland Stanford?" she began. "That E. H. Harriman and Jay Gould were both high school dropouts? That Collis P. Huntington started out in his teens as a clock peddler? They all began life dirt-poor, Trace, not with silver spoons in their mouths. In fact, poverty was no doubt one of the motivating forces that drove those men to lust after wealth and power."

He folded his arms over his chest. "And once they had wealth and power?"

"Well, it's said that 'absolute power corrupts absolutely,' " she reminded him.

"Maybe you're right," Trace conceded, somewhat mollified.

"Pax?"

"Pax," he echoed. "I think we've had enough philosophical debate for one morning."

"So do I," she agreed.

He gave her a meaning-filled glance. "Do you want to talk about the other night?"

"Which night?"

Trace wasn't fooled by her air of innocence. "The night we met in the gazebo."

Schuyler's next breath stuck in her throat. She finally managed, "No."

Frowning, he uncrossed his arms. "We'll have to discuss what happened sooner or later."

"Let's make it later," she proposed.

Trace laughed, and this time there was amusement in his laugh. Then he slowly shook his head. "In that case, do you have any questions you'd like to ask me about Cora's will?"

Schuyler was genuinely relieved. At least Cora's legal affairs were a safe topic of conversation. "I don't have any questions, but I wish I understood what she meant in her note by 'lay the ghosts to rest.' Do you have any ideas?"

Trace rubbed the palm of his hand up and down his forearm. "Maybe Cora left some kind of clue for us. The trick, of course," he admitted, his dark brows forming a quizzical arch, "will be to find it."

Schuyler agreed with him. "Grantwood isn't a normal house. For one thing, it's huge. For another, it's like an intricate and obscure Chinese puzzle." She blew out her breath in exasperation. "We'll be looking for a needle in a haystack."

Trace considered their predicament. "Then I recommend that we speak to Mrs. Danvers. If anyone has a clue, it'll be her."

They found the housekeeper-cook sitting at the kitchen table, writing out her recipe for lobster salad onto a three-by-five index card.

Schuyler cleared her throat. "Excuse me, Mrs. Danvers."

The woman looked up and smiled. "Yes, Miss Grant?"

Their relationship had improved immeasurably since that first night, in no small part because of Schuyler's genuine appreciation for Elvira Danvers's superb cooking.

"I need your help," she said simply.

"Of course. What can I do for you?"

Schuyler wished to be discreet for Cora's sake, yet she also had to be candid and forthright with the housekeeper. "My great-aunt left a letter with Mr. Ballinger. In that letter she asked me to take care of a certain family matter for her." A small sigh unintentionally escaped Schuyler's lips. "To tell you the truth, Mrs. Danvers, I don't know where to begin. You spent more time with Cora than anyone else these past few years. Did she keep a diary or a personal journal or anything of that nature?"

"Not that I'm aware of. As you know, Mrs. Grant was plagued by arthritis, especially in the joints of her fingers. Writing was difficult for her. Why, sometimes she couldn't even hold a pen in her hand on account of the stiffness and pain."

Schuyler tried another approach. "Can you think of anything she especially enjoyed?"

Elvira Danvers answered somewhat modestly, "My cooking."

"Anything else?"

"Sitting by a sunny window. Smelling lilacs in the spring and roses in the summer."

Schuyler went at it from a different angle. "Was there anything unusual that she liked to do?"

Elvira Danvers put her pen down, folded her hands in front of her on the kitchen table—Schuyler noticed the woman's fingernails were cut short and blunt, and were devoid of any polish—and gave the matter her full attention. "I don't know as I consider it unusual, although I imagine some folks might."

Her ears perked up. "What?"

"Mrs. Grant stored a few keepsakes in a trunk in her closet. She told me there wasn't anything particularly valuable inside, but she loved to sit and look at her 'special treasures,' as she called them. When her arthritis was acting up, she would ask me to unlock the trunk and lift the lid for her."

"What was inside?"

"Oh, I couldn't say, Miss Grant," the housekeeper replied, measuring out her words. "I never really looked. I didn't think it was any of my business. I just opened the trunk and left. Mrs. Grant always called me on the house phone when she was done."

"Your discretion is to be commended," Trace piped up.

"Thank you, Mr. Ballinger."

Next, he said with an air of nonchalance, "Is the trunk still in Cora's closet?"

"Of course. Far as I know, none of Mrs. Grant's things have been touched by anyone but me in the seven years I've been at Grantwood." Elvira Danvers's bottom lip trembled slightly. She interlaced her fingers and squeezed them tightly together as if that would somehow hold her emotions in check, as well. "I dusted and tidied Mrs. Grant's rooms myself when she was alive. I saw no reason to change that once she was gone."

Trace waited a moment or two before inquiring, "Do you know where the key to Cora's trunk is kept?"

The woman's front teeth were sunk into her bottom lip. It was a moment or two before she could respond. "Yes, sir, I do."

"Where is that, Mrs. Danvers?"

"On a hook next to the trunk."

Schuyler gently prodded, "Can you think of anything else that may have been out of the ordinary recently?"

Gray eyebrows furrowed, emphasizing a permanent crease between the housekeeper's eyes. "Just one thing."

Schuyler waited.

Elvira Danvers drew a breath and spoke slowly. "On the last day of her life; of course, no one knew it was her last day on this earth, God rest her soul . . ." Here the woman had to pause and raise one corner of an immaculate apron to dab at her eyes. "Mrs. Grant mentioned the name Richie several times."

"Richie? Are you certain?"

"I'm certain."

Schuyler looked from Mrs. Danvers to Trace Ballinger and back again. "Who's Richie?"

The middle-aged woman seated at the table admitted, "I couldn't say, and it wasn't my place to ask. Mrs. Grant would have told me if she wanted me to know." After a moment, "I wish I could be more help to you, Miss Grant."

"You've been a great help, Mrs. Danvers." It was only after she and Trace had left the kitchen that Schuyler said to him, "Did you ever hear Cora mention anyone named Richie?"

His voice was final. "Never."

She spread out her hands in a gesture of resignation. "Well, at least we have a place to start."

"The trunk in Cora's closet," Trace said as they headed upstairs.

Chapter Fourteen

"You want the good news or the bad news?" Trace asked as he opened the door to the walk-in closet in Cora's bedroom and switched on the lights.

"The good news," Schuyler responded from behind him.

"Cora kept everything."

"What's the bad news?"

His mouth twisted. "Cora kept everything."

"Everything?"

"From the looks of it." Trace stepped aside and made a grand, sweeping gesture with his arm. "As they say: 'Ladies before gentlemen.' "

Schuyler peered around him and groaned. "How can one closet hold so much stuff?"

He was quick to point out, "Because the closet in question is the size of the average master bedroom and is stacked from floor to ceiling."

Schuyler gave him a sidelong glance. "That was a rhetorical question."

He flashed her a grin. "I know."

She wet her lips with her tongue and drew a deep breath. "I need a rubber band."

Trace dove into the pockets of his blue jeans. "Sorry, no rubber bands."

"There's one." She indicated the shoe box at his elbow (it was one of several hundred shoe boxes stacked in this section of the closet), its top secured with a thick rubber band.

Trace retrieved the rubber band and watched as Schuyler

pulled her hair back from her face and up into a ponytail.
She suddenly appeared younger, less sophisticated and sexy
as hell.

He had to keep his attention on what they were doing
and not on Schuyler Grant.

It was easier said than done.

The trunk was at the far end of the closet, which was
longer than it was wide. The key to the trunk was right out
in the open, just as Mrs. Danvers had told them.

"There's the trunk and the key," Schuyler said with a
notable lack of enthusiasm.

Trace began to roll his shirtsleeves up to his elbows.
"What's the matter?"

"Pandora's box."

"Pandora's box?"

"Do you know your mythology?"

"Vaguely."

There was apprehension in her voice. "Pandora was the
first woman, according to the Greeks. Her name meant 'all
gifts' because she given Aphrodite's beauty, Athena's feminine arts, and Hermes' cunning. She was also given Pandora's box, although it was actually a jar, and it contained
every human evil and sickness."

"Nice gift," Trace muttered.

"Anyway, Pandora had been cautioned not to open the
jar, but her curiosity got the better of her. She decided to
ignore the warning and take a peek."

Trace could see what was coming. "Bad move on Pandora's part, right?"

"You can say that again. When Pandora lifted the lid of
the jar, sorrow and misfortune were unleashed upon the
world." Schuyler sighed heavily. "By the time she managed
to close the lid again, only hope remained."

Trace knew a sardonic smile touched the edges of his mouth. "Is there a moral to this story?"

She gave him a quick look and added meaningfully, "Sometimes it's best not to go looking for trouble."

"What if trouble comes looking for you?"

Schuyler spoke to her hands. "Turn and run in the opposite direction."

He tried to be sympathetic. After all, it'd been a hell of a week for the woman. "I take it you're having second thoughts about opening Cora's trunk."

"Second, third and fourth thoughts," she confessed, gripping her hands together until the knuckles were white.

"The past can be a tricky place to go," were his only words of wisdom.

Schuyler reached up and tucked an errant strand of hair behind her ear. "I learned a long time ago the past can't be changed. It simply is what it is."

"Or what it was."

She seemed to make up her mind about something. Then she straightened her back and said, "Let's do it."

"Would you like me to do the honors?"

"Please."

Schuyler stepped aside while he retrieved the key, unlocked the trunk and lifted the lid. Then he stood back and let her have the first look.

She swallowed. "I'm going to feel odd pawing through Cora's personal belongings."

Trace was pragmatic. He'd had to be. He'd rarely had the luxury of not being pragmatic. "I don't know any other way to fulfill her final request."

Still, the woman beside him hesitated. "Will you help me?"

There was only one answer as far as he was concerned. "Of course."

Schuyler reached out and lifted a piece of tissue paper that covered the contents of the trunk. She appeared to be holding her breath, almost as if she were afraid of what she might find underneath.

It was anticlimactic.

"It's a"—Schuyler lifted out the piece of material that was yellow with age—"tablecloth?"

Trace rubbed the back of his neck with one hand. "That's what it looks like to me."

She shook her head. "I don't know the significance of keeping an old tablecloth."

Cora, Cora, what were you up to? Trace asked silently. Aloud he said, "We'll probably never know now."

Schuyler laid the material aside and went on to the next item. It was a scrapbook. She carefully opened the cover and then leafed through the pages. "Newspaper clippings."

Trace bent forward from the waist and placed his palms on his thighs. He peered over her shoulder. "Looks like wedding announcements, births, social functions."

"Obituaries," she added.

He watched as his breath stirred the tiny hairs on Schuyler's nape. He wondered if she was as aware of him as he was of her. "What are the dates?"

"Fairly recently." There was a certain breathless quality to her voice. "The last ten or fifteen years."

"What's next?" he inquired, taking the scrapbook and putting it on the floor behind them. He drew up a small chair and Schuyler sat down. He went down on his haunches beside her.

She lifted out another shoe box and opened the cardboard lid. It was filled with colorful ribbons and bows. All used, faded, frayed at the edges. She turned her head slightly and looked at Trace. "What would you call this?"

He shrugged. "Junk."

"So would I."

The next item was a velvet box with three drawers down the front. Schuyler pulled open the first drawer. Inside was a jumble of jewelry. She picked up a broach; the stones formed a bunch of red and yellow flowers.

"Rubies?"

"Glass."

"Valuable?"

"Costume jewelry, and not even very good costume jewelry at that."

Schuyler's expression evolved into a frown. "So far none of this makes sense, does it?"

"Nope."

"Surely this doesn't qualify as anyone's 'special treasures,' " she went on to say.

"Maybe Cora had recently moved her so-called treasures. Why don't you keep sorting through the contents of the trunk and I'll take a look-see around the closet?" he proposed.

"Good idea."

It didn't take long for Trace to determine that Cora had kept everything from at least the past three or four decades. There was row after row of dresses, skirts and blouses, even fur coats. Shelves from floor to ceiling held every handbag she had probably ever owned and every pair of shoes. The task of sorting through her belongings was going to be monumental. There was nothing that shouted "special treasures" at him, however.

Trace gave a sigh, folded his arms across his chest and turned to watch Schuyler. Her face was intent, intelligent, patrician and sweet as she sorted through a stack of old books.

It was a minute or two before she happened to look up. "What are you doing?"

At first he wasn't going to tell her. He changed his mind. "I'm watching you."

"Watching me?"

"Yes."

She was briefly disconcerted. "Why?"

Honesty was nearly always the best policy. "I like watching you."

"You're supposed to be searching the rest of the closet," she pointed out.

"I tried."

"Well, try again."

Trace noticed that she checked up on him when she thought he wasn't looking.

He stood there for another minute or two without moving, hands buried in the pockets of his jeans, one leg crossed over the other at the ankle, one shoulder propped against a wall divider.

"Somehow I don't think you're trying very hard," Schuyler concluded.

He pushed off from the wall and retraced his steps, stopping a foot or two from where she sat in front of the open trunk. "Trust me, it'll take a small army to sort through Cora's belongings. Besides, I'd rather look at you."

"Is that a compliment?"

"Yes, it is." He added, "You have very nice legs."

"Nice legs?"

"Actually, you've got great legs."

"Thank you."

Trace glimpsed a smile behind the diaphanous scarf Schuyler was holding up in front of her. "I noticed your legs that first night as you got out of your Jaguar. Trace, I said to myself, now, that's a hell of a pair of legs." He thought about confessing that he'd been dreaming about her legs and then decided it might be best if he skipped the specifics. "You're a lovely woman, Schuyler."

"So are you." She quickly amended her statement. "I should say you're a lovely man."

"I knew what you meant." He opened the cupboard door at his elbow, discovered it was filled with dozens of small boxes and quickly closed it again. "We should talk."

"I thought we were," was her reply.

"About that night," he said.

Schuyler's expression, and apparently her mind, appeared momentarily blank.

Trace wasn't fooled. "The night we met in the gazebo."

"What about that night?"

He crossed his arms. "We kissed."

"Yes. We did."

He took a step toward her. "Do you know what's intriguing about kissing?"

She shook her head from side to side. "No."

"It's never the same twice."

Her hand went to her throat. "I hadn't really thought about it like that. I suppose you're right."

"Of course I'm right." He moved closer still. "Wasn't our first kiss different from the second or the third or the fourth?"

"I only kissed you once."

Trace made a small clicking noise with his teeth and tongue. "That isn't altogether true."

"It isn't?"

"You may have kissed me on only one occasion, but we kissed a number of times."

Schuyler swallowed hard. "I couldn't say."

"Well, I could." He went on. "I have a theory. Would you like to hear it?"

"I think you're going to tell me, whether I want to hear your theory or not," she said with the faintest smile.

He ignored her attempt at humor. "I believe the most common mistake men and women make is confusing the impact of a kiss with their surroundings. They allow themselves to be too easily swayed by a romantic setting like a garden, soft music playing in the background, the scent of flowers in the air."

"Moonlight," she said.

"Moonlight," he echoed. "But there is a simple test that clears up any confusion."

"A simple test?"

He ignored her question and forged ahead. "What do you think is the difference between kissing in the middle of the day compared to the middle of the night?"

"The amount of light?"

"I mean emotionally."

Schuyler gave him a speculative glance. "Generally speaking, one feels less inhibited at night."

"A valid point." Trace returned her gaze unflinchingly. "Anything else?"

Schuyler brought the scarf in her hands up to her chest and held it against her as if it would somehow provide her with a degree of protection. "Whether it's true or not, I think most people feel a greater sense of freedom."

"Another valid observation."

"There's something about the night that is sensual, seductive, erotic."

"Precisely my point."

She breathed in and out. "What's your simple test?"

Trace closed the space between them. "To kiss in the most *unromantic* setting one can imagine in the middle of the day. It's the only way to be sure."

She blinked.

"Otherwise, how will we ever know if it was the garden, the music, the scent of flowers, the—"

"The moonlight?" she finished.

"Exactly. The moonlight or just us?"

Schuyler sat up straighter. "You, sir, have a devious and cunning mind."

Trace tried to appear wounded.

She was curious. "Do you win most of your courtroom cases with arguments like that?"

He admitted, "I don't do a lot of trial work."

She persisted. "But when you do, do you win?"

This was no time for modesty or dishonesty. "Always."

"I thought so."

Trace brought his teeth together. "Are we going to put it to the test, then?"

Schuyler relaxed her grip on the scarf in her hands. "I suppose I've been wondering about that night myself."

"There's only one way to find out," he insisted.

Schuyler hesitated for another heartbeat. Then she put the scarf down, got to her feet and took a step toward him, murmuring, "Wasn't it curiosity that killed the cat . . . ?"

Trace nodded. "And I believe it was satisfaction that brought it back."

It started out as curiosity, not just on Trace's part but on hers as well. After all, she'd had her doubts about the night they had met in the gazebo and the way she had reacted when he'd kissed her.

There was an additional test that Trace knew nothing about, of course. She had been kissed by Johnny in the middle of the day and, while his kiss had been pleasant, agreeable and rather nice, nothing beyond that had happened.

Nice, Schuyler decided, was faint praise for a man's kiss.

Had her reaction to Trace been a fluke? Had it been the cool night—after all, she'd been chilled to the bone—or the stars overhead or the smell of the dew on the grass or the scent of spring flowers?

There was a difference in the fragrance of flowers at night. Why wouldn't there be a difference in the way it felt to be kissed by a man at night?

On the one hand, it made absolutely no sense to Schuyler that she should reach the age of thirty—well, nearly thirty; her birthday was at the end of the summer—and suddenly discover passion in the arms of a stranger.

On the other hand, she realized that there was precious little common sense or logic involved when it came to an emotion like passion.

One minute she was standing in Cora's closet, watching Trace come closer and closer, and wondering what the enigmatic expression on his face meant. The next minute he was kissing her. And she was kissing him back.

It was like night and day.

She realized that she loved the taste of him, the feel of his mouth on her mouth, the way his lips moved against her lips, lightly brushing back and forth, and then more, so much more.

She loved the way he held her in his arms. She loved the strength she could feel in him and the stroke of his hand as he held her with fingers splayed at her nape.

She loved the way her body felt pressed to his, her breasts flattened by his chest, her thighs against his muscular legs.

She loved the indisputable fact that she aroused him. That he wanted her. That she wanted him. That whatever was happening between the two of them, it was wild and wonderful and definitely mutual.

He tasted her with the tip of his tongue, then delved deeper and deeper into her mouth until she was no longer certain who was giving and who was taking.

He was devouring her with his lips and teeth and tongue. She felt herself absorbed by him, almost as if she could become a part of his flesh and bone, his very blood. She went willingly, eagerly, mindlessly.

He filled his hands with her hair and she wondered if he said, "Silk," aloud, or if she'd only heard it in her mind.

He filled his hands with her shoulders, her arms, her waist, her hips, her derriere, wanting her nearer, urging her nearer, demanding she come nearer to him as he lifted her, parting her thighs and thrusting his pelvis forward.

There were only his blue jeans, and whatever he wore under them, and the thin layer of her slacks and the even thinner layer of her panties separating them. Schuyler could sense his heat, taste his desire, feel his need. And her own.

Then she heard her name spoken as she had never heard it spoken before: softly, deeply, intensely, passionately, as if both the question and the answer were contained in a single word and the word was her name: "Schuyler."

The middle of the day or the dead of night, Trace discovered, in the end it made no difference. When he kissed Schuyler it was like putting a match to dry kindling: He went up in flames. And she went with him.

Self-discipline, common sense, intelligence, even a modicum of his usual caution, all vanished in an instant, the instant he covered her mouth with his.

It was ironic. No, it was more like some kind of absurd joke he was unintentionally playing on himself: He had no self-control when it came to this woman.

He heard her name spoken in a voice he didn't recognize as his own: "Schuyler."

"Trace," came her whispered response.

His attention wasn't focused on what she was saying to him, but on what she was doing to him. She dropped the scarf that she'd been clutching in the hands wedged between them. It fluttered, unnoticed, to their feet. Reaching up, she wrapped her arms around his neck. Her touch was cool on his heated flesh.

Trace wanted her touch. He needed her touch. But he needed far more than the innocent caress she was giving the cord at his nape, or the brush of her fingertips through his hair, or the way she made the faintest impression circling his ear. He needed her hands on him.

"Schuyler," he breathed into her mouth, "touch me."

"I am touching you," she murmured against his lips.

He backed off an inch or two, stared long and hard into her eyes and repeated the request. "Touch me."

"How?"

"As if you wanted me."

"I do want you." Then, as if the word had been stuck in her throat: "Where?"

Trace's gut tightened. "Here." He placed a hand on his chest. "Here." He moved lower, stopping somewhere in the vicinity of his rib cage. "And here." His palm came to rest on his abdomen.

Without another word, Schuyler granted his wish. She ran her hand along the line of his shoulder, down the entire length of his arm to the tips of his fingers and back up again.

Then she made a detour and leisurely trailed her fingers across the expanse of his chest, hesitating when she encountered the hard nub of a male nipple beneath his shirt, then curiously going in search of the other.

Trace shuddered.

She splayed the fingers of both hands, covering as much of him as she could, then deliberately and slowly caressed him—from his shoulders to his chest to his rib cage and finally to his waist, where she paused.

They both were well aware of his aroused state. It was there between them: unmistakable, indisputable, substantial, undeniable, rigid.

Trace couldn't speak. Instead, he raised both his hands and brought them down gently on Schuyler's shoulders. Then, at an excruciatingly slow pace, he traced the outline of her figure.

She had a lovely body: trim, firm, slightly muscular, yet soft and supple in all the right places. He realized that he wanted to see her naked, that he wanted to touch her in ways and in places that he would have to be content to only dream about for now.

His hands were resting on her hips when they heard a door slam somewhere nearby. Probably it was one of the small army of women who came in every day to clean and scrub Grantwood under the watchful eye of Mrs. Danvers.

Immediately the sensual spell was broken.

Trace swore under his breath and dropped his hands to his sides. Then he turned and started to walk out of the closet.

"Where are you going?" Schuyler asked him.

"To take a shower before we leave to have tea with the Miss Fricks." He was suddenly annoyed with her, annoyed with himself, annoyed with the whole damned world. "A cold shower," he muttered under his breath.

Chapter Fifteen

The creature that answered the door of the large Victorian cottage reminded Schuyler of an exotic bird. Ida Frick was a vision in purple, from the sprig of silk lilacs arranged in her hair to the amethyst broach pinned to the front of her purple polka-dotted dress to the purple shoes on her feet.

"Our guests are here, sister," she announced before she had even greeted them. "Good afternoon, Miss Grant. Mr. Ballinger. Please come in."

Trace Ballinger was solicitous. "Good afternoon, Miss Frick. I hope we're not late."

"Late?" The woman was suddenly flustered. "I shouldn't think so. I haven't checked the time in the past few minutes, but I'm confident that you aren't late." She paused and followed that statement with another. "I don't suppose you're early, either."

"No need to fuss, Ida," came the deeper and calmer voice of Ellamae Frick. The tall woman appeared behind her shorter sibling and looked straight at Schuyler. "We heard your car pull up in the driveway." Her attention transferred to Trace. "You're precisely on time."

At least that matter was settled to the satisfaction of all four.

"We mustn't keep Miss Grant and Mr. Ballinger standing on our doorstep," scolded Ida, with a click of her tongue and a hint of disapproval.

Her sister smoothed over the moment. "We're having tea in the parlor this afternoon. It's this way."

Miss Ida Frick fluttered her hands in the air—the motion

was rather like a bird flapping its wings in an attempt to become airborne—and chirped, "I do think it's nice to entertain company in style, don't you?" She seemed especially pleased with herself. "I've baked a special cake in honor of your visit. I hope you like coconut cream."

Trace reassured her that they did.

Meanwhile, Schuyler wondered how many visitors the Frick sisters entertained on a regular basis.

Ida twittered excitedly. "We used to have such lovely teas when we were girls. Mother would bake all manner of cakes and special confections. There would be tea for the ladies in the parlor and lemonade for the children in the kitchen or sometimes on the back porch, weather permitting." She turned to her sibling. "Do you remember Mother's teas, sister?"

Ellamae straightened her already ramrod-straight spine. "Of course I remember."

Ida reached out and took Schuyler's hand in hers. Then she gave it a soft rat-a-tat-tat with the tip of her index finger. "You didn't forget your promise, did you, Miss Grant?"

Schuyler hesitated. "My promise?"

The woman lowered her voice to a confidential level. "To share your recipe for lobster salad with me."

"As a matter of fact, I have it right here." Schuyler reached into her handbag. "Mrs. Danvers was kind enough to make a copy."

"Thank you," exclaimed Ida Frick as she clasped the three-by-five recipe card in her hand as if it were the worm and she was the early bird. "I can't thank you enough."

Trace held out a distinctive gold gift box. "I thought you might enjoy some chocolates."

Ida's eyes lit up with interest. "Godiva. How delicious. How thoughtful." She accepted the offering on behalf of herself and her sister. "I'll take these to the kitchen and put on the kettle. Why don't you get our guests settled, Ellamae?"

"This way," the tall, thin Frick sister indicated.

"I'll join you in a few minutes," Ida flung over her shoulder as she disappeared down a long passageway—although the floors of the house were covered with an array of area rugs, underneath they were wood and polished to a rich patina—and through a door into what Schuyler assumed was the kitchen.

"What a charming house, Miss Frick," Schuyler said as they walked into the formal parlor and entered a world where time seemed to have stood still.

The richly colored and busily patterned carpet on the floor, the ornately rendered oversize furniture, the bric-a-brac cluttering nearly every available surface and the lace doilies were all typical of a bygone era.

"Thank you, Miss Grant. Ida and I have lived in this house all of our lives. In fact, we were born in the front corner bedroom at the top of the stairs," she informed them, taking a seat on a maroon velvet sofa with a tufted back and an assortment of similarly tufted velvet pillows. "Little Hollows was originally the family's summer cottage." After a pause she went on to add, "Six up and six down."

"Six . . . ?"

"There are six rooms on each floor," the woman explained. "During the stock market Crash of 1929 and the Great Depression that followed, we Fricks suffered a reversal of fortune, like so many other families at that time in our nation's history." She indicated a pair of slightly shabby straight-backed chairs done in the Queen Anne style. "Please sit and make yourselves comfortable."

They could manage the former if not the latter.

Ellamae Frick chattered on. "Grandfather lost all of his

money in the Crash. Every last cent of it. He was never the same again. Of course, neither was Grandmother after he put a bullet in his brain. Anyway, the family was able to salvage this summer cottage and it became our year-round residence."

"We've been very happy here," piped up Ida as she rejoined them several minutes later. "One thing has always puzzled me, however. Why is the house called Little Hollows?" she said, blinking owlishly behind her bifocals. "We don't live in the country. In fact, we're in the middle of town."

"I don't believe the cottage was situated in the middle of town in those days," Ellamae pointed out.

The light dawned for Ida Frick. "Good gracious. Why didn't I think of that before? The town has grown up around Little Hollows, hasn't it?"

It was some time later that Schuyler gazed out a window and said, "I see you have a lovely flower garden."

"Do you enjoy gardening, Miss Grant?" Ellamae inquired as they sat sipping a cup of tea and eating their cake, too.

"I love fresh flowers," Schuyler answered enthusiastically. "Regrettably, I've never had the time or the opportunity to garden."

Ida Frick balanced her cup and saucer and cake plate on her lap like an expert. "You live in Paris, I understand."

"Yes, I do. I have an apartment in the city, so all my flowers are grown in window boxes."

The sisters were curious about her. "How do you spend your time?" one of them asked.

"I do what most people do. I work. I play. I spend time with my friends. And I have two cats."

Ida Frick seemed taken with the notion that Schuyler worked. "You have a job?"

"Yes, I'm a consultant for the Louvre."

Ellamae Frick set her teacup on the rococo table at her elbow and leaned toward her. Two small red spots suddenly appeared in the center of her otherwise colorless cheeks. "The Louvre," she repeated with something akin to reverence.

Schuyler put her fork down. "I research the history of ownership, specifically provenances, of paintings that were assumed lost or stolen during the last World War."

"How fascinating," claimed Ida Frick, although it was obvious the woman had only a limited grasp of what Schuyler was talking about.

It was Ellamae Frick's pale gray eyes that lit up with intense interest. "I wanted to study painting when I was younger," she blurted out. "I used to dream of going to Paris and strolling along the Seine with my canvas and paints."

"Sister has talent," Ida stated as she helped herself to another piece of coconut cream cake.

Ellamae exhaled on a wistful sigh. "Very little talent, if the truth be told."

"I don't have any artistic ability, myself," Schuyler admitted, "but I do have a keen eye for talent in others."

"We have a few paintings in the house that you might find worth your attention," the tall, thin Miss Frick shared with her. "Not the Great Masters, of course, but several wonderful artists of the Hudson River School."

Schuyler's curiosity was immediately piqued. "Whose paintings do you have?"

"Let me see, there is a small Frederick Church, a Thomas Cole and a Jervis McEntee."

"We had to sell a painting or two and a silver tea service just last year," Ida volunteered. "Now with all the lovely money Cora has left us, we won't have to sell any more paintings or pieces of Mother's silver."

The red spots on Ellamae Frick's cheeks spread out to cover her entire face, her ears and her neck. "Miss Grant and Mr. Ballinger aren't interested in hearing about Mother's silver, sister." She awkwardly cleared her throat. "I see we need more hot water. I'll get it this time, Ida."

"I'll help you," Schuyler volunteered.

". . . and it's rumored that on the anniversary of her death she wanders the pathway along the river, searching for her long-lost love," Ida Frick was recounting to Trace with what sounded suspiciously like dramatic license when Schuyler and Ellamae Frick rejoined them in the formal parlor.

"Our apologies," Schuyler extended to the other two. "I'm afraid we got caught up in a discussion of paintings and painting techniques." She only hesitated briefly before adding, "Time got away from us. Here's fresh tea."

"Thank you, my dear girl," Ida Frick responded. "However, we didn't miss you and Ellamae at all, did we, Mr. Ballinger?" She didn't give him an opportunity to respond. "Mr. Ballinger and I have been discussing the history of the Hudson River Valley, especially its restless spirits."

Schuyler was fairly certain Ida had been the one talking and Trace had been the one listening.

Ellamae was quick to admonish her sister. "I hope you weren't boring Mr. Ballinger."

"Of course, not." The woman came to an abrupt halt, cleared her throat, took a sip of tea and began again. "It's not every day I find so sympathetic a listener as Mr. Ballinger." She peered at her sibling over the rim of her spectacles. "He may not be a complete believer, but he does maintain an open mind."

Schuyler couldn't resist. "We all know that a mind is a terrible thing to waste."

Trace seemed to be biting the inside of his mouth against a smile. "I agree."

A myopic gaze scanned those gathered around the tea table. "I was just telling Mr. Ballinger that thirty million people in this country have seen a ghost."

Ellamae nodded her head and made a particular kind of sound with her teeth. "Even more claim to have experienced some kind of psychic phenomena, whether it's clairvoyance, telepathy or communicating with the dead."

Trace spoke up, adding, "You both have amazing statistics at your fingertips. Miss Frick"—he was referring to Ida "—informed me that nearly five million people in the United States have been abducted by aliens."

Schuyler decided it wouldn't be polite to allow her skepticism to show. "You don't say."

"I do say."

Miss Ida Frick bent over at the waist, extended her head and neck rather like a pecking and chirping bird and confided in a stage whisper, "It seems likely that number is grossly underestimated, since even more don't remember the experience." Then she sniffed and touched a dainty handkerchief, embellished with crochet work, to her nose.

"Ida would know," Ellamae stated unequivocally. "She has the gift."

"The gift?" Schuyler echoed.

The artistic Miss Frick moved her head up and down. "My sister hears voices."

"Hears voices?" This time it was Trace who repeated her words. "What voices?"

"The voices of those who can no longer speak for themselves," was the explanation given to them.

Based on what the Frick sisters had said to her the day

of Cora's memorial service, Schuyler had a hunch she knew. "Would that be voices from the other side?"

Ellamae Frick nodded.

"In that case, may I ask a question?" Schuyler said, putting her teacup down on the table.

"Well, of course you can, Miss Grant," the two women replied practically in unison.

"You knew my great-aunt for a number of years," she began, determined to speak clearly.

"Indeed we did," confirmed Ellamae Frick. She turned to her gifted sister. "How many years did we know Cora?"

Ida's answer was vague and inconclusive. "More years than I care to count."

Ellamae grew a bit impatient with her sibling. "Well, please do count them, Ida."

The white-haired woman put her teacup down and began to move her fingers as if she were doing precisely that: counting. "My best guess would be fifty-one years."

The gray-haired Miss Frick was quick to dissuade them of that impression. "No, Ida, not fifty-one. More like fifty-two or even fifty-three."

"Fifty-four years," declared her sister.

Trace appeared to be biting the inside of his mouth against another smile. "A long time," he concluded.

Schuyler was determined to find out what the Fricks knew about her great-aunt's penchant for building. "Did Cora always make"—here she paused for a moment and searched for the right word—"improvements to Grantwood?"

The answer to her question was apparently going to take some thought on the part of both sisters.

Ellamae was the first to speak. "Well, it started out when we were little more than girls. Remember, Ida, we went to see Uncle Gus in Minnesota one summer and when we returned home there was scaffolding erected over one end of the big house?"

"I remember," claimed Ida.

"Then there was the spring everyone in town was talking about the architect Cora had brought up from New York. He actually lived at Grantwood for the better part of several years."

"He was very handsome," her sister recalled.

Ellamae Frick turned to Schuyler. "I believe Cora felt she *had* to make changes to the house."

There was a rather pensive sigh from the rounder Miss Frick. "Sometimes I wonder if she was simply lonely and wanted the company."

Schuyler sat and waited while the exchange between the sisters continued.

Another possibility occurred to Ida. "Perhaps it was like the story we heard about Oliver Winchester's widow."

Ellamae was the one who explained. "When Oliver Winchester died in the early 1880s—and yes, he was *that* Winchester, the inventor of the rifle that bore his name—he left his widow more than twenty million dollars."

"That was a great deal of money in those days," piped up Ida Frick as she reached for another tea cake.

"That's a great deal of money today," her sister announced, deadpan.

"Go on," Schuyler urged.

"Sarah Winchester, his widow, had an obsessive fear of the spirits of the dead."

Ida swallowed and insisted upon putting in her two cents' worth. "Specifically the thousands of souls who were killed by the Winchester rifle."

Ellamae nodded gravely. "Desperate, Sarah sought help from a world-renowned psychic. She was told that the spirits of the dead were going to haunt her and the only way to save herself was to build a structure large enough to house them all. So she started adding rooms to her home."

Schuyler felt the hairs on the back of her neck stand on end. "How long did Sarah build?"

"Every day for thirty-eight years. By the time the Widow Winchester died, her house contained one hundred and sixty rooms."

"And ten thousand windows."

"Two thousand doors."

"Forty-seven fireplaces. But only one ballroom," said Ida.

"The house still stands today." Ellamae Frick paused and considered the matter. "Somewhere in California, I believe."

Chapter Sixteen

"There's Teddy now," Ida announced as a door slammed somewhere in the back of the cottage.

Footsteps could be heard, and then another door opening and closing. "He's gone to work. I don't think you'll meet him today," Ellamae said without apology. "Once Theodore's in his laboratory, he frequently doesn't come out again for hours and hours."

Trace frowned. "His laboratory?"

"It's a kind of greenhouse filled with plants and scientific experiments and expensive equipment. We never go into the lab. Not even to dust or sweep. Teddy wouldn't like that."

Ellamae picked up the conversation where her sister had stopped. "Theodore is a botanist. His specialty is mosses and fungi. He spends a good deal of his time in the field."

"That means he tromps about in the woods, collecting specimens and transporting them back to his laboratory," Ida explained to their guests. "Our brother is a brilliant man. World-renowned in his field. He gets mail from as far away as Russia and China." She went on, "Teddy didn't always live here with us."

Ellamae Frick translated. "Theodore went away to the university, of course, and then traveled all over the world. He returned to Little Hollows just last year."

"It's nice to have a man around the house," Ida declared. "And not as much trouble as we thought it would be."

"No, indeed."

A guileless smile appeared on a surprisingly wrinkle-free

and rather round face. "That's why it's so lovely having you come for tea, Mr. Ballinger. We don't often have gentlemen visit us. Will you come again soon?"

"My plans are somewhat indefinite," Trace replied, giving no particular implication by his answer.

Miss Ellamae Frick was all pale skin again, the excitement of the moment having passed. Her dress was an unflattering mustard yellow with small nondescript flowers scattered across the front. There was a serviceable barrette in her salt and pepper hair. She turned her head and abruptly changed the subject. "What is your favorite tea cake, Mr. Ballinger?"

He tried not to grasp the handle of his cup too tightly for fear the delicate china would shatter in his hands. "Tea cake?" Since there was no way around it, he might as well come clean. "I don't usually take tea," Trace confessed.

"You don't take tea?" The thought had obviously never occurred to either of the Miss Fricks. Although it was Miss Ellamae who had inquired, they were both equally astonished by his answer.

"Whyever not?" she inquired.

A man was damned if he did and damned if he didn't.

"I live and work in a large midtown Manhattan office building. I'm usually traveling to see a client or in my office at this time of the afternoon," he said by way of an explanation.

Schuyler took another sip of tepid tea and listened to the exchange between Trace and the Frick sisters.

"What kind of clientele do you have, Trace?" inquired his nearest companion.

"I handle a little bit of everything, but I specialize in estate planning," he responded.

"Is that what you did for Cora?"

"Yes."

It was Ellamae Frick who asked the questions. "Are you from a family of lawyers?"

Schuyler sat and waited, along with the others, for his answer. She realized she knew very little about Trace when it came right down to the facts.

His reply was almost immediately forthcoming. "I was born and raised along the railroad tracks in Pittsburgh, Pennsylvania, otherwise known as Steel Town. My grandfather was a coal miner. My father was a steelworker. I was a steelworker myself until I was twenty."

"You're self-made, then?"

"Yes."

"I like that in a man," Ellamae Frick proclaimed.

Ida Frick wiped at the corners of her mouth with a fine linen napkin. "What do you like in a man, sister? I didn't know you knew any men. That gentleman down the street hasn't been pestering you again, has he?"

There was a long-suffering sigh. "No, Ida. He hasn't. And I was speaking of men like Mr. Ballinger, who have the brains and the guts to know what they want in life and then go after it."

Ida seemed scandalized. "What was the word you used?"

"Guts."

The rather round Miss Frick was all apologies. "I don't think that word has ever been spoken before within the walls of Little Hollows. Mother and Father must be turning over in their graves."

Ellamae didn't mince words. "I seriously doubt that, Ida. Besides, I was expressing my admiration for someone who has the wherewithal to do what they want to do. I wish I had."

This apparently was news to Ida Frick. "What would you have done?"

"Lived a little more. Feared a whole lot less. Painted. Gone to Paris." The woman's voice dropped. "Spent a whole day, maybe two whole days, wandering through the Louvre and experiencing all those magnificent works of art."

"It's never too late," Schuyler interjected gently. "After all, Paris is the city of lights and enlightenment."

Ellamae Frick was silent for a small space. Then she looked up and said, "I can do whatever I want with my share of the inheritance from Cora, is that right, Mr. Ballinger?"

"Yes, Miss Frick, that's right," Trace assured her.

Ida suddenly burst out with an unexpected question of her own. "I wonder if French cooking is as wonderful as everyone always say it is."

Trace set his teacup down on the table in front of him. "Miss Grant would know the answer to that. After all, she's lived in France for nearly a decade."

Schuyler backed him up. "There's no better place on earth than France for a gourmand like yourself, Miss Frick."

Ida Frick, silk purple flowers drooping over one ear, turned to her sister. "Ellamae . . ."

"Yes, sister?"

"We should start packing."

"Packing, Ida?"

The pink, plump woman drew herself up and stated, "We are going to Paris."

The sudden and amazing transformation in the two women was a sight to behold.

Schuyler's head came around. "That's a wonderful idea, Miss Frick. If you like, I can give you the names of some friends who would love to introduce you to their Paris and their France."

It was some time later that Schuyler and Trace took their leave of Miss Ida and Ellamae Frick, soon-to-be world travelers.

"You've been most gracious," Schuyler enthused. "Your tea and cakes were delicious, Miss Ida. The floral arrangements in the house must come from your garden, Miss Ellamae. I don't believe I've ever seen such wonderful flowers. You've both made me feel welcome."

Ellamae Frick was effusive. "We should be thanking you, Miss Grant. I never thought I would see Paris. It's going to be a dream come true for me."

"Thank you for sharing your recipe for lobster salad," joined in Ida Frick. "I'm sure I'll be bringing back all kinds of wonderful recipes from across the ocean."

As their guests traipsed across the lawn to their car, the sisters called out, *"Au revoir."*

Ellamae Frick chewed on her bottom lip in an uncharacteristic and nervous fashion as she watched the elegant Miss Grant and the handsome Mr. Ballinger walk toward their automobile. She finally voiced aloud what was on both their minds. "I wonder if we should have told them, sister."

Eyes of pale blue—far too often they gave the impression of being vague of thought and intent—followed the retreating figures. "I don't know."

Ellamae heaved a sigh. "Perhaps it's best that they find out for themselves."

"Perhaps."

They stood side by side for another minute or two. Then Ellamae remarked, "Cora's right, of course."

"She usually is," Ida agreed.

Ellamae nodded her head.

Ida added, "They do make a handsome couple."

Ellamae Frick noticed her hands were trembling slightly

as she opened the screen door and waited for her sister to precede her into the house where they had lived together all their lives. "Yes, my dear, they do." She turned back for a moment. "If they can only weather the storm ahead."

Chapter Seventeen

"Where is the woman?"

Jonathan Grant sat back in the upholstered leather arm-chair and, with far more forbearance than he was feeling, repeated, "I told you, Elaine. Mrs. Danvers said Schuyler is having tea with the Fricks this afternoon."

Elaine Kendall sniffed in that indignant manner as only she could, and voiced her complaint. "I don't see why she would go off to have tea with a couple of old ladies when she's expecting me to show her house. It's not every day you find someone interested in an estate like Grantwood. Clients with the Plunketts' kind of money don't grow on trees, you know."

The beautiful woman—far too beautiful for her own good, in Jonathan Grant's opinion (he believed it had resulted in a certain deficiency in her character, which naturally he kept to himself)—paused, muttered under her breath, paced back and forth in front of the library fireplace and glanced at her watch for the tenth time in as many minutes.

He offered what little consolation he could. "Schuyler must have forgotten you were showing the house this afternoon."

"Of course she's forgotten," Elaine snapped, "or she'd be here, wouldn't she?" As she paced the floor, he noticed her high heels made no sound on the thick carpet. "We agreed that your cousin would be an invaluable asset in selling this place." She threw up her hands in frustration.

"Well, we'll just have to start without her if the Plunketts arrive first."

Johnny shrugged his shoulders.

Elaine had done her homework. "Thank goodness I've brushed up on the history of Grantwood. The house has some beautiful features and its idiosyncracies just might appeal to Mr. and Mrs. Plunkett."

Johnny intended to set the record straight. "Schuyler may not want to sell."

Elaine Kendall rarely took no for an answer. "Of course she'll want to sell. You told me yourself this is the first time she's been back to Grantwood in nearly a decade."

He restated his disclaimer. "You never can tell about my family. They tend to be eccentric."

Elaine, exquisitely turned out from the top of her head—her black hair was shorn in the latest ultra-short style—to the tips of her perfectly manicured fingernails to the cropped jacket of her designer suit to the pointed toes of her stiletto heels, said, "You mean like Crazy Cora."

He casually crossed one leg over the over. "So you've heard about Cora."

"Everyone has heard about Cora. As a matter of fact, I know a great deal about Cora LeMasters Grant." Elaine Kendall smiled a smug kind of Cheshire cat smile. "Almost as much as I know about you, darling."

Never let them see you sweat.

Johnny managed not to let the woman see his reaction to her implied threat. "Ancient history," he declared as he nonchalantly plucked a speck of nonexistent lint from his pant leg.

Red lips protruded, then pouted. "Is that what we are, Johnnykins? Ancient history?"

He hated Elaine's nickname for him and she damned well knew it, too.

"Anything between us was over and done with a long time ago and you know it," he said testily.

She knew it.

Still, Elaine enjoyed reminding Jonathan Tiberius Grant of the fact that at least for a short time they had been more than simply business associates.

"Have you told Schuyler Grant about us?"

"There is no us," the handsome man stated.

She attempted a bluff. "I could make her believe there still is an us."

Johnny's delicious masculine laughter filled the library. "Behave yourself, Elaine."

"I don't want to behave," she answered honestly. She never wanted to behave herself when she was around Johnny. She was in love with him.

Not that she had ever breathed a word of her true feelings to Jonathan Grant, of course. A man with Johnny's looks and charm had women—literally dozens of women— falling over themselves to capture his attention.

She refused to be one of them.

"You don't have any choice," he reminded her. "This is business. Big business."

"There's more to life than money," she stated.

A blond eyebrow arched in a skeptical fashion. "Is there?"

She sauntered closer to his chair, leaned over the arm and lazily drew an imaginary line with her index finger back and forth across his mouth. "We're good together."

"We *were*."

It was better—and far safer—for Johnny to think that all she'd cared about was the sex. "We're great together in bed."

"I repeat: We *were*. Past tense." He couldn't have made his disinterest any more obvious..

Elaine Kendall wasn't a stupid woman. She knew when it was to her benefit to back off.

She directed their conversation to the one thing she and Johnny always had in common: the real estate business. "Doesn't it seem odd to you?"

"Doesn't *what* seem odd?"

"The fact that we show up for our appointment and discover that Schuyler has blithely gone off to have tea."

A frown appeared on Johnny Grant's handsome-as-sin face. "As a matter of fact, it's damned odd. Who did you say called to arrange the showing?"

"A man who identified himself as Cora's attorney. Funnily enough, I can't seem to recall his name."

Johnny got an expression of distaste on his face. "I can tell you his name. It's Trace Ballinger."

"I don't think that was the name given to me over the telephone," Elaine said to him.

"Well, that's the name of Cora's attorney. Unless someone else from his law office made the call."

"Does it matter?"

Johnny shook his head. "I wouldn't think so."

Suddenly Elaine latched on to a possibility that had just occurred to her. "My God, Johnny, what if the lawyer forgot to tell her? What if Schuyler isn't even aware of our appointment to show Grantwood to the Plunketts?"

"Bloody hell," he muttered under his breath.

"It would explain why the housekeeper acted surprised when we showed up at the door."

"Yes, it would."

"What do we do now?"

It was a minute or two before he suggested, "Brazen it out." Then he went on, "It's a dog-eat-dog world out there,

Elaine. You of all people should understand the concept of seizing an opportunity when it presents itself."

"So Schuyler Grant is going to return later this afternoon and discover that strangers are traipsing through Grantwood. Of course, she'll be too polite, or too bowled over by our audacity, to throw us out on our arses."

"Something like that."

She held her breath. "Do we dare?"

Johnny shrugged his elegant shoulders. "No guts, no glory."

"No sale. Is that it, Johnny?"

"I'm just trying to figure a way out of a potentially awkward situation. Have you calculated what the commission is going to be on this place?"

Naturally she had.

"Still, I have my reputation to think of," she hedged.

He hooted in her face. "Your reputation? Shall I tell you what your reputation is in the real estate business? You're known as Elaine the ball-buster."

"Stop it!"

"Why?"

She knew her face was flushed with color. "I don't like being called names."

The handsome man laughed again. "If the shoe fits . . ."

She decided not to argument with him. "What if Schuyler decides not to sell?"

He answered her only indirectly. "She will sell."

"And if she refuses?"

Johnny got a look on his face that she had seen there before: determination. "That's my department."

Suddenly she was suspicious. "What are you up to?"

"It's none of your business."

"You've got plans for you and Schuyler Grant, don't you? I should have known."

All he said was, "We're perfect for each other."

"Does she agree with you?"

"She will." Then Johnny mused aloud, "It's time I got married."

Her eyes widened appreciably. "You?"

"Yes, me."

"I thought you were of the school of thought that every woman should marry, and no man," Elaine said, paraphrasing some famous quote she had once heard.

"I've had a change of heart. It's time I settled down, made a home for myself and had children." He steepled his fingers under his chin. "Schuyler and I are two of a kind."

Elaine frowned. "What about us?"

"Like I told you before: There is no us."

That's where Johnny was wrong.

Elaine made a generally inconclusive and vague movement with her hand. "I wish you all the best, of course."

He was suddenly on guard. "What's going on inside that devious mind of yours?"

Elaine lowered her voice to an intimate level. "I mean it, Johnny. I wish you both all the best in the world."

Johnny reached up and patted her hand. "I'm sure Mr. Right will come along one day."

For a moment Elaine Kendall was uncertain whether the devilishly handsome man was teasing her or whether he was serious. Then she smiled. "In that case, I'll be Mrs. Right."

Chapter Eighteen

Mrs. Danvers was waiting for them in the front entrance—the housekeeper was pacing the floor, practically wearing a pathway in the black-veined Brescia marble, and jingling her household keys—when Schuyler and Trace returned from having tea with the Fricks.

"You had callers while you were gone this afternoon," Schuyler was informed the instant she walked into the house.

"Callers?" A frown creased her brow. "Do you mean there were visitors?"

The housekeeper nodded her head and wrung her hands. "Yes. As a matter of fact, you just missed them."

"How long ago did they leave?"

Elvira Danvers consulted the antique clock in the hallway. "Ten minutes ago."

"Who were they?"

Mrs. Danvers forced each word from her mouth as if she really didn't want to say them. "Mr. Jonathan Grant for one, and that real estate agent for another."

Schuyler felt as if they were speaking a different language. "What real estate agent?"

The woman's spine was as straight as a board. It was also apparent she was trying to keep a stiff upper lip. "Ms. Kendall left her business card on the table."

Schuyler made her way across the great hall, picked up the business card that had been left on the silver salver and read aloud to no one in particular, "Elaine Kendall, residential and business real estate development."

The housekeeper's thin lips grew even thinner. "Ms. Kendall was quite put out. She claimed that you'd forgotten about your appointment with her."

Schuyler was at an utter and complete loss. She made a futile gesture with her hand. "What appointment?"

Mrs. Danvers answered for her. "To meet with the couple interested in buying Grantwood."

Schuyler handed Elaine Kendall's business card to Trace. "What couple?"

Mrs. Danvers summed up the interested party in one word. "Foreigners."

Schuyler was more than a little perplexed. "Foreigners?"

"From Texas." Elvira Danvers folded her hands together at her waist. "I had trouble understanding them because of their accent, but the so-called gentleman warned me not to squat with my spurs on. I told him I never wore spurs. For some reason he seemed to think that was funny. He couldn't stop laughing."

Schuyler managed not to laugh now. "Did they go through the house?"

"Yes. I didn't know what to do. They insisted they had your permission to show Grantwood to qualified buyers, as Ms. Kendall referred to the couple. I wished you'd told me, Miss Grant."

Spreading her arms in a gesture of futility, Schuyler confessed, "I'm at a loss to understand how this happened without my knowledge or consent."

Trace spoke up for the first time since their return. "Did all four of the visitors traipse through the house?"

"Yes and no, sir. At one point I believe the gentlemen excused themselves and went into the billiard room, while the ladies strolled outside to look over the gazebo. Later on, Mr. Grant disappeared upstairs while the others were in the library."

"So he spent some time separate from the others?"

"Yes, sir." Mrs. Danvers recalled, "Then Ms. Kendall came to the kitchen to ask for a glass of water for one of her clients."

"So the couple were left alone in the library."

"Now that you mention it, I suppose they were, Mr. Ballinger."

Schuyler was astonished that strangers had been allowed to wander through a private residence. "Where would a real estate agent gain the impression that I wanted to show my house?"

Mrs. Danvers had more facts. "She said the appointment was made through your attorney."

"Not this attorney," Trace said, his mouth thinning.

Schuyler encouraged her by saying, "Tell us what else you recall about the couple."

"The man's name was P. G. Plunkett and I heard him tell Mr. Grant that he was in oil. His wife was introduced as Wilma. She had pink bouffant hair. At one point Mrs. Plunkett remarked to Ms. Kendall it was best not to try to teach a pig to sing. She said it was a waste of time and it annoyed the pig. Ms. Kendall obviously had no idea what the woman was talking about."

Schuyler speculated, "Surely you've seen those television commercials that claim Texas is a whole different country." She shrugged. "I guess they meant it."

Trace seemed to find that vaguely amusing. "Have either of you ladies ever been to Texas?"

"No."

"Well, I have. It's not *that* different." He took Schuyler by the elbow and suggested, "Let's see if our unexpected guests were up to anything special while we were out." Once they reached the library, Trace stood in the middle of the room and did his thinking out loud. "I wonder if it was coincidence or if they deliberately asked for a glass of water to have a few minutes alone in here." He turned to Elvira Danvers. "Would you recognize if something was missing?"

"No, sir," she admitted. "But I know someone who would."

"Who?"

"Annie Barker."

Schuyler turned to the housekeeper. "Any relation to Geoffrey Barker?"

"Annie's his niece by marriage. In fact, she and her husband live in one of the estate cottages with Mr. Barker. Anyway, Annie has been coming in to clean the library for a lot longer than I've been here. If anything is out of place, she'd be the one to know. Would you like me to telephone her?"

Schuyler answered, "Please do, Mrs. Danvers."

"What do you think, Annie?"

"Ah, here's what you've been looking for." The middle-aged woman removed an oversize leatherbound volume from a shelf above her head and placed it on the library table. "This book has recently been moved, Miss Grant, and then put back in the wrong place, to boot. I know because I dusted these shelves myself just this morning."

"What kind of book is it?"

Annie opened to the first page. "Maps."

Schuyler didn't understand. "Maps?"

"Old maps of the estate, miss. They go back right to the beginning when Mr. William Tiberius Grant built the house." Annie Barker ran her hand along the binding. "That's odd."

"What's odd?"

The woman's expression was one of concentration. "The edge is jagged. It looks like a page has been torn out."

That got Trace's immediate attention. "Do you have any idea what might have been on that page?" he asked.

Annie scanned the maps to either side of the one missing. "Best as I can figure, it was an architectural rendering of the grounds from the 1940s."

Schuyler looked from Trace to Annie Barker and back again. "Why would anyone want information that is more than fifty years out of date?"

"I couldn't say, Miss Grant," the woman admitted, shaking her head. "But my husband's uncle can tell you all about the old days at Grantwood. At least Uncle Jeff can on a day when his mind is clear, if you know what I mean."

Schuyler thought of the memorial luncheon and her conversation with Geoffrey Barker. The retired head gardener had been lucid one minute and then had drifted into another time and place the next.

"Thank you, Annie. You've been a tremendous help," she said to the woman. "I would like to stop by and talk to Mr. Barker one afternoon soon, if I may."

"He'd like that, Miss Grant. Uncle Jeff doesn't get a lot of visitors these days."

Chapter Nineteen

"Welcome, welcome," greeted Geoffrey Barker as he proudly ushered Schuyler into the living room of his cottage. "It's good to see you again, Miss Grant."

"Thank you, Mr. Barker," she responded politely. She noticed the old man was leaning heavily on his cane. "I've brought you a few treats from Mrs. Danvers's kitchen." Schuyler indicated the shopping bag she was carrying. "She made me promise to tell you that she's included some of your favorite cookies."

"Mrs. Danvers never forgets to send over something for my sweet tooth," he said, obviously pleased that the housekeeper had remembered him.

"And I've brought you a bottle of whiskey. I hope you won't think it presumptuous of me."

"No, no, not at all, miss." Geoffrey Barker glanced up at the grandfather clock in the front entrance and observed with a hint of regret, "A bit early for a whiskey."

It was the middle of the afternoon.

"I'm afraid it is," Schuyler agreed.

Geoffrey Barker licked his lips. "Unless it was for medicinal purposes, of course."

She didn't crack a smile. "You seem well."

"Oh, I am. A spot of rheumatism now and then, and sometimes my memory comes and goes a bit, but I can't complain, Miss Grant," the elderly gentleman said, motioning her to one of two overstuffed La-Z-Boy chairs.

Apparently Geoffrey Barker felt that age had its privileges. He didn't waste any time. He came right out and asked, "So, miss, are you going to sell up?"

"Sell up?"

"Sell Grantwood?"

Schuyler settled in the chair beside him and said, "I haven't decided."

"I heard there was a couple in to look the place over," came the unadorned statement.

There was no reason to try to argue otherwise with Geoffrey Barker. "There was a couple in, as you say."

"I don't know what will happen to folks like me if Grantwood's sold." He looked around the comfortable cottage. "I've lived in this house for nearly fifty years. It's in good repair, too, thanks to Mr. Ballinger."

"Mr. Ballinger?"

The retired gardener nodded his head. "Since Mrs. Grant got too old to take care of things, Mr. Ballinger has made certain that all of the staff cottages are kept in excellent condition."

It seemed there was a thing or two she still had to learn about her attorney.

The old man smacked his lips together several times. "Mrs. Grant used to come by regular-like back in the old days. Sure do miss her visits." His eyes narrowed. He peered at her. "I do believe you look like her, after all. Maybe it's the hair."

Schuyler fingered the piece of protective plastic covering the arm of the chair. "Did Cora have red hair?" She only remembered her great-aunt as having white hair.

"When she was younger . . . much younger. Turned white overnight, it did."

"What did?"

"Her hair. It went from red to snow-white overnight,"

the elderly gentleman claimed, repeating himself, but making his statement no less *un*clear.

Schuyler folded her hands in her lap. He obviously couldn't mean literally. "I was wondering if I might ask you a question or two, Mr. Barker."

"Fire away," was his reply.

She took the roundabout way of getting to the point. "Your niece, Annie, works up at the house."

"Has since she married Fred."

"Fred?"

"My nephew. He came to work for me back in 1955 right out of high school. Annie and Fred moved in here with me when they were married a few years later. That's when Annie went to work for Mrs. Grant. Annie has a very important job."

"Yes. I know."

He stared out the window for a few minutes. "She sees to the cleaning of some valuable pieces, especially in the library. Got to know what you're doing or a priceless painting or book could be ruined forever." He took another moment to consider that daunting prospect, then declared, "Wouldn't want the responsibility, myself."

Schuyler seized the opportunity. "As a matter of fact, Annie was showing me a book of maps in the library only a few days ago. We were surprised to discover a page was missing."

"Missing?"

She nodded. "Someone had recently torn the page from the book, according to Annie, and we couldn't imagine why."

Geoffrey Barker tapped his cane on the floor. "Who would want to tear up a map book?"

"I don't know." Schuyler decided to keep her suspicions to herself.

"What was taken?"

"Annie thinks it's an architectural drawing of the grounds as they appeared half a century ago."

"Wouldn't think that'd matter to anyone nowadays."

Schuyler disagreed. "I would very much like to know what was on that page."

Geoffrey Barker fell silent for a minute. His gaze seemed to fix on the horizon. "I might be able to help you."

"I would appreciate it."

The old man raised one finger—Schuyler noticed the skin on the back of his hand appeared to be tissue-paper-thin and freckled with age spots; his veins bulged just beneath the surface of his flesh—and pointed to his head. "It's all in here."

"What is?"

"The way Grantwood looked in its glory days."

She blinked several times in rapid succession. "I wish I could see inside your head, Mr. Barker."

He raised his cane and gestured toward the big house. "There must be photographs somewhere."

Schuyler gave a sigh. "Cora kept everything, but I haven't found any old photographs yet." At least not the ones she needed. She was still looking, but it was a monumental task. "Do you remember what the original layout of the gardens was?"

"'Course I do."

"Would you describe it for me?"

He settled back in his chair and cleared his throat. "Well, now, missy, you know as you come up the drive?"

"Yes."

"The English rose garden was on the left." His weathered face brightened. "Come summer 'twas a sight to behold, I'll tell you. Roses of every size and color and variety in bloom." He took in a breath. "I can still smell them."

Schuyler knew that Geoffrey Barker would get around to telling her in his own time and in his own way.

"The formal garden and the gazebo are pretty much as they were in those days. Not so nice, of course. There used to be a Persian carpet on the floor and fancy furniture and such."

"Now it's benches."

The old man's tone changed to one of disapproval. "Some builder added them back in '62."

"Did Cora know?"

His lips formed a thin, tight line of disapproval. "Can't say that she did." He went on. "Anyway, how far back do you want me to go?"

Schuyler kept her voice even. "Could you go as far back as Mrs. Grant's private garden?"

"I can try." A sweet smile appeared on the elderly gentleman's face. "Sometimes I remember the old days better than I do yesterday or even today," he confessed.

"Then I hope your memories are happy ones," Schuyler said in a soft voice.

He sat back and closed his eyes. "Happy and sad," he added with a sigh.

"Cora's private garden," Schuyler nudged.

"It wasn't big." Geoffrey Barker opened his eyes. "But it wasn't small, either. We planted all of her favorite flowers in her favorite colors. There was a pathway of smooth stones that meandered through the garden, and a bench under a shade tree where she liked to sit on a sunny afternoon."

"She must have loved the garden."

"Yes, she loved her garden." His voice trailed off. "And she hated her garden."

"Hated it?"

The retired head gardener stopped and dug around in the

pocket of his cardigan sweater. He removed a handkerchief and wiped his mouth. "She grew to hate it," he said, more to himself than to Schuyler. "Not that any of us could blame her, after the tragedy."

Schuyler could suddenly hear her own heart beating. "What tragedy?"

There was no indication by his words or actions that the old man had heard her question. "The garden was closed, of course," he stated. "No one ever went there again."

"What happened?" she asked, needing to know.

"He made a mistake." Geoffrey Barker's gaze was fixed on some distant point where Schuyler realized she couldn't go. "He believed it would be a wonderful surprise."

"The wishing well?" she ventured.

"Mrs. Grant wished for it and he gave it to her. Only it didn't turn out as they thought it would. That's what happens, doesn't it? You wish for something without knowing what you're really getting." He fell silent again. "She paid a terrible price."

"What was the price?"

He was lucid enough to relate to her, "The life of the man she loved."

Schuyler realized her mouth had dropped open. "Cora's husband? Mr. Grant?"

There was the slightest nod of the old man's head. "The master took to drink." Almost as an afterthought, Geoffrey Barker added, "He died the next year."

Schuyler sat and watched the late afternoon sunlight streaming in the living room window. She'd always known that Cora had tragically lost her husband, but since no one in the family was allowed to speak of it, the details hadn't been known. At least now she had one small piece of the puzzle.

Unfocused eyes stared straight past her. "Have you been to Cora's garden?"

"No," she answered.

"Then you haven't seen the wishing well."

"No. I haven't."

"Has anyone ever told you about wishes and dreams?"

She shook her head.

"Don't ever let yours go, no matter what," Geoffrey Barker warned. "No matter what."

Schuyler's voice was strangely hoarse. "Can you tell me where Cora's garden is, Mr. Barker?"

He nodded. "Gone. Gone long ago." And he kept nodding his head.

It was a minute or two, maybe longer, before Schuyler said to him, "I must go home now, Mr. Barker, but I'd like to come visit you again if I may."

"You do that, Miss . . ." He'd forgotten her name.

"Grant."

Her aged host insisted on rising from his La-Z-Boy chair and walking her as far as his own front door. "I've seen her," he suddenly blurted out.

"Who?"

"Lucy." He leaned heavily on his cane. "She was there at the river's edge, there by Lucy's Lookout."

Schuyler wasn't about to insult the old gentleman by contradicting him.

He pursed his lips. "Sometimes you can catch sight of her at twilight if you know where to look."

Schuyler chose diplomacy. "Thank you for talking to me, Mr. Barker."

"You're welcome, missy. Next time come for tea and we'll have a shot of whiskey."

Schuyler started along the well-trodden pathway that led from his cottage to the main house. She stopped, turned around and waved to the old man. But he'd already turned his back and begun the short walk to his cottage door.

It was a perfect May evening. The view across the river was magnificent: high bluffs and a springtime forest, and below, the water, all gold and silver in the fading light. It was a view that had changed very little in the past century or two.

Schuyler put her head back, shaded her eyes from the setting sun with her hand and gazed up at the house. This wing of Grantwood had been changed greatly from its original construction. There was a castlelike turret built of solid stone. There were dozens of windows of nearly every shape and size. Sometimes they were positioned at angles and irregular intervals.

Schuyler knew from family stories that her great-aunt had been building and renovating for decades. Perhaps, like the Winchester widow, Cora had thought to appease restless spirits, even if it was her own restless spirit.

Skirting the woods, Schuyler strolled toward the wing of the house that she was pretty certain contained Cora's rooms. She looked up and then turned to gaze out over the stretch of green lawn and the manicured formal garden.

"Why would anyone want a map of the grounds as they once were?" she wondered aloud.

She bent over, plucked a wildflower and straightened again. What was she going to do about Grantwood?

For that matter, what in the world was she going to do about Trace Ballinger?

She wasn't going to think about that now.

Schuyler sighed and closed her eyes. She could smell the damp earth, the green grass, a hint of burning wood and the fragile scent of the flowers at her feet.

She opened her eyes. The sky was clear overhead; there

would be stars tonight. The trees were green with new leaves. The woods were growing dark. There wasn't another human being in sight.

It was by sheer chance that Schuyler happened to glance up again at the house.

There!

There in a window was a woman's face!

But it was the face of no woman that Schuyler had ever seen before.

"Who are you?" she whispered.

The window was in the same wing where Cora's rooms were located. She counted from the corner of the building. In fact, the window was exactly where Cora's should be.

But the window was shuttered. There weren't any shutters on Cora's windows.

Then something occurred to Schuyler. Something she should have thought of before.

Rooms without windows.

Windows without rooms.

Chapter Twenty

Revenge was a dish best served cold.

That had been one of Trace Ballinger's mottoes for his thirty-eight, almost thirty-nine, years.

He'd been many things in those thirty-eight years: high school dropout, teenage rebel and all-around hellraiser, Pittsburgh steelworker, Harvard scholar and, for the past decade, high-powered attorney to the rich and sometimes ruthless.

Hell, he had been a little ruthless himself on occasion.

A number of his well-heeled and well-connected clients lived in the historic mansions along the Hudson River; an equal number were elderly, alone and lonely.

Despite his current success and elevated social standing, Trace never forgot where he came from: a working-class neighborhood in Pittsburgh, Pennsylvania. To his way of thinking (it had been true twenty years ago when he'd been working in the steel mills and it was still true today), the world was pretty much divided into two kinds of people: bluebloods and blue collar.

Them and us.

Schuyler Grant was one of them.

Trace was well aware that he was from the other side of the tracks.

He had told Cora the first day they'd met that there were worse things in this world than being a fool. Still, he was *not* a man who suffered fools willingly. He knew he was smart—perhaps even brilliant—and tough.

Very tough.

He came by it naturally.

Trace's grandfather had been forced to quit school in the sixth grade: If he'd wanted to eat, he'd had to work. So Jack Ballinger had gone down into the coal mines of western Pennsylvania (which was, in truth, part of Appalachia economically if not geographically) at the age of eleven.

Jack Ballinger had been a man old before his time, a bitter man, a real bastard when he drank. Trace remembered his grandfather lying in a tiny back bedroom of a too-small house beside a railroad track, the air gray with smoke—he still smoked three packs of cigarettes a day; a habit he had no intentions of quitting whatever the goddamned doctors had told him about his lungs.

If Trace had one lasting and vivid impression of his grandfather, it was the sound of a hacking cough and a hoarse whisper as he cursed the name of Grant.

The year Trace was ten, Jack Ballinger had died of black lung disease.

His father had wanted a better life for himself. Wes Ballinger had waited until he was sixteen to drop out of school. Eventually he had gotten a job in the Pittsburgh steel mills. It was hard work. Dirty work. Dangerous work. But the pay had been good and the work steady until the bottom dropped out of the market for domestic steel.

The year Trace was nineteen—he'd already been working alongside his father at Grant Steel for five years (sometimes it seemed like twenty-five)—Wes Ballinger had suffered a heart attack.

His father had lived by steel, and before the age of fifty, he'd died by steel, cursing the name of Grant.

From that day forward, all of Trace's energies had been focused on getting out and getting even. He was his father's son and the third generation of Ballingers who hated everything and everyone associated with the name of Grant.

Them and us.

Schuyler Grant was a descendant of Dutch patroons and English land barons who had first built their mansions along the Hudson River in the eighteenth and nineteenth centuries. Her pedigree was long and distinguished. She had attended private schools, studied in Paris and traveled the world: all in first-class style.

Schuyler was a true blueblood from the top of her head to the tips of her toes.

There were those, of course, who claimed Schuyler was too good to be true.

There were those who whispered that dark secrets must lurk somewhere behind that famous Grant facade, behind the walls of the palatial estate.

Grantwood: the home—the obsession—of an eccentric woman who had endured the tragic loss of everything she'd held dear.

Grantwood: one of the most magnificent mansions ever built along the Hudson River and, unlike many of the estates, which were quickly becoming a fading and crumbling memory of aristocratic luxury and a bygone era, still occupied by its founding family.

Up and down the river, ruins were visible through the trees and dense undergrowth: ruins that had once been great houses with their turrets and spires, rambling porticos, gleaming columns and glaring gargoyles, and inside, vaulted ceilings, spacious ballrooms and huge libraries that reflected the river elite's historic obsession with books.

Trace had walked for miles along the river one afternoon. He'd glimpsed an abandoned castle through a thicket of trees and decided to investigate. What he'd found was a savage display of destruction and decay holding its secrets in deserted attics, hidden passageways and weed-choked gazebos.

Them and us.

Trace frequently found himself thinking back to his first chance encounter with Schuyler on that dark and rainy night when they had both arrived at Grantwood, soaked to the skin and in something of a state of shock after their near miss on the road.

They'd met again the next morning in the library: he the attorney and executor of Cora's estate; she the beneficiary who was about to inherit Grantwood and the Grants' money.

Them and us.

But Schuyler wasn't what she had first appeared to be. And now Trace Ballinger found himself caught between the devil and the deep blue sea.

He couldn't forget that the Grants had made their millions on the backs of hardworking blue collar families like his who, generation after generation, had worked themselves to death in the Grant coal mines and the Grant steel mills.

Them and us.

He thought he would have enjoy—hell, he thought he'd relish—getting his revenge at last. But it turned out that revenge was a dead-end street.

Who was he going to take his revenge on?

A little old lady who had been rather frail and eighty years old when he'd met her?

Schuyler? The woman he couldn't keep his hands off of? The woman who haunted his dreams every night? The woman he was afraid might be all of his dreams come true?

Yup, when you got right down to it, revenge wasn't all it was cracked up to be, Trace Ballinger decided.

Chapter Twenty-One

Revenge was a dish best served cold.

Ice-cold.

He knew all about revenge. He had lived, breathed, plotted, and dreamt his revenge night after night, week after week, month after month, even year after year. Now it was coming to fruition, and the anticipation was sweet, indeed.

Revenge had been the one overwhelming, driving, *secret* force in his life. He was determined to have it whatever the cost. In fact, he had done it all in the name of exacting his revenge.

His retaliation would be complete, absolute and utterly without mercy. There would be no room for pity. There would be no appealing to his better nature; he had none. There would be no invoking his nobler side; he knew himself to be without nobility.

He took no prisoners.

He licked his lips as he watched Schuyler Grant stroll across the grounds of Grantwood. His plans were progressing even better than he could have hoped.

When the time was right, when the players were in place, he would strike like a cobra: swiftly and deadly.

He smiled and licked his lips again, savoring every morsel of gratification.

It was delicious.

He must be careful not to smile too quickly or give himself away too soon. After all, his so-called partners weren't completely stupid. He was counting on their avarice. It would make his revenge that much sweeter.

He looked around nervously. He didn't like being out during the day, even when he was concealed behind a thicket of underbrush and low-hanging branches as he was now.

He was a creature of the night. He loved the darkness. He always had, even as a child. While other children feared the dark and the unknown, the unnamed, the terrifying monsters that lurked beneath their beds, behind closed doors, down cellar steps and along dark hallways, he had been fascinated by that darkness, that unknown, that terror.

There was something comforting about the night. It was quiet. It was private. It was solitary. It was aloneness.

He preferred being alone.

He preferred to be awake when everyone else was asleep. He often worked late at night. Reading. Thinking. Plotting and planning. Poring over his collections, savoring his latest find, contemplating what his next move would be.

He needed the night like most men needed air to breathe. He thrived on it. He craved it. He had to have it for his mind, his body, his very soul.

Yes, the night was his.

The night could also be seductive. The very same man or woman could become quite a different human being once the sun had set and the moon had risen.

There were more things done, said, performed during the dead of night that would never see the light of day.

He frequently had no need for a flashlight. He had the eyesight of a nocturnal animal; he saw more clearly in the dark than he did in the daylight.

He knew the woods in this region well. They were the place in which he spent most of his waking hours. He stood in the woods now, breathed in the air and waited for the night.

Yes, revenge was best served ice-cold, and it was best executed under the cloak of darkness.

Chapter Twenty-Two

On tiptoe.

Schuyler slipped in a side door of the conservatory. The glass-sided and glass-roofed orangery smelled of humus and vegetation and sweet-smelling—almost overpoweringly sweet-smelling—blooms. She skirted towering palm trees and sprawling tropical plants and quickly, yet quietly, made her way up the back staircase to the wing of the house where her own room was located.

She had deliberately avoided Mrs. Danvers and any other staff that might still be working in the house at this hour of the early evening. And Trace.

Especially Trace.

There wasn't time to explain to anyone what she thought she'd seen and why she was hurrying to investigate. Perhaps if she moved fast enough, whoever—*whatever*—she had glimpsed in the half-shuttered window would still be there.

As she paused for a handful of seconds to catch her breath, another possibility suddenly occurred to Schuyler. That first morning in the library Trace had told her that Cora believed Grantwood was haunted. She had assumed her great-aunt's reported sighting of Lucy was the basis for her claim.

But what if it was something else altogether that had led Cora to declare there was a ghost?

What if Cora had seen the face in the window, too?

Schuyler heaved a sigh.

Assuming there had been a face, of course. Assuming

that it wasn't some kind of optical illusion, or the fading
sunlight reflecting off a pane of glass, or even one of the
local women who came in on a regular basis to scrub and
polish and dust and vacuum under Mrs. Danvers's watchful
eye; a woman, for example, like Annie Barker.

Schuyler glanced down at her wristwatch. It was nearly
five-thirty. Most of the local staff would already be on their
way home by this hour.

Nevertheless, she intended to satisfy her own curiosity
about the matter.

The first thing Schuyler did on arriving at the hallway
where her great-aunt's bedchamber was located was to
double-check the rooms to either side of Cora's. She was
confident there weren't any shutters on Cora's windows,
but she wasn't as certain of the other windows in this wing
of the house.

The bedroom suite to the left of Cora's was definitely
decorated in a masculine style, from its massive pieces of
furniture—there was a large sleigh bed, an oversize French
armoire, a bombé bureau and several overstuffed leather
chairs—to the rich woods on the mantelpiece to the dark
colors on the walls.

There were no shutters at the windows.

Next, she explored the chamber to the right of Cora's.
This turned out to be a far more modest room. It was also
significantly smaller in size than either of the others. The
furniture was of good quality, but fairly plain and unadorned. The walls were painted a pale neutral shade rather
than wallpapered or paneled. There were two standard windows on the far wall.

There were no shutters.

Noiselessly Schuyler closed the door again and turned
to Cora's bedroom.

What was she missing?

She had to be missing something. There must be an important detail that had escaped her attention. A fact that had slipped her mind. A necessary observation that she'd failed to see. A vital connection she just hadn't made.

What was it?

Schuyler gave herself a gentle slap alongside her head. *"Je suis tout imbécile."*

She'd been looking for a logical explanation. She had been expecting the totally expectable. Yet Grantwood was famous for its eccentricities. Just as her great-aunt was famous, even infamous, for hers.

Rooms without windows.

Windows without rooms.

Schuyler crossed the room, opened the door to Cora's closet and groped for the light switch around the corner. There was a fixture overhead and a solitary bulb that gave off a dim yellowish tinge of light. The other bulbs must have burned out. She'd have to remember to replace them in the morning.

In the past week or two Schuyler had spent hours in Cora's closet, sorting through the woman's belongings, looking for clues, trying to piece together the story of a life and a lifetime.

It was all there: the glittering and expensive ball gowns from the 1930s and 1940s, with matching evenings bags and imported, handmade Italian shoes; the beautifully tailored travel suits with fur collars and fur cuffs; the delicate and fragile hand-stitched lingerie, packed away in layers of tissue paper; lacy things, silky things, exquisite things.

There were drawers filled with gloves in every imaginable color: long evening gloves, summer Sunday gloves, kid gloves and fur-lined gloves for winter.

There were hat boxes stacked from floor to ceiling. Inside were veiled concoctions, stylish chapeaux with exotic—

and possibly extinct—birds' feathers decorating the crowns, banded hats, straw hats, even bejeweled hats.

There were special shelves displaying cashmere sweater sets, silk blouses in every style and every shade of the rainbow, with silk scarves dyed to match.

In another area of the closet hung a row of fur jackets and coats: mink, sable, lynx, even leopard.

The section closest to the bedroom door contained the clothes of an older woman, an aging woman. There were several dozen dresses, all of the same style but in a variety of colors and materials. There were plain but good leather handbags and low-heeled shoes and serviceable cardigan sweaters.

Schuyler went to the rear of the closet where Cora's trunk was shoved against the wall. She reached behind the trunk and felt along the wall itself, and then bent over to examine the woodwork. She finally discovered what she suspected she might find. It was subtle—in fact, almost imperceptible—but there was a small crack in the plaster and the slightest gap in the woodwork.

She preferred to work in silence, but now she had no choice. Schuyler lightly tapped the wall with her knuckles and listened for the slightest variation.

There!

A slight hollow sound.

There was something, even if it was only a small gap or space, behind the wall of Cora's closet.

Schuyler licked her lips and whispered so softly the words scarcely carried to her own ears, "There weren't any 'special treasures' locked away in your trunk, Cora. So what did you do when you retreated to your closet? Where did you go?"

It couldn't be that difficult to figure out. Cora had been in her eighties, painfully arthritic, poor of eyesight and hard of hearing. If her great-aunt had a hiding place behind the wall, Schuyler could surely find it.

It was so simple.

It was almost too simple.

Schuyler gave the crack in the woodwork a nudge with the toe of her shoe and the wall swung open. It was a concealed door: a cleverly concealed and virtually invisible door.

"Well, surprise, surprise," she murmured, leaning forward slightly and peering into the space.

It was more of a corridor than a small room, and longer than it was wide. There didn't appear to be any doors—other than the one she was standing in—and there certainly weren't any windows, shuttered or unshuttered.

She couldn't see any light fixtures on the narrow walls or detect any switchplates. The faint cast given off by the single light bulb behind her was little help. The corridor was dark at both ends and filled with shadows.

Stepping forward ever so slightly, no more than an inch or two, Schuyler squinted for a better look.

She took another small step.

That's when it happened.

Her shoe slipped on something wet and slick on the floor. Her feet were suddenly threatening to go out from under her. She had no choice but to reach out and grab whatever she could get her hands on to keep herself from falling.

She braced herself against the opposite wall, and that quickly the concealed door swung closed behind her.

She immediately turned around and gave the area a shove. But nothing happened. It wouldn't budge. She nudged, then kicked, then kicked harder at the woodwork—or where she assumed the woodwork was—with the toe of her shoe.

Nothing.

Nada.

Rien.

"Bloody hell," she muttered into the silence, not caring for a moment if someone did hear her.

It was a good thing she wasn't claustrophobic, Schuyler reflected with something less than her usual good humor.

Then, very carefully she felt her way along the walls of the corridor.

There were no windows.

There were no doors.

Not even the door she had originally entered through.

The area's approximate size was four feet in width and twelve feet in length. She couldn't tell the height of the ceiling. It was certainly taller than she was with her hand and arm stretched straight over her head.

There was nothing on the walls. There was nothing on the floor, except for that damned slippery spot, of course. There was nothing, period.

She was trapped.

Nonsense.

Schuyler put her shoulders back and raised her chin a fraction of an inch in the air. She'd been in far tighter spots than this in her life: figuratively, if not literally. She absolutely refused to believe she was trapped, and she always rejected the idea of conceding defeat.

There were times when the famous Grant stubbornness— it was especially true of the females in the family and, as she'd told Trace during their initial business meeting in the library, the preferred term was *strong-willed*—was an asset.

Well, right about now she could use all the assets she could muster, Schuyler acknowledged.

Funny things happened in the dark.

Time was distorted: It seemed to stand still. Then it seemed to cease existing altogether.

Size was distorted, as well. First, Schuyler felt larger than the confining space. Then, at some point, she felt very small and the corridor loomed large.

The air around her felt stale, at a standstill, a little suffocating. Then there seemed to be a slight change in the air and the faintest hint of a breeze.

Suddenly the hair on the back of Schuyler's neck stood straight up on end.

Was someone there?

Could she hear the sound of breathing?

Did she sense a presence?

She opened her mouth and whispered hoarsely, "Who are you?"

Chapter Twenty-Three

Schuyler went perfectly still.

"Trace, is that you? Have you been searching for me? You mustn't scold me," she called out, and then felt a little foolish for having done so.

There was no reply.

There was no warning.

Before she could turn around, someone—*something*—put its hands in the middle of her back and gave her a shove. She fell against the wall of the corridor, hitting her right elbow. Instantly she broke out in a cold sweat. Pain shot down her arm. She wondered briefly if a bone had been broken.

Before she had the time or opportunity to recover from the first assault, another even more forceful shove landed between her shoulder blades.

The wall in front of her gave way and she stumbled forward into some kind of chamber. Then the opening behind her immediately closed again.

She was no longer in the dark, narrow corridor, but neither was she back in Cora's closet. She groped for a doorknob, a handle, for any means to get out. She pushed with her left arm; the right was still throbbing and of little use. She threw the full force of her weight against the wall.

It didn't budge.

There was a slightly musty, decayed smell in the air. She tried to ignore the sound of something underfoot skittering across the floor. She brushed away what she assumed was a cobweb.

Schuyler finally found her voice. "Hello."

Silence greeted her.

She raised her voice. "Hello! Is anyone there? Could you please help me? I'm inside . . ."

What was she inside?

Dead silence.

That was when a small feeling of panic began to creep into her heart and mind. Perhaps she was trapped.

Darkness.

There was only darkness . . .

Her arms and shoulders ached with fatigue. Schuyler had been calling out for help and intermittently pounding on the walls since first finding herself trapped wherever she was trapped.

She couldn't see a thing.

There wasn't any light. As a consequence, in the dark, she had lost track of time.

She was cold and tired, hungry and thirsty. She recalled reading somewhere that a human being could survive for days, even weeks, without food as long as water was plentiful. The thought only made her realize how thirsty she was.

Surely someone would come to her rescue soon. Surely Mrs. Danvers or Trace would realize by dinnertime that she hadn't returned from Geoffrey Barker's.

She pulled her jacket more closely around her. She permitted herself a small sigh. Just one. Under the circumstances, there wasn't room for self-pity. Besides, Trace would come for her. She believed that with every ounce of her being.

She froze. Had she heard something? Or was her imagination playing tricks on her? She cocked her head and listened intently with her ear to the wall. Then she called out again: "Hello! Please, is someone, anyone, there?"

There was no answer.

A minute or two later there was a scrape followed by a thud, as if a large, solid object were being moved. Adrenaline shot into her bloodstream. Her heart began to beat faster.

No one came.

She was going to have to try something else, Schuyler realized. She stumbled over furniture, banged her shins several times and finally found her way to what she assumed was a window. It was shuttered and nailed shut.

She pulled at the edge of the wooden shutter until it began to give way in her hands.

Through the crack she could see it was evening. The setting sun was behind the trees, and a blue mist was forming over the river in the distance. There was no sign of another human being. She had never felt so lonely in her entire life.

"Don't be morose, Schuyler Grant," she lectured herself. "This isn't the first time you've found yourself alone, and it won't be the last."

Somehow the sound of her own voice cheered her. She rubbed her arms and hobbled about, stomping her feet. The evening was warm, but she was thoroughly chilled to the bone. Why shouldn't she be? She had been locked in a dark room for what seemed like hours.

She stood at the window and watched through the crack. Suddenly she spotted someone below in the yard. She raised a hand and was about to call out again when something made her stop.

Better the devil she knew . . .

She couldn't see the man's face, but there was something about the way he moved that made her hesitate.

Schuyler squeezed her eyes tightly shut and intoned a heartfelt prayer. She opened her eyes. The evening mist was thicker still, but the man had vanished. Breathing a sigh of relief, she leaned her cheek against the shutter.

The next time she peeked out, she saw a familiar figure beneath the window. She moved her lips. "Trace. Buddy."

Trace Ballinger looked up at Grantwood, but she wasn't at all certain that he saw her.

Chapter Twenty-Four

Trace was about to finish up for the evening when a knock sounded on the library door. "Enter."

It was Mrs. Danvers.

"I know. I know," he began apologetically. "Dinner is ready and I'm not."

There was a short pause.

The woman poised on the threshold announced, "I need to speak with you, Mr. Ballinger."

"In that case, please come in."

Elvira Danvers took two measured steps—mo more, no less—into the library and stopped. "I'm not an alarmist by nature," she said in preamble.

He was well aware that the housekeeper was a woman who kept her wits about her. "Go on," he urged.

"I'll get to the point."

"Please do," he agreed, nonchalantly crossing his arms and leaning back against an enormous secretary filled with pens and antique inkwells, every manner and style of writing paper, and slightly top-heavy with books.

"She's not back."

His voice was perfectly calm. "Who's not back?"

"Miss Grant."

Trace dropped his arms and slid noiselessly to his feet. "What do you mean?"

"I mean just that: Miss Grant hasn't returned home." Mrs. Danvers sniffed several times, took a handkerchief from somewhere on her person—Trace didn't see exactly where—and dabbed at her nose. "In fact, no one has seen her since she went to visit Mr. Barker this afternoon."

Trace cautioned himself not to jump to conclusions. "Have you checked her room?"

"That was the first place I looked."

"Cora's closet?" Sorting through her great-aunt's belongings had turned into a full-time job.

"That was the second place. I rang up Annie Barker, as well. I didn't want to raise the alarm prematurely, so I made some excuse for asking what time Miss Grant had left their cottage." The housekeeper took a deep breath and delivered the bad news. "She left three hours ago, Mr. Ballinger."

A chill ran down his spine. "Where else have you checked?"

"I've been to all of her favorite places." Elvira Danvers began to list them aloud for his benefit, checking them off on her fingertips as she went. "The formal gardens, the gazebo, Lucy's Lookout, the old rose garden—"

"The old rose garden?"

"Miss Grant has shown a recent interest in the rose gardens. She's been talking about having them restored."

"I see." Trace stroked his jaw thoughtfully. "Did she have any appointments scheduled for this afternoon?"

"Only informally with myself and certain members of the household staff."

"Would she have gone to visit a friend or someone in town without telling you?"

Elvira Danvers shook her head. "She knows I would worry, and she has grown very thoughtful about my feelings. Besides," she added, "the last place I checked was the garage."

"Her car's still there," he concluded.

"It is."

There might yet be an innocent explanation, Trace reminded himself. "Maybe someone telephoned her and picked her up in his car." He was specifically thinking of slick Johnny, of course.

"That doesn't seem very likely to me," countered Mrs. Danvers. "She doesn't know that many people in the area and Mr. Grant has returned to the city."

"And you've checked the house from top to bottom."

"From top to bottom. I didn't wish to raise a false alarm and possibly embarrass her, so I made my inquiries discreetly." Concerned eyes studied him intently. "As far as I can ascertain, the last person to see Miss Grant was Geoffrey Barker."

The skin around Trace's mouth grew taut. "I told myself I had to stay here and finish this blasted work, but my gut instincts told me not to let her go alone," he said, blaming himself. "I should have known better."

He had known better. But he'd been too damned preoccupied with his own business to drop everything and walk with Schuyler to the row of tenant cottages.

"It's not out of the question that she may have suffered a sprained ankle or some minor injury on the walk back," the housekeeper speculated.

Trace hoped and prayed it was that simple. "It's not out of the question," he agreed.

Mrs. Danvers continued to stand at attention. "What do wish me to do, sir?"

"Stay here. Stay by the telephone. I'll return just as soon as I can."

"Where are you going?"

"I'm going to hike to the cottages just as Miss Grant would have done this afternoon." He gave a sharp whistle. "Buddy!" That quickly the golden retriever was at his side.

Trace was out the kitchen door in record time and headed straight for the path that wound through the woods.

Buddy trotted along in front of him. As soon as the house was behind them and out of sight, they broke into a run.

A sense of urgency drove Trace. He hadn't wanted to say anything to Elvira Danvers, but it was possible that Schuyler's disappearance was no simple matter of lost and found.

He pounded his fist against his thigh as he ran and muttered under his breath, "Damn. Damn. Damn." If anything had happened to Schuyler, it would be on his conscience.

His heart was pounding, but his mind was clear. His senses were razor-sharp. His hands were steady. He had always been this way in times of danger. It was one reason he'd been such a damned good street fighter and an even better lawyer. They said that he had ice water in his veins.

They were right.

If this incident had anything to do with the strange goings-on at Grantwood, he would get to the bottom of it if it was the last thing he did, Trace vowed.

And if even one hair had been harmed on Schuyler's head, he would make someone pay . . . and pay dearly.

She was nowhere to be found.

He called out her name and nothing came back to him. A wave of impotent fury swept through Trace. Schuyler brought out some very primitive instincts in him, he realized. She needed him to protect her, and, by God, that's what he intended to do. In fact, he would do whatever it took to keep her safe.

Just as soon as he found her.

Where was the woman?

"Where are you, Schuyler?"

Buddy whimpered beside him, put his head down to sniff the path and then barked.

Trace retraced his steps from the point where he'd entered the woods. He stood for a moment, put his head back and gazed out over the landscape. Then, just at the outer edge of his field of vision, he thought he saw something—or someone—move.

He quickly turned and looked up at the house. There, in a second-story window behind a half-opened shutter, he thought he caught a glimpse of a woman's face. He couldn't remember any windows with shutters on that side of the house.

Trace looked up again. Cora's bedroom was somewhere in that vicinity.

"C'mon, Buddy."

He took off again at a dead run across the lawn, in the back door, and up the staircase. He took the stairs two at a time. He entered Cora's room.

Someone had been here.

Someone was here now.

Trace could feel it.

The distinctive squeak of a door slowly opening registered in the back of his brain. It seemed to be coming from Cora's closet. He glided across the room and opened the door.

Nothing.

He raised a hand, drove his fingers through the hair at his nape and muttered under his breath.

Where was she?

Where could she have gone?

He opened his mouth. "Schuyler, are you there?"

There was no answer. Not a sound. It was as though the woman had vanished into thin air.

He planted himself in the middle of the room, his feet a good eighteen inches apart, his hands forming fists on his hips, and glared out at the night.

Then he thought of the shuttered window. He counted

the windows in Cora's room. He went into the bedrooms on either side of hers: None of the windows had shutters. Yet he was certain that the face he'd seen had been at a shuttered window.

Maybe, just maybe . . .

He went back to the closet and began to tap along the wall, listening for the distinctive hollow sound that would tell him whether his hunch was right.

Then he noticed that Buddy was sniffing the woodwork.

"What is it, pal? Do you smell something? Do you smell Schuyler?"

Buddy gave a low growl.

Trace pushed against the closet wall. Then he got down beside Buddy and spotted the crack in the woodwork. He stood and gave it a good tap with the toe of his boot.

The wall opened.

Trace reached back and dragged the trunk into the breach to keep the trapdoor from closing behind him.

"Stay," he commanded Buddy.

He stepped into the dark and narrow corridor beyond. Then he put his mouth to the opposite wall. "Schuyler?" He raised his voice another notch. "Schuyler, can you hear me?"

There was a faint and muffled cry, "Trace!"

She was behind the corridor wall. There must be a way in. Yet he couldn't detect one, even after careful examination. That usually meant some kind of fulcrum point moved an invisible door.

"Stand back!" he shouted, hoping she could hear him. Then he put his shoulder to the wall and pushed with all his might.

Nothing happened.

He tried again several more times and in several different places, but it was to no avail. Then, in sheer frustration, he raised his fist and brought it down on the blasted thing.

The wall moved.

There was a room concealed behind the corridor wall. It was pitch-black inside.

"Schuyler."

"Trace."

Her face appeared. She was as white as a ghost.

"Christ, I've been worried to death," he exclaimed as she propelled herself into his arms.

Trace held on to her for dear life. She was caught up in his embrace, her head buried against his chest, her arms wrapped around his waist.

She finally raised her head, leaned back and confided, "I knew you would come."

"Did you?"

She nodded. "I told myself it was just a matter of time." She seemed to ponder the subject of time for a moment, then inquired, "Why did it take you so long?"

"I only realized you were missing when it was brought to my attention before dinner by Mrs. Danvers," he admitted with what sounded like chagrin. "She'd been searching for you everywhere. Naturally she became concerned."

She nestled closer to his warmth.

"What happened?"

She frowned. "I'm not sure. I thought I saw something in the window. I came up to investigate. I discovered a concealed corridor and took a step inside, slipped on something wet and the opening closed behind me. Then I think I was pushed and ended up in this room."

The muscles in his forearms tensed. "You were pushed?"

"I think so," she said wearily.

"The important thing is you're safe now," Trace said in a deceptively mild tone.

"I'm safe now."

"I should never have let you go alone this afternoon." His voice was heavy with self-reproach.

"Good God, it's not your fault. I've traveled the world alone. I can certainly visit a cottage on my own estate without a bodyguard," she told him.

His tone was grim. "I'm not so sure about that."

"I'm perfectly capable of taking care of myself. I've been on my own, after all, for the past nine years."

He wasn't going to argue the point with her now. But some changes were definitely in order, Trace decided as he held the woman against him.

Chapter Twenty-Five

"Where are we?" Trace asked.

Despite the size of the room they were in, his voice didn't bounce off the walls and echo back to them. In fact, his usually resonant baritone had a hollow ring to it.

Which Schuyler found strangely disconcerting, since she was fairly certain they had stumbled into a large room with a high ceiling. She'd done some exploring during the past several hours—under the circumstances there had been little else to do—only calling a halt after she'd bumped into the sharp corner of a piece of furniture for the fourth time. She would have bruises on her shins tomorrow, and plenty of them.

"I don't know exactly where we are," she admitted. "I haven't been able to locate a light switch that works." Then she sneezed. "I can definitely smell dust."

"So can I," Trace concurred. "Windows?"

"I got one partially uncovered. They seem to have shutters on the inside that are nailed shut. It's as if someone was deliberately trying to keep out the sunlight."

"The sunlight, the moonlight and everything else," he observed. "I'm going back to my room for a flashlight. Will you be all right for another couple of minutes?"

"Sure," she said, but it was all bravado.

Trace gave her hand a reassuring squeeze. "I promise I'll be back before you can count to one hundred. And Buddy will be standing guard nearby."

Wisely they had decided the golden retriever should stay outside of the concealed room.

Schuyler began counting to herself as soon as Trace disappeared through the secret door.

One.

Two.

Three. . . .

Ninety-eight.

Ninety-nine.

"I'm back," came Trace's voice from directly behind her.

She finished aloud, "One hundred."

Switching on the high-powered flashlight in his hand, Trace asked, "Now, where's the window?"

Schuyler pointed.

He headed in the direction she'd indicated. He stood in front of the boarded-up window. "Would you hold the flashlight and direct the beam right there?"

"Déjà vu all over again," she murmured. "Isn't this where I came in?"

"At least it isn't raining this time," Trace said with an attempt at humor. He managed to get a firm grip on the edge of the shutter and yank it toward him. There was the sound of wood cracking and hinges snapping, then the whole apparatus came apart in his hands. "The wood's rotten."

"That's good, right?"

"That's very good," he replied, making some kind of movement with his head that Schuyler assumed was a nod. "It makes the job a whole lot easier."

Trace made quick work of the wooden shutter. Even then there wasn't enough moonlight coming in the window to illuminate the room. Still, with the help of the flashlight they could see far more than they'd been able to before.

The man beside her looked around and speculated, "I think this used to be a kid's playroom."

Schuyler discovered the air was trapped in her lungs and her heart was pounding in her ears. "I think it used to be the nursery, as well," she said in a whisper.

A thick layer of powdery dust and more than a few cobwebs covered everything, from the child-size furniture arranged around the room to a hobby horse on wheels in one corner to a crib against the far wall. There were shelf after shelf of toys and books, and a trunk painted with a circus theme, its lid propped open to reveal a menagerie of stuffed animals inside: a long-necked giraffe, a spotted leopard, an elephant and a zebra.

In a corner cupboard was a collection of tin soldiers neatly lined up in rows and a grouping of small metal cars and trucks, including what had once been a bright red fire engine.

In another area of the spacious room was a game table with a checkerboard imprinted on its surface. The playing pieces were still in position.

There were pictures on the walls and sports equipment organized in a corner rack: a baseball glove, several bats and a ball with some faint scribbling on it.

Trace shone the flashlight on the baseball. Then he exclaimed in a hushed tone, "My God, Schuyler, this ball was autographed by Babe Ruth himself." He returned to the center of the room and made a slow turn, spotlighting one object after another. "This place is every boy's dream come true."

"Yes, it is."

"At least every boy who lived some fifty or sixty years ago," he amended.

That's when Schuyler spied a table in a recessed alcove. She made her way toward it. "Trace . . ."

He came to stand beside her. "What is it?"

She circled the table and the architectural model that

SUZANNE SIMMONS

took up the greater part of its surface. Then she moistened her lips. "It looks like a model of Grantwood."

His brows came together in a studied frown. "Grantwood the way it was?"

Noting the castle turret, the oddly shaped windows and the other eccentric characteristics of the current house, she suggested another alternative. "Or Grantwood the way it would become."

"I'm not sure I understand," Trace said, rubbing one hand along the back of his neck.

"I'm not sure I do, either," Schuyler admitted. An idea was beginning to take shape in her head. "How long would you say this model has been here?"

"Judging from the dust and cobwebs, about the same amount of time as everything else in this room."

"Precisely."

Trace focused the beam of light on the architectural model. "Interesting, though."

"What's interesting?"

"Maybe *curious* is a better word," he muttered under his breath.

"Curious?" she repeated.

"Would you say that's a professionally rendered model of the house?"

Schuyler bent over and took a closer look, although the dust and the cobwebs—a small brown spider was busily spinning its web even as they watched—discouraged her from getting too near. "No, I wouldn't."

Trace appeared puzzled. He stood there for a minute, frowning. "What's your first impression?"

She closed her eyes, then opened them again. "It's like something a child would make out of bits of scrap metal and wood."

"Exactly," he said.

Schuyler straightened. Then she asked him, "Are you thinking what I'm thinking?"

Trace placed his hand on her shoulder with apparent casualness. "That depends on what you're thinking."

Her voice fell softly on the silence of the tomblike room. "What if this model served as the inspiration for Cora's renovations to Grantwood?"

He was skeptical. "Doesn't that strike you as a little too fantastical?"

"Grantwood is a little too fantastical," she pointed out.

"True," came Trace's one-word response.

"It was just an idea," Schuyler went on to say, opening her arms and letting them fall in a classic gesture of bewilderment. "I suppose like everyone else I've always wondered why Cora felt compelled to make continuous changes to the house."

Trace turned his attention to something by the secret doorway and made a sound like "Hm."

"Hm, what?"

"What does that mean?"

Schuyler approached the table and chair. There was a silver candelabra in the center of the table—a half dozen candles were burned down to mere stubs of wax—and a box of matches. "I wonder . . ." she said in a preoccupied tone.

"Penny for your thoughts."

She glanced up at the man standing beside her and posed a question. "What's different about this table and chair from the other objects in the room?"

It didn't take Trace long to figure out the answer. "No dust," he concluded. "Well, at least only a little dust. Nothing like the thick layer coating everything else."

Schuyler was starting to get that funny feeling in the pit

of her stomach; the one that always began with butterflies fluttering about. "And I know why."

"Why?"

"Because this is where Cora came to gaze at what she called her 'special treasures.'"

Trace snapped his fingers and followed her line of reasoning. "Which explains why the so-called treasures in the trunk appeared to be junk."

She couldn't conceal her excitement at their discovery. "Because it *was* junk."

He took logical thinking a step further. "The trunk in Cora's closet was a decoy."

Schuyler nodded. "This is where Cora really came, and this is where she sat after putting a match to those candles."

Trace directed the powerful beam of the flashlight on the electric fixtures that were positioned along the walls and in the ceiling overhead. "I don't think the problem is the electricity. I'll wager the bulbs are burned out, and as she got older and more frail, Cora simply couldn't replace them."

"I'll bet you're right." Schuyler turned and stared into the heart of the ghostlike room. "Why did she come here?"

"To relive her memories," was Trace's conclusion.

"And perhaps her dreams: dreams of what might have been, dreams of what was sadly never to be."

"This was the room of a young boy."

Schuyler agreed.

"It seems reasonable to conclude that he was somehow related to Cora." Trace took in a breath and then slowly exhaled. "I wonder what the hell happened." After a pause he inquired, "Did you find out anything from Geoffrey Barker?"

"Mr. Barker slips in and out of reality." Schuyler raised

one hand to brush a cobweb from in front of her face. "Or perhaps I should say he slips back and forth in time."

"What did he tell you?"

She sighed. "That Cora's hair went from red, like mine, to snow-white overnight."

"Overnight?"

She nodded. "He didn't say why. But he did mention that Cora's husband had arranged a surprise for her thirtieth birthday and that the surprise went tragically wrong."

Trace raked his fingers through his hair. "I guess the old gentleman wasn't as much help as we'd hoped he would be."

"Wishes and dreams," Schuyler murmured.

"What about them?"

"Geoffrey Barker was talking about wishes and dreams this afternoon as if they were the real treasures."

Trace repeated a question he'd asked Schuyler before. This time he hoped she would give him an answer. "What did you dream about when you were a girl?"

She hesitated, then apparently decided to tell him. "I dreamed of doing so many things, of being so many things."

He waited for her to go on. He wasn't going to hurry her, but he wasn't going to let her hide behind the protective barrier she put up between herself and other people, either.

She continued quietly, "As a little girl I thought I wanted to be a ballerina." There was the sound of soft, almost childlike laughter. "And like so many little girls before me, it soon became apparent I was too tall and too awkward."

Trace thought she was one of the most graceful women he'd ever seen walk across a room.

"Then I decided I was going to be a famous explorer

and tramp through the jungles of the Amazon or study a long-lost tribe of indigenous headhunters à la Margaret Mead. I was going to join the Peace Corps and save the world, or at least one small corner of it. I was going to be the first woman to walk on the moon or the greatest actress who had ever performed on the stage or the scientist who cured cancer."

Trace smiled down into her sweet face. "At least you were a world-class dreamer."

"Oh, yes, I was a world-class dreamer," she admitted in an unselfconscious moment.

"By the way," Trace said as they left the nursery, "You never told me what gave you the idea of looking behind Cora's closet for a secret room."

Schuyler swallowed hard. He wasn't going to like her answer. "I was walking back from the Barkers' cottage when I happened to glance up at the house. I realized this was the location of Cora's bedroom, but I knew there weren't any shutters on the inside of her windows. That's when it occurred to me that there might be more here than met the eye."

"Anything else?"

"Well . . ."

She may as well confess everything to him. Trace was very good at recognizing when she was keeping something—anything, for that matter—from him, anyway. It was downright uncanny.

"I thought I saw a woman's face in the window," she finally blurted out.

Trace stopped dead in his tracks. "So did I."

"I didn't recognize her," Schuyler stated.

"Neither did I," he said.

"Gave me the creeps."

"Me, too."

Then, as he brushed the dust and cobwebs from the front of his shirt, Trace suggested to her, "Why don't we get cleaned up, have a bite of supper in my room and talk over everything that's happened so far?"

"But that could take all night," Schuyler pointed out.

Trace flashed her a meaningful look. "Yes, it could."

Chapter Twenty-Six

It was over an after-dinner cup of French roast coffee that Schuyler mentioned to him, "I've been thinking about the woman I spotted in the upstairs window."

Trace's head came up. "What about her?"

Schuyler only hesitated briefly before saying to him, "I don't believe she was an apparition, Trace. I think she was a flesh-and-blood person."

"So do I."

She seemed surprised that he readily agreed with her without a single word of argument. "Then how do you explain the fact that we saw a face at a window we're both certain was shuttered and nailed shut from the inside?"

Trace leaned forward in his chair, coffee cup in hand. "The key word is *inside*."

A studied frown formed a soft crease between her eyes. "I don't understand."

"We assumed all of the shutters on the windows in the nursery were nailed shut using the same method. But we don't know that for sure, do we?"

"Don't we?"

Trace shook his head and leaned back in the overstuffed easy chair, making himself comfortable. "The room was dark. We were working by what little light we had available."

"Your flashlight."

He nodded. "We weren't looking for any indication that someone had been there before us and pried a shutter partially away from a window, or that there may have been another way altogether of opening the shutters."

"I hadn't considered that possibility," Schuyler admitted to him with a degree of chagrin.

"To tell you the truth, I didn't think of it myself at the time. It was only once I was back here in my room taking a shower that it dawned on me someone could know something about the shutters we didn't."

"It's a reasonable assumption," she said.

"It's also reasonable to assume somebody might know how to get in and out of the nursery-playroom and the hidden corridor without being detected."

"Of course," came a hoarse whisper.

He went on. "That's when it occurred to me that the face in the window and the person who shoved you from behind are undoubtedly one and the same."

Schuyler shivered and wrapped her cashmere bathrobe more closely around her. "It was no ghost who pushed me."

"Exactly."

"Who was it, then?"

"That's what I'm going to find out, come hell or high water," Trace vowed.

"We," she immediately corrected him. "*We* are going to find out."

He'd have to see about that.

Aloud, Trace suggested, "Let's consider what we know and what we don't know so far."

That got Schuyler's undivided attention. "Let's," she agreed, setting her coffee cup down on the table in front of her. (The table and the two overstuffed armchairs made up a small, intimate sitting area in one corner of the Blue Room. There was a similar arrangement of furniture in the Yellow Room.)

Playing devil's advocate was a natural role for Trace. "What was the first incident?" he asked.

Schuyler supplied the answer. "Someone forced my car off the road on the drive to Grantwood."

The analytical side of his brain took over. "Actually, that wasn't the very first incident."

Her face lit up. "You're right. The very first time was when Cora thought she saw and heard odd things going on outside her window."

"Bingo."

Schuyler kicked off her slippers and tucked her legs up under her. "Do you remember when my great-aunt initially mentioned the flickers of light or the strange sounds?"

"I can do better than that," Trace told her. "I can give you the exact date."

"When was it?"

"Two months ago."

"So it was just a few weeks before Cora died."

"Yup."

Crossing her arms in front of her, Schuyler gazed off into space for a moment or two, then brought her attention back to him. "Why would you know the exact date?"

He recalled the chain of events. "At Cora's request I had driven up for the weekend. In order to avoid the Sunday night traffic heading back into the city, I usually waited until Monday to return home. But on that particular occasion I decided to leave early. Cora telephoned me first thing Monday morning at Dutton, Dutton, McQuade & Martin. She was apologetic, but I could also tell she was pretty badly shaken by what had happened."

"What did you do?"

"I dropped everything at the office, got into my Jeep, stopped at my apartment long enough to collect Buddy and headed right back to Grantwood."

Schuyler sunk her teeth into her bottom lip. "That was very kind of you, Trace."

He looked directly into her eyes. "I liked Cora. In fact, over the past eight years I had grown quite fond of her." This is no time to get maudlin, Ballinger, he reminded himself. "Anyway, the first few suspicious occurrences took place even before you returned to the States."

Schuyler picked up the thread of their conversation. She ticked the episodes off one by one on her fingers as she related them. "Since I've been back there has been the mysterious car following me on the highway, the flickering lights near the gazebo, the strange sounds in the woods, the face in the window and now the incident in the closet corridor."

"What do they have in common?"

"They were all directed at me."

"What else?"

"While some of them appeared threatening, no real harm was done." She moistened her lips with her tongue. "That is, if you discount the close call with the car and then the bruises I got tonight when I was shoved up against the secret panel into the playroom."

His mouth thinned. "What bruises?"

"It's nothing to concern yourself about," Schuyler hastened to reassure him. "Mrs. Danvers put an ice pack on my injured arm and I'm fine now."

Trace tried to control the sudden shot of adrenaline pumping through his veins. "Maybe someone is trying to warn you off," he said.

Schuyler appeared to give that suggestion serious consideration. "Warn me off *what*?"

"Coming back to Grantwood."

"Legally I had to come back after Cora died," she said in a low, earnest voice.

"Staying on at Grantwood, then?"

"As far as anyone knows, I'm only staying long enough to take care of Cora's business affairs and put the estate up for sale. In fact, locally that seems to be the consensus of opinion," she said, tightening the cashmere belt around her waist.

He was curious. "Would you sell your ancestral home to a couple like the Plunketts?"

"If—and it's a big if—I decided to sell, Grantwood would have to go to a buyer with enough money to keep up the place. The taxes alone would bankrupt most people."

"I know." He was privy, after all, to Cora's financial affairs. "By the way, what did Johnny say about the misunderstanding with Elaine Kendall and her clients?"

"She still insists that a man who identified himself as Cora's lawyer called her office and made the appointment. Johnny has assured me that Elaine Kendall is a highly respected professional in her field. She was very apologetic. He was very apologetic. Since nothing was missing from the house—"

"Except the page out of the map book," he interjected, although he knew full well she hadn't forgotten the incident the day they had returned from tea with the Fricks.

"Except one page missing from one book, and since Grantwood is filled with valuable antiques and priceless treasures—none of which were even touched as far as we can ascertain—I've decided to drop the matter."

Trace stared at her profile. "What about Johnny?"

"What about Johnny?"

Schuyler sat and waited for the man beside her to explain. She warned herself not to read anything into Trace's question until he'd made it clear why he was asking about her cousin.

He gave her a speculative glance. "Have you decided what you're going to do about him?"

She spread her hands. "Why would I have to do anything about Johnny?"

Trace gave her a long, hard look. "Jonathan Tiberius Grant's pedigree is no doubt as impeccable as your own. He enjoyed the same privileged upbringing and the same private school education. He travels in the same elevated social circles. He's no doubt just as stinking rich. In short, you're like two peas in a pod."

"Are we?"

Dark brows snapped together in a frown. "Some people seem to think you'd make the perfect couple."

"Some people?" Schuyler repeated. Then she asked, "Does 'some people' include you, Trace?"

He gave a short, humorless laugh and pushed himself to his feet. "Good God, no."

For the past decade Schuyler had told herself there was nothing left for her to fear. Was that true? Or was she simply paying lip service to the notion?

She watched the man as he paced back and forth across the small expanse of the sitting area. "What do you recommend I do about Johnny, then?"

"Send the man packing." Trace came to a dead stop in front of the overstuffed chair and stared down at her. "Tell him to get lost. Make sure he understands you're not interested in him. At least not in that way."

Schuyler realized she wanted—needed—to have it spelled out for her. "And what is *that* way?"

"As a man."

She sunk her teeth into the tender flesh on the inside of her mouth and made every effort not to smile. "I'd scarcely be interested in him as a woman."

Trace went on to ask her, "Is Johnny Grant one of your personal ghosts?"

Schuyler responded with what she hoped was a casual air. "He was a long time ago."

Dark blue eyes speared her to the spot where she sat. "How long ago?"

"I had a crush on my cousin when I was thirteen and he was twenty-two."

Trace exhaled and then appeared to breathe somewhat easier. "Kid's stuff."

"In my case, yes." She immediately turned the tables on him. "Were you a kid at thirteen?"

Trace returned a guarded answer. "No."

She'd guessed as much. "Who—or what—were your ghosts at thirteen, Trace Ballinger?"

For a minute, maybe longer, he didn't give any indication that he'd heard the question. Then, just when Schuyler was about to give up hope, Trace opened his mouth and the words came tumbling out. "When I was thirteen I ran away from home."

She went very still. "You were a runaway?"

"Yup," he said with a stoic laugh.

The pounding of her heart was deafening in her ears. "Why did you run away?"

His voice was hard and unforgiving and edged with steel. "My grandfather had died a couple of years before. Then my mother that winter. That left just my father and me. He was a sick man, himself. It was his heart." Trace Ballinger tapped his chest. "Wes started drinking again against the doctor's orders." Trace's eyes grew so dark they appeared to be black rather than blue. "My dad got real mean when he was drunk."

Schuyler's whole body was suddenly shaking. Her skin

became oddly damp. She drew a deep breath and spoke slowly. "Was he abusive?"

"They didn't use words like *abusive* in my old neighborhood back in Pittsburgh."

"What words did they use?"

"Strict."

Her tongue was thick in her mouth. "Strict?"

His voice was soft and ice-cold when he went on. "Spare the rod, spoil the child. Beat some sense into a smart-ass kid. Teach him who's boss."

She couldn't move. "I'm sorry, Trace."

"No pity, Schuyler."

"Why not?"

"I wasn't the only one getting beat up. In the summertime, when it was sweltering hot outside and the windows were thrown open, you couldn't help but hear what was going on behind your neighbors' closed doors." His voice faltered for an instant. "Don't kid yourself, it still does go on."

Schuyler heard herself saying carefully, "So you ran away from home."

He nodded. "I ran."

"Where did you go?"

He shrugged his broad shoulders. "Anywhere. Everywhere. I got as far as Texas before the authorities picked me up and sent me to juvenile hall."

"And . . . ?"

"And then they sent me back to my father in Pittsburgh. Only I'd had a growing spurt in the six months I was on the road. I was too big for Wes to pick on anymore. So he left me alone."

"Did you go back to school?"

Trace shook his head from side to side. "I went to work in the steel mills."

"How old were you?"

"Fourteen."

Something else occurred to Schuyler. "Were those the Grant Steel Mills?"

"Yes," he stated, his voice matter-of-fact.

Somehow she suddenly knew. She couldn't have explained why or how; she just did. "When you were growing up, did you hate my family's name?"

"Yes."

"Did you want to take your revenge?"

He nodded.

Her eyes grew huge. "Have you?"

"Have I what?"

"Have you taken your revenge?"

He walked toward her and held out his hand. She trustingly placed her hand in his and rose to her feet. "Revenge isn't all it's cracked up to be, Schuyler."

"It isn't?"

His voice had a note of acceptance to it. "I remember my first trip to Grantwood eight years ago. I confess that revenge was somewhere in the back of my mind, but then I met Cora." Trace smiled. "Dear, sweet, slightly dotty and surprisingly generous Cora. And you know what?"

"What?" she asked, looking up into his face.

"I liked her."

"I'll bet she liked you, too."

Trace nodded. "We hit it off right from the start. Before that afternoon was over, Cora had asked me to be her attorney and I had accepted."

"I guess it can be like that sometimes."

"I guess it can." Trace gazed long into her eyes. "I took one look at you and I knew."

Schuyler couldn't seem to catch her breath. "What did you know?"

"We're the ones who are perfect for each other."

*   *   *

Sometimes, Schuyler realized later, a moment, a thought, a simple, seemingly insignificant act could change someone's life forever. When Trace had bent his head, perhaps he had intended to tuck an errant strand of hair behind her ear, or whisper something to her about the night—perhaps he had not intended to kiss her at all—but he did, and she did not turn away.

In fact, she raised her face to his and waited.

His eyes never left hers. His breath was fresh and sweet, yet masculine, with a hint of the strong coffee they had drunk after dinner; it stirred the tendrils around her cheeks. His hands were on either side of her head as he backed her up against the wall.

"Trace." The voice didn't sound like hers.

"Schuyler." His was different, somehow, as well. Husky. Guttural. Intense.

He muttered, "Maybe this isn't a good idea."

She moved his head. "Maybe it is. Maybe it isn't." She pushed at his chest; it was an ineffectual, halfhearted gesture at best. "Then why are we . . . ?"

He eliminated the space between them. "Because we have to. I've known that since the first afternoon we kissed in Cora's closet." A heartbeat, then two. "So have you."

"Yes." The shadows closed around them. "I feel as if things are about to change."

"They are."

"Change can be frightening," she admitted.

"Change is inevitable."

She tried to collect her wits. "I suppose you're right."

Trace looked down at her. "I know I'm right."

Held close to him as she was, she found his eyes unavoidable. "I don't look up to many men."

The corners of his mouth, his beautiful mouth, curved. "Literally or figuratively?"

Schuyler swallowed. "Both."

Quick fingers closed on her wrist. Trace raised her hand to his mouth. Then he brushed his lips back and forth across the sensitive skin at the base of her thumb. She sucked in her breath. His eyes darkened.

Her heart was racing.

The last inch between them disappeared.

Kissing Trace Ballinger was a paradox. He was exactly what she had expected, and he was far more than she had bargained for.

It was abundantly clear from the way he kissed her, the way he caressed her, the way he used his body to pin her against the wall, that he wanted her.

Chapter Twenty-Seven

It wasn't the smartest thing he had ever done.

In fact, inviting Schuyler to his bedroom at this hour of the night ranked as the least intelligent course of action he could have taken under the circumstances.

To make matters worse, he had lost control. He'd hauled her into his arms and started kissing her as if he were a starving man and she was the feast.

Damn slick Johnny!

Damn his own jealousy!

And damn his stupidity, his foolhardiness and his pathetic lack of self-control!

Trace tore his mouth from hers. His breathing was ragged. His hands were shaking. His blood was on fire. His body was slick with sweat.

He knew there was a wild look in his eyes. He wouldn't be surprised if he had frightened the woman half to death. No apology was going to make up for what he had done, but at least he could try to make amends.

"Christ, I'm sorry," Trace began, determined to regain control of himself and the situation.

Schuyler tilted her head to one side and said a little breathlessly, "About what?"

Bile rose in his throat. "For jumping you like that."

She dug her teeth into her bottom lip. "Jumping me?"

Trace almost said: *For jumping your bones, lady.* Instead, he muttered in self-disgust, "It's not my style to assault a woman, any woman, under any circumstances."

"You didn't assault me. You took me into your arms."

222   SUZANNE SIMMONS

He had *forcefully* taken her into his arms.

Schuyler went on, "You kissed me passionately."

Several times. More than several times. He had nearly eaten the woman alive.

She had that enigmatic, Mona Lisa–like expression on her face; he'd seen it before and marveled. "And I kissed you back."

She *had* responded to him. He'd been so damned busy feeling guilty that he had failed to notice she wasn't struggling to break free. As a matter of fact, she'd wrapped her arms tightly around his waist, pressed her breasts against his bare chest and returned his kisses with genuine ardor.

He should have known she would respond differently than any other woman of his acquaintance.

Schuyler *was* different.

Trace recalled that first night in the gazebo. He had kissed her—simply kissed her, nothing more—and yet he had nearly lost control then.

It had happened again earlier tonight. He had touched her, caressed her and, again, he had been the one to lose control.

It was the damnedest thing.

Schuyler licked her lips nervously and looked up at him. "Do you remember that night in the gazebo?"

The woman was a mind-reader. "Yes," he answered warily.

"You gave me the shirt off your back."

"I did."

She nodded. "I was wishing you'd kiss me."

He tried nonchalance. "I did kiss you."

She looked up at him with eyes of molten gold. "I know, and it was the single most passionate moment of my life."

"Mine, too."

She reached out and with her fingertips touched his

mouth. "Since then I've been having the same dream every night."

"Same dream, huh?"

She nodded. "I dream that you make love to me, Trace."

He trapped her fingers. "God knows I want to, Schuyler, but you have to understand there won't be any drawing back this time."

"I understand."

His dark brows drew together. "Are you sure?"

"I'm sure." She whispered softly but distinctly, "I want you."

"I want you, too," he said fiercely.

Schuyler understood the significance of what she was about to do. She was going to give herself to this man here, now, tonight. Because she loved him. Because whatever the future held for her, she would always have this night.

Trace turned off the lights one by one until only a small lamp in the corner was still lit. He led her to the open window. He stood behind her while they gazed out on the expanse of green grass and beyond to the formal garden.

It was not quite a full moon tonight. The scent of flowers and the river drifted up from somewhere below. A soft breeze stirred the diaphanous curtains.

Schuyler turned and went into Trace's arms.

His mouth was on her mouth. His hands clasped her by the waist and brought her up against him. She was aware of the changes in his body. His heart was pounding. His skin was sleek to the touch. His penis was fully erect and pressing against her.

This was the way it was meant to be. She'd recognized that on some instinctive level that night in the garden when he'd offered her his shirt, his warmth and his passion.

She soon had her hands on his bare chest, caressing his

skin, tugging at his hair, trailing her fingers over his masculine nipples, feeling his reaction as she did so.

Trace untied the belt of her bathrobe and the garment fluttered to the floor. She stood there in her nightgown, aware that the fine material did little to conceal what was underneath.

He gazed down at her. She recognized the look in his eyes. She knew he could clearly see the outline of her breasts and the rose-tipped peaks at their centers. His hands came up to cup her, cover her, caress her. Then he grasped her nipples between his thumbs and fingers and squeezed.

"Trace . . . ?"

"What?"

"I'm . . ." Schuyler tried to swallow.

"Are you nervous?"

She quickly passed her tongue over her lips and admitted with a small, self-conscious laugh, "Yes."

"Me, too."

"You?"

"It's been a long time for me." He spoke low. "And you're like a dream."

"I'm not a dream. I'm a flesh-and-blood woman," she reminded him.

"I know." He went perfectly still. "If you want me to stop, Schuyler, all you have to do is say so."

"I don't want you to stop."

He brought his hands up to rest lightly on either side of her collarbone. Then his fingers delved under the thin spaghetti straps of her nightgown. The inconsequential straps slipped off her shoulders and down her arms until the silky material was bunched up around her waist, leaving her breasts bare and exposed.

"I imagined you like this," Trace confessed, his voice husky and a little thick.

Schuyler was amazed to hear herself say saucily, "So, you've been thinking about my breasts."

"And your legs," he admitted with a crooked grin, "and a few other parts of your lovely body."

She put her palms on his chest. "You're lovely, too. All smooth skin, hard muscle and masculine hair."

With his index finger Trace drew a line from her shoulder, down her back, around to her rib cage, across her abdomen and up between her breasts. "Your skin is like fine porcelain."

She quivered with awareness.

He began again, tracing a slow, sensual circle around the outside of her breast. Then he traced a slightly smaller circle, and then another, and another, each diminishing in size until the last circle encompassed only her nipple.

Schuyler felt the fine hairs at her nape stand straight up on end.

He lightly plucked at the tips of her breasts and she felt an erotic shiver all the way down her body to her toes.

He bent his head and used the tip of his tongue on her nipple, flicking back and forth across its sensitive surface, licking her, nipping at her, biting her, creating a need, a desire, a longing that she had never experienced before.

He tugged on her with his lips. He pulled her into his mouth, and he suckled her. Then his attention went to the other breast, and he gave it the same attention as he had the first. "Your breasts are perfect," he muttered hoarsely.

Schuyler's knees buckled beneath her.

Trace turned her around until she faced the garden again. As she gazed out on the moonlit night, he drew the wispy material of a curtain across her skin. She watched her body respond.

Then he placed his hands on her. She glanced down and there were his wonderful, strong, long-fingered, tanned hands covering her breasts, caressing her breasts, giving her pleasure such as she had never known.

He stepped away from her and quickly pulled off his jeans, kicking them aside with his foot.

"We'll take this slow and easy," he promised her.

"Slow and easy."

His eyes blazed. "I want you more than I have ever wanted anyone or anything before in my life.

Schuyler couldn't take her eyes off him. Trace's body gleamed in the moonlight. His hair was like dark silk. His skin was a rich golden brown.

He was fully erect. His penis was large and hard. She had the most incredible urge to reach out and touch it, to kiss it, to take him into her mouth and literally bring the man to his knees.

"May I . . . ?" she stammered, licking her lips.

"If you wish to," came the strained response.

She reached out with her finger and touched the very tip. "You're so soft."

His laugh was ragged, edgy. "Soft, huh? Just what a man wants to hear."

She traced a random pattern down one side of his cock and back up the other. "You're so hard."

Through gritted teeth, Trace managed to tell her, "That's better."

She wrapped her hand around him. "I wish . . ."

"You can do anything you wish, sweetheart. Just remember to be careful what you wish for . . . you just may get it," he said, teasing her.

Schuyler stared down at the swollen penis she held in the palm of her hand. She brushed a fingertip back and forth across the satiny head and watched as a drop or two of moisture glistened near the opening. She gently squeezed.

Trace sucked in his breath.

Schuyler was instantly concerned. "Are you all right?"

Tension emanated from him. And heat. Suddenly there were tiny beads of perspiration on his upper lip. "Yes." He rocked back on his heels. "No."

She wasn't sure what to believe. "You look like you're in pain."

His laugh was hoarse. "I am, but I'm not. Like I said, it's been a hell of a long time for me."

She understood. "You're afraid you'll lose control."

He was blunt. "I believe the correct terminology is premature ejaculation."

There was going to be nothing premature about it, Schuyler mused as she began to touch him again, caress him, study the length and the breadth of him, even the nest of soft dark curls that encircled the base of his penis.

"May I kiss you?" She finally voiced the question at the forefront of her mind.

He blinked one, twice. "Kiss me?"

"There."

He sucked in air and didn't release it.

She eyed him with a certain amount of apprehension. "Don't you want me to?"

Trace nodded but didn't speak.

Her cheeks were hot. "Have I shocked you?"

He shook his head.

"Why don't you say something?"

He finally exhaled. "Yes, I want you to."

She smiled then, and sank to her knees in front of him. He placed one hand gently on the back of her head. He ran his thumb back and forth along her bottom lip until her mouth opened. She needed no further encouragement.

She scored his sensitive flesh with a fingernail and felt his body flinch. Then she licked her lips as she kissed him there and received a small taste of his essence, of those glistening drops on the soft, smooth crown.

He'd had enough.

He hadn't had nearly enough.

Trace was at his wit's end. Well, at the limit of his patience and self-control, anyway. It was time he took command of a very explosive situation.

He reached down and drew Schuyler to her feet. "You are amazing."

"Thank you."

"Now it's your turn."

She gave him a look of polite inquiry. "What do you mean, it's my turn?"

He unleashed a knowing, masculine smile. "You'll see soon enough."

She appeared bemused. "Will I?"

"Yes," he told her.

Hot molten eyes blinked several times in slow motion. "Is that a promise?"

"Yup."

He went down on his knees in front of her and removed her slippers. Then he eased the silky nightgown over her hips and watched as it fluttered to the floor.

The moonlight shone in the window behind her, outlining her figure in a soft white glow. The lamp in the corner of the bedroom was turned down low, yet he could see every curve, every shape, every line of her body.

"You are beautiful," he exclaimed.

Schuyler never moved a muscle. Indeed, she appeared to be holding her breath. "You're beautiful as well," came rushing out of her mouth.

He flashed her a smile. "First, lovely. Now, beautiful. What's a man to say to such praise?"

"Thank you?" she suggested.

"Thank you," he echoed.

"You're welcome."

He straightened and took a step toward her. His chest was mere inches from her breasts. Starting at the top of her head, he gently ran his hand down one side of her body and back up the other.

She shivered.

He was totally focused on her. "Do you like my touch?"

She nodded but didn't say a word.

He started again. This time he used his mouth instead of his hands, raining a shower of kisses along her forehead, the curve of her cheekbone, that delicate place at the base of her throat, the sensitive spot below her ear, her bare shoulder, her elbow, her rib cage, her breast, where he lingered, before moving on to her slender waist, her thigh, her knee, her ankle, even her foot. Then he began again, returning up the other side.

This time he paused and placed his mouth on that soft feminine mound with its sprinkling of auburn hair, that sweet, delicious mound that was already damp and swollen.

Trace touched her with his tongue.

She jerked.

"Ohmigod," she whispered.

"If you'll just separate your legs a little more," he urged, placing one hand on each side of her inner thighs.

Schuyler did as he requested, parting her feet perhaps five or six inches. It gave him enough room to do what he was hungering and thirsting to do. He flicked her with his tongue, taking first a sip, then a gentle nibble and finally a sensual bite.

Then he entered her with the arrowed tip of his tongue and she came utterly undone in his hands, crying out his name softly, intensely: "Trace!"

He could feel her quivering with need, with desire, with unnamed cravings. By the time he returned to take her mouth in a long, drugging kiss, they were both unsteady on their feet.

She reeled. "I feel so odd. . . ."

"I know," he murmured reassuringly.

"I don't think . . ."

"There's no need for you to think, Schuyler. There's no need for either of us to think."

"I can't stand up any longer," she admitted.

He gathered her up in his arms and carried her to the bed. He threw back the covers, placed her on the mattress and stretched out beside her.

"Now you won't have to worry about standing up," he said as he leaned over her, touching his lips to her mouth, the tip of her breast, her soft white belly.

"This is how I dreamed of you," she murmured, gazing up at him with golden eyes.

"And this is how I imagined making love to you," he replied, parting her thighs, slipping his hand between her long, lovely legs, threading his fingers through the thatch of womanly hair—it had its own texture, its own color—and finding the erotic nub hidden there.

Schuyler gasped.

Trace moistened his hand with her musky essence. Then, as he captured her mouth, driving his tongue between her lips, he eased a finger into her.

She arched her back and raised her hips off the bed. Trace swallowed her cry of arousal as his finger was driven deeper and deeper into her body. He slid it in and out, faster and faster, sensing his own body was approaching that inevitable point of no return.

Schuyler moved against his hand, moaning her need, her head thrashing back and forth on the pillow. Then, when the moment was upon her, Trace could feel her climax as she convulsed around his finger.

He'd intended to wait until her spasms had ceased, but his own body had been denied its release for too long already. As Schuyler called out his name, he softly shouted hers in return and ejaculated on the bed beneath them.

It was some time later—he could not have said how much later, and if it had come to that, neither could she—that Schuyler opened her eyes and gazed up into his.

Her voice was still a raspy whisper. "Now it's your turn."

A tiny crease formed between his dark blue eyes. "I don't understand."

"You will," she promised, pushing him over onto his back.

She sat up straight, her shoulders posture-perfect, and proceeded to swing one long, lovely leg across his lower torso. She straddled him. Being on top apparently gave her the impression that she was in control, he realized.

The lovely creature above him, hovering over his body, was well aware that he was positioned directly between her legs and that his erection was pushing against that sensitive female aperture where it so longed to be allowed to enter.

Her hair fell forward around her face. Her lips were already swollen from his kisses. Her complexion was a rosy shade of pink, whether from pleasure, or anticipation, or embarrassment—perhaps a little of all three.

She leaned over him and began to rain a succession of kisses upon him, from his forehead to his nose, from his nose to his mouth, from his mouth to his chin, from his chin to the hollow at the base of his throat, from his throat to his chest to his belly: teasing kisses, cruel kisses, wondrous kisses.

She gradually slid down his body, taking her remarkable

kisses with her. Kisses that trailed across his abdomen,
along his waist, to his leg and hipbone, burning his flesh
wherever her lips touched him. Kisses that lingered at his
navel, a tongue which dipped into the tiny indentation.
Kisses that barely avoided his erection—he was harder than
ever, dammit—and went first to one thigh and then the
other.

He groaned out loud.

Schuyler separated his legs several inches and placed her
mouth on his inner thigh, nipping at his sensitized flesh,
tugging on the random smattering of manly hair, caressing
the bone and muscle so near to his sex that he felt himself
swell in reaction.

Enough was enough.

He raised her up for a moment and held her there suspended above his body. His arms, strong as they were,
trembled with the effort as he slowly, oh, so slowly, lowered her onto him.

She took just a little of him at first, the very tip and
perhaps only an inch or two.

He felt the sweat break out on his skin.

Her eyes closed and then opened again. She stared
straight down into his and whispered, "Our turn."

Gradually she was impaled on his hard flesh. She managed, in the end, to take every last bit of him into her. They
paused and savored the sensation of his body buried deeply
inside her. Then they began to move together, slowly at
first, seeking to discover what pleased and what pleasured.

"God, you feel so damned good," he exclaimed as he
finally rolled over, staying inside her all the while, and
found himself gazing down into her eyes.

"So do you, Trace," she whispered fervently as he began
to thrust inside her again and again.

Then there was only the two of them. And there was
only here and there was only now.

All a wonder and a wild desire.

Trace was kissing her, urging her lips apart, teasing her
with his tongue, delving into her mouth as if he were trying
to meld their lips and teeth and tongues into one.

He was touching her, using his strong hands and his long
fingers to steal the very breath from her lungs, the strength
from her bones and muscles.

He was caressing her, making her blood sing in her
veins, making her body sing with a wild, hot song she had
never heard before, making her heart sing within her breast.

This was passion.

This was a fever in the mind.

This could make a woman forget everything but the way
a man made her feel.

His handsome face was before her, and his broad shoulders were blocking out everything but him. He made love
to her utterly, completely, asking no quarter and giving
none.

And when he thrust into her for the last time and shouted
her name over and over again, seeking his release, finding
his satisfaction, Schuyler felt a sense of belonging that she
had never known before.

Trace awakened with a start.

He hadn't meant to fall asleep. He glanced at the clock
on the mantelpiece. He gazed down at the woman in his
arms, snuggled against his side as if she had been made for
him. He would like nothing better than to awaken her with
the passion that had exhausted both of them into a sound
sleep.

There wasn't time.

"Schuyler," he said her name as he gently shook her.

"Trace," she murmured, still in that netherworld between sleep and wakefulness.

"You have to wake up."

"No."

"Yes. It's nearly four o'clock. You should return to your own bedroom."

Her eyes opened and stared up into his. For a moment he felt as if he were drowning in a sea of gold. "What time is it?" She formed the words with difficulty.

He repeated. "Four A.M."

She quickly sat up in bed. "It can't be."

"It is."

She seemed to suddenly realize that she was naked and the bedcovers were down around her waist. Her breasts were bare. Trace found himself unable to keep his eyes from them. As if it had a mind of its own—he was convinced that it did—his penis began to harden against her leg.

"Oh, no, you don't," she scolded, but she was laughing lightly and her cheeks were pink. "You implied time was of the essence. That will have to wait for another time."

He wanted to ask her if there would be another time. But this was no time to be discussing their future.

"I need to find my nightgown, bathrobe and slippers," she said, scooting out of bed and dropping to her knees on the floor.

Trace propped himself up on his elbow and watched the tantalizing view of Schuyler's derriere. He gave himself a shake. "I'll escort you back to your room."

"No," she said in a word.

"Yes," he countered.

"It's just down the hall. If I go alone I can always pre-

tend I was out for a late-night or an early-morning stroll if
I encounter anyone along the way."

"In your nightgown?" he said sardonically.

"I'm known for my eccentricities," she claimed. "The
staff already thinks I'm a little odd."

"No," Trace repeated, throwing back the bedcovers and
stretching before he reached for the jeans he had tossed
across a chair last night—well, in the middle of the night.
"I am going to see you safely to your door."

"You are a stubborn man," she declared, finding her
nightgown and slipping it on over her head.

"I like to think it's more a matter of strength of character," he told her as he thrust his arms into his shirt.

"Call it any fancy name you wish," she said saucily. "It's
still pigheadedness."

He made a slight grimace as he pulled on his jeans,
certain Schuyler couldn't miss the telltale bulge in his
pants. She blushed, but it was with pleasure. "You are insatiable."

"As are you," he said by way of a playful reminder.

She fumbled with the tie of her bathrobe and glanced
toward the door.

His hand was on the doorknob. "Are you ready?"

Schuyler nodded.

They were out the door of his bedroom and moving
along the corridor as silently as ghosts in the night.

As far as Trace could tell, the staff was still asleep, but
they wouldn't be for long. There would be women cleaning
the house, working in the kitchens and doing the myriad
tasks that kept a large estate running.

They had reached Schuyler's bedroom and gone inside
when something caught Trace's attention. His arm came out
and flattened Schuyler's back to the wall.

He held his index finger to his lips and softly whispered, "Shhh."

Schuyler obeyed. She kept very still and didn't say a word or make a sound.

Trace had always had the eyes of an eagle and excellent hearing. His senses, including his sixth sense for danger, had been very useful back on the streets of Pittsburgh. He used them to his advantage now. He waited and he watched.

There it was again.

He crossed to the window and looked out. Despite the fact that his room was only down the corridor from hers, the view was slightly different. There was a sound, a scraping sound. Then he saw the faint glow of a light in the distance.

It lasted only for a moment or two, but he was certain he hadn't imagined it.

"Speak softly and don't turn on a light," he whispered.

She nodded.

He put his mouth next to her ear. "You remember that night I followed you out to the gazebo?"

"Of course."

"Well, I want you to tell me exactly what it was that you saw and heard that made you decide to investigate."

A crease formed between her eyes. "What is it, Trace?"

He attempted to dismiss the whole business offhandedly. "It's nothing."

"Nothing?" Her tone was one of disbelief. "Somehow I think it must have been something." She gently scolded him. "After all we've been through together in the past several weeks, this is no time to start having secrets from one another."

He wanted to have his secrets. He didn't want her to read his mind. He put his hand on her shoulder with apparent casualness. He took her by the elbow and drew her into the shadows.

He peered out the window.

"You did see something, didn't you?"

Trace nodded. "A light," he finally said. "It lasted only for a moment or two, but I'm pretty sure I didn't imagine it."

Chapter Twenty-Eight

Trace pushed off from his stance leaning against the eighteenth-century Thomas Chippendale writing desk, decorated with Chinese lacquer and exotic landscapes— suddenly this room, this house, made him feel like a caged tiger—and, keeping his voice low, repeated, "You're *not*— I repeat—you're *not* going with me."

A frown formed between Schuyler's eyes. "But you said you saw something."

"I did see something," he confirmed.

"Did you hear anything?"

There was no way he was going to lie to her. "A kind of scraping noise."

Obviously her mind was made up; her voice became matter-of-fact. "Then I'm going with you," she stated, pulling on a pair of slacks and reaching for a dark pullover sweater.

Trace pointed to his head. "Do I look like I'm crazy?" He flashed her a sardonic smile and said, "On second thought, don't answer that question."

A pair of flat shoes were slipped onto her feet. "I'm going. Period. Nothing you can say or do will change my mind."

Somehow he had to make Schuyler understand the potential danger involved. "Look, honey, I literally grew up on the streets in one of the roughest neighborhoods in Pittsburgh. I had to learn how to take care of myself at a very young age if I wanted to survive. No offense, but you're soft."

"And you're hard," she countered with an unintentional double entendre as she pulled her hair back into a ponytail. "I suppose that's why they say opposites attract."

"This is dead serious, Schuyler."

"I realize that."

"I'm asking you to stay here, to leave this business, whatever it is, to me."

She reached out and took his hand in hers. "I can't do that, Trace."

He swore softly under his breath. "Dammit, I don't want you to get hurt."

Schuyler threw his words right back in his face. "And, dammit, I don't want you to get hurt." Then she pleaded, "Trust me, Trace. I'm tougher than you think I am."

His frustration reached the boiling point. "But Schuyler—"

"We're in this business together, or we aren't in it at all." She meant every word.

"You are a stubborn, headstrong young woman," he declared, and he didn't mean it as a compliment.

"You are a stubborn, headstrong man," she returned in kind. "Now let's discuss our plans."

He didn't like it one damned bit, but he didn't have to, Trace realized. "The first step is to sneak outside without being seen by anyone."

She listened intently. "I understand."

"We'll make our way along the back of the house, using what's left of the darkness and the shadows as cover. Then we head directly for the woods." He added, "No flashlights."

"No flashlights," she reiterated.

"Do you have any questions?"

Schuyler's face was white. "Only one."

"What is it?"

"Do we have any weapons?"

"Weapons?"

"Guns? Knives?"

Trace noticed that her hands were trembling ever so slightly. He tried to lighten the mood. "You've got your deadly umbrella handy, haven't you?"

She tried to smile. "I have."

"And you've got me," he reminded her. "What more could any woman need?"

She turned to him with a determined air, put her chin up a notch, then reached over and patted him reassuringly on the arm. "You're absolutely right."

Trace blew out his breath expressively. "Ready?"

She gave a single curt nod of her head. "Ready."

His mind was racing. "Remember to move quietly."

"I will. I've sneaked out of this house before in the middle of the night and no one was ever aware of my absence," she reminded him with a certain feminine pride. "Except you just happened to look out your window and see me, of course."

He couldn't argue with her near success.

He broached another subject altogether. "Once we reach the woods, we talk only when it's absolutely necessary, and then in whispers. In order to communicate at other times, we will devise a series of simple hand signals."

She looked at him challengingly. "What if it's too dark to see each other's hands?"

"Then you stick to me like glue," he declared, grimly amused.

"I can do that," she said, seemingly innocently.

Trace shook his head. "You are an amazing woman."

She could give as good as she got. "You are an amazing man."

"You're quick, too."

"So are you."

"I meant quick-witted."

"So did I."

He paused with his hand on the doorknob. "I'm a bit rusty at this kind of thing."

"I'm sure it's like riding a bicycle," she reassured. "You never really forget how."

With Trace in the lead and Schuyler close behind, they slipped downstairs and, without a sound, disarmed the alarm system and let themselves out the kitchen door.

They moved quickly, quietly, without speaking, without making a single unnecessary sound.

Darkness was their friend.

They moved from shadow to shadow along the rear of the great house. They skirted a hedge of waist-high yews and made their way to a spot directly across from the woods.

They moved stealthily. They blended in with the night. They saw no one and no one saw them. There were deep shadows cast by the first of several large chestnut trees. Trace and Schuyler made a run for cover and flattened themselves against the trunk, its rough bark scraping against their backs.

They both held their breaths.

As they crept from tree to tree, they realized they were getting closer and closer to both the faint sound Trace had heard earlier and, there through the underbrush, a faint flicker of light.

But the loudest sound, Schuyler realized, was the thrumming of her heart.

They were about to cut across a small clearing when her hand shot out to stop Trace.

There!

Trace saw it, too. Someone—or something—was lurking in the cover of darkness provided by the forest.

They improvised. Instead of heading straight for the mysterious flicker of light, they took the circuitous route. The going was rough. Every now and then Schuyler felt a branch scratch her face and she tasted blood on her lips.

Her own blood.

They crouched behind a fallen tree and slowly brought their eyes level with its surface. At that moment the moon emerged from behind a thin stratus of clouds. They could make out a lantern and the shape of a shadowy figure.

The ground was damp. Trace tugged on the pant leg of her slacks and Schuyler hunched down beside him. He dipped his fingertips into the mud and began to smear the stuff in broad strokes down the side of his face, across his cheekbones and along his forehead. Then he did the same to Schuyler before giving her the thumbs up. She nodded her head in understanding.

Schuyler shook her head.

"What's this?" Trace whispered directly into her ear, imitating her action.

She mouthed, "No."

He mouthed back, "No?"

Something bothered her about this whole setup. She put her lips against his face and said, "What if there is more than one person out there?"

Trace drove his hand through the hair at his nape. He pulled her down behind the log again and said, "We'll cross that bridge when we get to it."

It looked like they were going to have to cross that bridge. The first person they recognized as they crept through the underbrush toward the source of the light was Johnny Grant.

The second was a woman.

Schuyler moved her mouth and silently formed the words, "Elaine Kendall?"

Trace nodded.

What was a real estate agent doing in the woods on the Grantwood estate in the middle of the night? Schuyler had always heard they worked long hours, but this was ridiculous.

She glanced up at the silvery circle in the sky. It was close to a full moon tonight, which both helped and hindered them. Adrenaline shot through her veins. She was out of her element, but she had no intentions of letting Trace do this alone.

So what in the hell were Johnny Grant and Elaine Kendall doing here?

She could hear them whispering nervously to each other. Then the young woman asked, "Deeper?"

Johnny answered her cryptically. "He says it goes down about eight or nine feet."

Her tone was one of disdain. "And I suppose *he* gives the orders around here."

Johnny gave his accomplice a dirty look. "I give the orders. He just thinks he does."

Chapter Twenty-Nine

It wasn't the smartest thing he had ever done.

In fact, it might even rank right up there with the top ten dumbest stunts he'd ever pulled in his life.

Trace Ballinger swore under his breath and tried to think as quickly as he could on his feet. Not that he was on his feet, exactly. He and Schuyler were still hiding behind the fallen tree.

The truth was he hadn't been paying attention when Johnny Grant disappeared into the shadows beyond the clearing, making some inane remark over his shoulder to Elaine Kendall about needing to answer the call of nature.

The next thing he knew, slick Johnny had been directly behind where they were crouched in the bushes. Not the ideal position to be in when surprised by an enemy. Especially when that enemy was clutching a small black revolver in his hand.

"Well, well," came the smooth, cultured tones, "what—or should I say *who*—do we have here?"

"What the hell are you doing out here in the middle of the woods, Grant?" Trace demanded to know, as if he had every right to be asking the questions and requiring the answers.

"I was about to ask you the same question, Ballinger," came the slightly amused reply from the handsome blond man. Then he speculated, "I don't suppose the two of you are out for a romantic stroll at this hour." He peered at the streaks of mud camouflaging their faces. "No, I didn't think so."

"What we're doing is none of your business," Trace stated as he got to his feet.

The revolver was brandished by a soft, manicured, yet surprisingly steady masculine hand. "Let's all step out into the clearing, shall we? And don't try any funny business, Ballinger, or my lovely cousin will pay the price."

Trace held out his hand and helped Schuyler to her feet. Then he motioned for her to precede him through the underbrush and into the open.

"I suppose some kind of introductions are in order," Johnny went on to say when the four of them were gathered within the circle of light cast by the kerosene lantern. "Elaine Kendall. Trace Ballinger. And Schuyler Grant, of course."

When Schuyler finally spoke up, her voice was impervious, even regal, in tone. "What, pray tell, are you doing trespassing on my property?"

"Your property?" Johnny repeated with a well-modulated laugh. "I've got to hand it to you, cousin. You do the lady-of-the-manor bit rather well. Cora would be proud of you."

Schuyler's whole demeanor showed an increasing disdain for her distant relation. "Which is certainly more than I can say for you, Johnny."

"Tut-tut, let's not go slinging mud, now. Although, from the looks of it, I gather that is precisely what you and Mr. Ballinger have been doing."

"Trés amusant," Schuyler muttered in French, but she didn't mean it.

"I thought it was rather amusing." Johnny Grant was suddenly deadly serious. "I was always Cora's favorite, anyway. And I was here for her, which is more than you can say, Schuyler. Where were you the past nine years?"

They assumed his question was a rhetorical one.

He went on, "The fact that I was smart enough to keep my eyes and ears open and seize an opportunity when it presented, itself—" here Johnny paused and shrugged his shoulders—"well, to the victor belong the spoils, I always say."

"I always suspected you were an opportunist," Schuyler flung back at him.

Trace needed facts, and he needed them fast. "What opportunity might that be, Grant?"

Elaine Kendall bent over the handle of her shovel and speculated, "They don't know what this is all about, do they?"

"Of course they know," Johnny argued with her. "Why else would they be tramping around the forest at this hour and sneaking around in the bushes?"

Trace could bluff with the best of them. "Did you hatch this half-baked scheme all on your own, Grant?"

"Good heavens, no, of course he didn't, Mr. Ballinger," came the woman's throaty laugh as she answered for her accomplice. Elaine Kendall propped her shovel against the trunk of a nearby tree and added, "Johnny and I are partners in everything. Aren't we, Johnnykins?"

"I suppose we are," he agreed without looking around at the woman who came up to stand beside him.

They were both dressed in serviceable jeans, jackets and sturdy hiking boots. It was no accident that the pair had appeared when and where they did.

Elaine Kendall's voice dropped to a sultry purr. "So you know about the treasure, too?" She took several steps closer to what appeared to be an old well.

There was a pickaxe leaning against the crumbling stone structure, Trace noted.

"Shut up, Elaine," snapped her accomplice.

Elaine Kendall wasn't a stupid woman. In fact, Trace had a strong hunch the woman was a survivor. And survivors usually had excellent instincts. They had to. Hers appeared to be finely honed.

"Sometimes Johnny forgets his manners," she said, dispensing with discretion, as if she ever bothered with it anyway. "But believe me, he does have his redeeming qualities." She turned her green-eyed gaze on Schuyler. "Would you like me to share some of the—shall we say—more interesting and *explicit* details about Johnny?"

"No, she wouldn't," Johnny interceded.

"I think Miss Grant is quite capable of speaking for herself," the dark-haired woman stated.

"I hate it when you talk about me as if I weren't standing right here next to you, Elaine," he griped.

"Then don't listen," she said to him sweetly.

Trace wondered just how far and how long Elaine Kendall and slick Johnny would go in exchanging insults. Would it be far enough and long enough to create a diversion so he could wrestle the revolver away from Johnny Grant?

Unfortunately Elaine foiled his plans.

"Let's not argue, dearest," she said in a conciliatory tone of voice. "This isn't the time or the place. Not when we were about to retrieve the motherlode itself."

"Too bad you weren't around to help all those nights when we were digging," Jonathan Grant said to Trace. "You seem to be the brawny type. Ah, well, as long as you're here now, Ballinger, I believe we'll have you climb down into the well and retrieve what we're after," he said, flaunting the small yet deadly weapon.

As he slipped over the side and dropped to bottom of the well, Trace wondered what he was supposed to be looking for. "I can't see anything."

"Why not?"

"Well, for one thing it's dark down here. I'll need a lantern or a flashlight."

A flashlight landed in his outstretched hands.

He flipped the switch on and shone the pale yellow beam around the man-made structure and the crushed stone floor. "I don't see a damned thing, Grant."

Well, nothing except what appeared to be a piece of wire, some tinfoil and a few bits of colored glass.

Jonathan Grant's head appeared at the top of the well. "Then you'll just have to dig a little deeper, won't you? The shovel is right there next to you."

Trace picked up the shovel and began. He'd excavated another foot of dirt and stone and sand before he reported, "There's nothing here, I tell you."

"How far down have you dug?"

"At least another eighteen inches," he said, exaggerating just a little.

"Well, now what the bloody hell are we to do?" Johnny demanded of no one in particular.

Trace stuffed the piece of wire, the tinfoil and the colored stones in his shirt pocket, found a foothold halfway up the stone wall and climbed out of the well.

"Maybe somebody got to the treasure before you," Trace suggested, dusting off his jeans with the back of his hand.

It was Elaine who went ballistic. "You don't suppose we've been double-crossed, do you?"

Jonathan Grant's dark brown eyes filled with rage. "He wouldn't dare."

Trace decided to try reasoning with the inept pair. "Why don't you put your weapon down and start acting like the rational human being you are, Grant?" he recommended. "There's nothing to be gained by waving a gun around. Somebody might get hurt."

Apparently Jonathan Grant wasn't interested in what Trace had to say on that subject, or on any subject, for that matter. "I'll do whatever I damned well feel like doing, Ballinger, and if that includes waving my revolver around, I will."

Schuyler wasn't certain when she put two and two together and came up with four, but she suddenly realized where they were standing and what the crumbling stone well was . . . or what it had once been, anyway.

She turned on her distant cousin. "It was you," she declared accusingly.

"What was?"

"You were the one who went into the library that day and tore the page from the map book."

Johnny smirked and suddenly his handsome face wasn't quite so handsome anymore. "What are you going to do, my dear cousin, sue me?"

"I should have my lawyer after both of you for criminal trespassing," she bluffed.

Elaine Kendall apparently didn't like the sound of that. "For what?"

Schuyler stared down the other woman. "You and Johnny made up that cock-and-bull story about showing Grantwood to qualified buyers, with one purpose in mind: so you could sneak into the library and steal a page from a book that didn't belong to you." Schuyler hoped she wasn't laying it on too thick. "What kind of jail time are they looking at for criminal trespassing, Trace?"

He played along with her. He stroked his jaw thoughtfully. "Two . . . maybe three years. Depends on the judge, of course. They could get out in half that time with good behavior."

Elaine paled. Her mouth opened and the words began to

spill out. "It wasn't my idea. It was Johnny's. It was all Johnny's fault."

Her accomplice gave her a dirty look. "If I'm in it up to my sweet ass, so are you, Elaine. Who claimed the lawyer—whose name you have conveniently forgotten—called and made the appointment to show the house? Who contacted the Plunketts? Who traipsed through Grantwood without the owner's permission?"

"I'm sure Miss Grant can understand an innocent mistake," the other woman said sweetly.

Schuyler shook her head. "And all because you didn't know where to find Cora's wishing well." She turned to Trace. "That's why they needed the layout of the grounds from the 1940s, in order to find her private garden."

"Well, aren't you the clever one, Miss Grant?" spoke up a distinguished-looking gentleman as he stepped from the woods into the clearing.

Chapter Thirty

"Mr. Theodore Frick, I presume," Trace said casually as he slowly turned to face the newcomer.

Theodore Frick straightened his back, relaxed his shoulders, spread his stance an inch or two as though making certain his balance was perfect and motioned with the hand *not* holding a gun. "At your service, sir."

"The brains of the outfit, so to speak."

"Naturally."

"I thought there was something about this whole situation that didn't ring true. Frankly, I couldn't imagine that Johnny or Ms. Kendall managed this scheme on their own." Trace added in a sardonic tone, "I suppose there's a method to your madness."

"What in the world are you talking about?" Schuyler finally got the question out.

"I assumed it was slick Johnny. In a way I suppose it was. I suspected he was the one who ran you off the road that first night." Trace turned to the usually immaculately dressed man. "You did, didn't you?"

Schuyler stared at Johnny. "I think you'd better answer that question, cousin."

Jonathan Tiberius Grant shifted his weight from one foot to the other and back again. "I meant no harm, Schuyler. I was just trying to frighten you a little."

"You could have killed me. Or Trace," she pointed out.

"I said I'm sorry," Johnny grumbled.

"Why did you do it?"

"So you wouldn't stay. So you'd go away. So I—we—could keep looking for Cora's tiara."

Theodore Frick swore at his dupe. "Shut your frigging mouth, Grant."

Schuyler looked from one to the other. "It's too late for that. What tiara?"

Teddy Frick gave a short, humorless laugh. "Do you honestly think any of us is going to tell you?"

"Yes. I do." She looked at Johnny and Elaine Kendall. "Mr. Frick may be beyond redemption, but you two still have a chance to make it right."

The handsome man shook his head slightly and finally said, "I can't tell you."

Elaine nervously licked her lips. "Neither can I."

Teddy Frick hesitated only briefly before speaking up, "In case you hadn't noticed, Miss Grant, I have a loaded revolver pointed at you and Mr. Ballinger, and I'm a very good shot."

"Why would you want to shoot us?" Schuyler blurted out without thinking.

Teddy laughed. "To get rid of you, of course."

She still didn't understand. "Why would you want to get rid of us?"

Once again, Teddy responded for all three of the coconspirators. "So we can have the tiara for ourselves."

"That is the most ridiculous, asinine, moronic thing I have ever heard," she shot back at him.

The man seemed taken aback. "I beg your pardon."

"That is the dumbest idea I've ever heard, and believe me, I have heard some pretty dumb ideas in my time."

Teddy Frick took her insult personally. "I don't care to have my ideas labeled as dumb, Miss Grant."

She bluffed. "Assuming you ever find this tiara, are any of you experienced in disposing of jewelry? Do you have any notion how or where to sell a valuable piece? Do you know how or where to sell a valuable piece? Do you know who would be on the list of buyers? Without proof of ownership, you can scarcely walk into Christie's or Sotheby's and have them auction it off for you."

There was no answer from either man or Elaine Kendall.

Schuyler went on, "Well, you'd better know what you're doing or you'll end up getting a fraction of its worth. I'm a curator at the Louvre, and believe me, if there's one thing I know, it's my priceless objects."

Trace added, "Not to mention the fact that if you try to sell it on the black market, you'll be dealing with some pretty unsavory types. Do you know how to deal with those kind of people? Or will you get robbed blind at best?"

"And at worst?" Johnny asked, swallowing hard.

"You'll be lucky to escape with your lives."

"How do you know so much about unsavory types, Ballinger?" the handsome man inquired.

"I grew up in a neighborhood where the motto was, 'If you're going to shoot someone, kill them.' You ever shoot anyone, Johnny?"

There was a soft gasp and an "Ohmigod" from Elaine Kendall.

Trace took a stance that was somehow forceful without being challenging. There was always a fine line between intimidation and stepping over that line, between sanity and insanity.

He decided to work on the weaker link first. Johnny was the weaker link. "Ever kill anyone?"

Johnny Grant seemed to pale. "Good God, no."

Trace sneered. "Never actually do the dirty work yourself, huh?"

"I don't have any idea what you're talking about. For

chrissakes, I'm not a criminal," Johnny said. "I went to Yale."

For some reason Elaine Kendall seemed to find that claim amusing. She laughed out loud. "Well, let's hear it for the Yaleys."

Johnny gave her a dirty look and wiped the back of his hand across his mouth. "Is that the kind of thing they taught you at Harvard Law, Ballinger?"

"In a way, yes, I suppose they did," he said with a hard-edged laugh. "Yale, huh? I shouldn't be surprised." He turned around. "You, on the other hand, do surprise me, Mr. Frick. I thought you were a botanist."

"I am. But I'm not rich botanist, nor am I a stupid botanist. I would like you to keep your hands where I'll be able to see them at all times."

Hands behind his head, fingers interlaced, Trace faced his adversary. "Teddy Frick," he said with an expectant tone in his voice, making certain that his expression gave nothing away. It was a technique he'd used to great advantage in the courtroom. "Why?"

"Why, what?"

"Why all this?"

Teddy made a noise that sounded like a snort. "You mean, why dig out here in the middle of this briar patch?" he answered as he brandished his revolver at them.

Schuyler made her disapproval known. "You're trespassing. This was Cora's garden, and now it's mine."

His reply was a sly one. "Possession is nine-tenths of the law, as I believe Mr. Ballinger will tell you. Cora hadn't been on this section of her land in decades and you would never have known it existed but for Johnny's stupidity."

Johnny didn't take kindly to the name-calling. "Hey, watch who you're calling stupid, Teddy."

"That's Mr. Frick to you."

Schuyler went on, "Johnny's stupidity—did that happen to include tearing the map out of the book in the library?"

"What map?" Teddy Frick wasn't a very good actor.

She said, "The map that showed this part of the garden as it used to be."

"Well, you figured it out, did you?" he said, looking down his nose at the small gathering of people.

Trace repeated his earlier question and diverted the man's attention. "You still haven't answered my question. Why?"

"Why, what?"

"Why all of this?"

Teddy took a step back, scowling. "I'll tell you why. That damned woman saw fit to leave something to everyone—everyone but me, that is."

Trace stalled. "What woman?"

"What woman do you think? Cora, of course."

"You weren't in her will."

"As you damned well know."

"Why did Cora leave you out of her will?" Schuyler spoke up, seemingly interested in the answer. "After all, as you said, she included everyone and anyone: the butcher, the baker, the candlestick maker."

"You're very amusing, Miss Grant," granted the man with the deadly weapon pointed at her. "Cora was *not* amusing, on the other hand." He appeared wounded. "She had made it clear a long time ago that she didn't like me."

"How long ago?"

He shrugged his professorial shoulders. "Thirty years. Maybe longer. Then when I returned home to Little Hollows last year she thought I was less than grateful for the home that Ellamae and Ida gave me out of the goodness of their hearts. She thought I failed to appreciate their charity. On top of that, she considered me a leech."

"You'd know all about the leech part, wouldn't you, Johnny?" Trace interjected with a insinuating glance at the other man.

Johnny's face blazed bright red. "I don't know what you mean by that remark, Ballinger, but you can shut your fucking mouth."

"Tsk-tsk. Such language in front of the ladies. I thought a Yaley knew better."

Johnny sneered. "What ladies?"

That earned him an appropriate accolade from Elaine Kendall. "Well, screw you, Johnny."

"You have, babe. And you're not even very good at it," was his parting shot.

"You're not good with women, either, are you, Teddy?" Trace proposed, using a very particular tone of voice, one that implied a certain inadequacy.

"That is none of your business," the man snapped.

Trace was not deterred. "In fact, I'd be willing to wager that you've never had a real relationship with a woman."

"Shut up. Just shut up."

"You hate your sisters. You resented Cora. You don't seem to like Miss Grant, and everyone likes Miss Grant."

Teddy licked his lips. "Especially you, Ballinger. You especially like Miss Grant, don't you? I saw you in the garden that night."

"So we can add Peeping Tom to your other virtues."

Theodore Frick's mouth disappeared. "We've wasted enough time on idle chitchat and exchanging personal insults," he declared meaningfully. "It's time to take care of business." He began to issue orders. "Johnny, you keep your gun aimed at your dear cousin, while I see to Mr. Ballinger."

"What's our plan?" Johnny inquired.

"We're going to arrange an accident."

Johnny and Elaine said in unison, "An accident?"

"Well, we can hardly let these two go free, now, can we?" pointed out their ringleader.

"Why not?" asked the real estate agent.

"Yes, why not?" Johnny echoed. "We haven't done anything wrong. Well, nothing really wrong. Why not just cut our losses and get the hell out of here?"

"Because I said so."

"But that's crazy," exclaimed Johnny.

Teddy's eyes glittered in the glow of his flashlight. "Who are you calling crazy?"

Johnny licked his lips. Trace noticed that the hand holding his gun was shaking ever so slightly. Johnny Grant was in over his head. He was playing a game—a very dangerous game—that was out of his league.

That would play right into Trace's hand, of course.

"Can't you see what's happening here, Grant?" Trace said to the handsome man. "He's going to go down and he'll end up taking you with him. Is that what you really want?"

"Don't listen to him, Johnny boy. The rest of the job is going to be a piece of cake, believe me," Teddy assured his two younger companions.

Johnny stood his ground. "Like I said earlier, Teddy, I don't know what the rest of the job is. We agreed to be partners and look for the treasure together, the object that Cora confided to me was her most priceless possession that had been lost down that wishing well years and years ago. Well, it turned out to be nothing more than a damned hoax."

"Not entirely a hoax," Trace interjected.

That got everyone's attention.

"What the hell are you talking about?" demanded Johnny.

"I did find something at the bottom of the wishing well. It's in my shirt pocket."

The handsome man snickered. "I don't believe you."

Trace looked at Teddy. "May I?"

"Yes. But slowly."

Trace reached down and took the tinfoil, the wire and the colored bits of glass from his pocket and tossed them on the ground where they could all see. "There's your tiara."

"What's the joke?"

"No joke. That's what I found."

"Not exactly priceless," Johnny muttered.

Schuyler spoke up. "Perhaps Cora simply had a different perception of what was priceless, of what was beyond the value of money. It was a lesson I thought we'd both learned, too, Johnny. But I was wrong, wasn't I?"

He looked at her. "I'm sorry about this, Schuyler."

"So am I," she said sadly.

"There never was a valuable tiara in the wishing well," concluded Elaine Kendall.

"I'm afraid not," Johnny commiserated.

"Ah, well, easy come, easy go," the woman said with a sigh. "I guess it's back to the real estate business for me."

"Not if Teddy has his way," Trace pointed out. "If you walk away and leave us to him, you'll become an accessory to a capital crime. Trust me, I know. I'm an attorney, remember?"

"He's right," Elaine said, gnawing on her bottom lip and looking sidelong at Johnny. "What are we going to do about those two?" she asked, glancing meaningfully at them.

"I think we should let them go," Johnny concluded. "Maybe we'll get away with a simple slap on the wrist for our part in this sorry business."

"They die," Teddy announced as if it were a foregone conclusion, as if he were judge, jury and executioner and the verdict was in. "If you want to switch sides and join them, then do so now."

Elaine Kendall and Johnny Grant seemed frozen to the spot where they stood.

"In that case, I'm afraid your luck has just run out, Ballinger. This is one jury you apparently couldn't sway to your way of thinking," came Teddy's final word on the matter.

Schuyler couldn't believe that evil would triumph over good. She couldn't believe that it would end like this: with a whimper and a crazy man holding a gun on them.

In fact, she absolutely refused to believe it. She would not give up. A Grant *never* gave up. Determination and pigheadedness were in the blood!

They would be saved. She and Trace would somehow save themselves and these two rather pathetic people who deserved little better than they were going to get. They would all be saved. Good would triumph over evil in the end. And all would be right with the world.

It was the least she deserved.

It was the very least Trace deserved.

"I thought I heard something," she suddenly announced in an urgent voice, glancing back over her shoulder.

"Nice try, Miss Grant," Teddy said with a disbelieving smile and without turning his head.

"I did hear something. Listen." She dramatically cocked her head to one side.

There it was.

An eerie sound coming from somewhere deep in the woods behind them. It wasn't quite a human sound. It sent chills down the spine and made the heart pound.

Teddy Frick laughed; it was a surprisingly chilling laugh. "Don't waste your breath, Miss Grant. I know these woods like the back of my hand. I wandered around in them for years as a boy. It will take a great deal more than a third-rate—and I am giving you the benefit of the doubt—performance to make me believe there's anyone out there."

"Or *anything*?" Trace speculated with what could only be described as a feral grin.

Theodore Frick pointed the weapon at Schuyler Grant's heart. "You might like to keep several things in mind, Mr. Ballinger. I am an excellent shot and I have virtually no conscience. I will do whatever needs to be done and I'll have no regrets. I will have my revenge."

"Revenge is a dead-end street, Mr. Frick. Believe me, I know," Trace stated.

"Revenge is sweet," countered the botanist. "I can almost taste its sweetness."

Trace shook his head. "Revenge is like a cancer that will crawl inside your guts and eat you alive from the inside out. There's no future in it. And, in the end, there isn't even any satisfaction. You're kidding yourself if you believe otherwise."

"I have spent months, even years, planning my revenge," Teddy Frick stated.

"And where has it brought you?" Trace asked. "You're standing in the middle of the woods in the dead of night. You're holding a gun on an innocent young woman who never did you a moment's harm. There is no priceless treasure. There is no great fortune to be dug up from Cora's wishing well. There is nothing here but empty and meaningless revenge."

"Don't bother trying to talk me out of what I must do, Ballinger," the man said in a deceptively mild tone.

Schuyler realized that Teddy Frick had no intentions of

setting them free. She and Trace might well never leave these woods. She looked at the man with the gun. "I'm deeply disappointed in you, Mr. Frick."

"Are you, Miss Grant?"

"You're nothing but a common thief."

The man glanced down his nose at her. "I'm not a common anything. In fact, I am a most *uncommon* man. I have the IQ of a genius."

She permitted himself a small sigh. "Well, you could have fooled me."

His brow crinkled into a genuine frown. "Would you care to explain that ill-advised remark?"

"I don't think you're very bright, that's all."

"Your opinion is of no consequence to me," he stated with an indignant sniff. "I'm used to people underestimating me. It's been true all of my life."

"I'm not surprised," she murmured.

"I surprised you on several occasions," the man said with a smug expression on his face. "By the way, how did you like the nursery?"

When Trace spoke, Schuyler could hear the underlying anger—and absolute determination—in his voice. "So *you* were the one who shoved Miss Grant."

Schuyler sucked in her breath.

"I see you finally put two and two together," Theodore Frick said, switching his attention to Trace.

"Finally." Then Trace speculated, "It wasn't a woman. It was you."

There was a long-suffering sigh. "Pity you discovered Miss Grant's whereabouts."

"Pity?" Trace repeated.

"It could have all ended there and no one would have found her. Perhaps not for years."

"She was supposed to die?"

Teddy Frick moved his head. "She was supposed to quietly disappear without a trace."

Trace stiffened beside her. "You bastard," he swore
harshly under his breath.

Cold gray eyes narrowed to two thin slits. "It's was
Cora's punishment."

"But Cora is already dead and beyond any punishment,"
Trace stated.

Schuyler had an odd feeling in the pit of her stomach.
"I'm not Cora."

"No, but you'll do."

Schuyler's heart was galloping. "Do?"

"As a stand-in." Teddy Frick grew agitated. "As I keep
telling all of you. Why won't you listen? I wouldn't want
to leave any evidence behind, now, would I?"

Schuyler was willing to reason with him, even plead
with him. "But Mr. Frick—"

"I'm sorry, Miss Grant. Enough is enough. No more
talking. I win, and you lose."

A voice from the darkness announced loud and clear,
"I'm afraid we win and you all lose. Drop your weapon,
Mr. Frick."

"No," he said belligerently.

A shot rang out. Theodore Frick dropped his gun and
grabbed his hand. Blood was dripping down his fingers and
onto the ground at his feet. "Somebody shot me."

A man and woman stepped from the shadows into the
clearing.

"I told you to drop your gun," the man stated. "That
should prove to the rest of you that we mean business."

Elaine Kendall's mouth dropped open. "Mr. Plunkett."

Mr. Plunkett did not smile. He nodded his head and said
in a businesslike tone, "Ms. Kendall."

The woman beside him wasn't wearing a smile, either.

"Mrs. Plunkett?" speculated Schuyler.

"What happened to your Texas accents?" Johnny demanded to know, his revolver dropping into the pine nee-
dles at his feet.

"We lost them," the woman snickered.

"That's enough, Wilma."

"What have you done to your hair?" Elaine asked her.

Wilma Plunkett said sweet as could be, "Why?"

Elaine Kendall swallowed the lump in her throat. "It was
pink the last time I saw you. Now it's . . . orange."

"Do you like it?"

Apparently Elaine chose diplomacy over the truth. "Yes,
I do."

"In that case, it's yours," the woman said, reaching up
and plucking the orange wig from her head and tossing it
into Elaine's hands.

"Rank amateurs," her male accomplice muttered.

"You can say that again."

"Who are you people?" Schuyler wanted to know.

"We're professionals," came the declaration. "Unlike the
rest of these bunglers who tried to take you to the cleaners."

"What did you intend to do?"

The woman known as Wilma Plunkett spoke first. "Originally we'd intended to get inside Grantwood and see if it
was feasible to make a job of it. But it didn't take us long
to discover two things: Your security system is too sophisticated and your real estate agent and your cousin had a far
more enticing and less dangerous scam up their sleeves."
She looked down her nose at Elaine Kendall and Johnny
Grant. "You two really should learn how to whisper if you
want to make it in this business."

"So we decided to hang around, let them do the work
and then reap the rewards of someone else's labor," piped
up the man known to some of them as P. G. Plunkett.

His female companion said, "I love it when a plan comes together, don't you, P. G.?"

"Yes, I do," he stated.

"So we win and you lose," the Plunketts declared in unison.

A strong, confident male voice rang out from the trees behind them. "I'm afraid *I* win, and *you* lose."

Seven heads snapped around.

A great crashing sound came through the woods from the opposite direction. Something was headed straight toward them. The group of people scarcely knew where to look.

"My God, it's a wild animal!" exclaimed Elaine Kendall.

"It's Adam Coffin," Schuyler cried out with relief.

"He's got a rifle," added Johnny Grant unnecessarily.

"No one speaks unless I give them permission," Adam Coffin's voice snapped with authority. "I've got you covered from the south. Moose has you covered from the north." The weapon he was pointing straight at the Plunketts spoke louder than any words. "Drop it, you two, or you'll be pushing up daisies."

Schuyler completely forgot about lowering her voice to a whisper. "It's Buddy, too!"

The great golden retriever snarled, showed his teeth and leaped.

His front paws landed squarely between P. G. Plunkett's shoulders, knocking the man to the ground.

It all happened very quickly. The revolver in the scam artist's hand went flying through the air and, as luck would have it, landed near Trace's feet. He picked it up with one hand and grabbed the man's arm with the other and twisted it behind his back.

Trace stood and glared for a moment. Then he issued his edict. "Listen up, people. From now on, we do this Mr.

Coffin's way." He looked at each of them in turn. "Understood?"

The Plunketts knew the routine, apparently. Their hands went into the air even as Trace released his hold on P. G. Teddy Frick's shoulders slumped forward like those of a defeated man.

"We're the innocent parties in this whole affair," whined Johnny Grant. "Elaine and I were just a couple of dupes who got mixed up in something we didn't understand."

"You can cut the crap, Johnny," ordered the usually shy man with the rifle. "I know who *and* what you are."

Chapter Thirty-One

Adam Coffin was hailed by one and all as a hero. In fact, the usually retiring gentleman had not stopped beaming since the unpleasant incident in the woods was successfully concluded and the authorities had come and gone.

At this very moment he was sitting at the kitchen table of Grantwood enjoying a cup of Mrs. Danvers's excellent coffee—as they all were. This time the strong black coffee was laced with a well-deserved and fortifying shot of brandy.

Moose was safely ensconced in Adam's coat pocket; the tiny creature was sound asleep after enjoying several small nibbles of filet mignon carefully fed to him by Mrs. Danvers.

Buddy had chowed down an entire steak and was now contentedly curled up at the housekeeper's feet. The golden retriever definitely knew which side his bread was buttered on.

The hour was late—well, the hour was early, it was morning and a yellow sun was already high in a clear blue sky—but none of the four were interested in parting company. The events of the long night had left them wide awake.

Adam Coffin cleared his throat. "I should have said something sooner, of course. But I was a coward."

Schuyler reached out and patted the man's hand reassuringly. "It's understandable why you hesitated."

He scowled. "When I first suspected something was going on in the woods, I didn't want to tell Cora for fear it would needlessly upset her."

Mrs. Danvers piped up and added her two cents' worth. "That was being thoughtful, not cowardly."

He went on, "I considered telling you, Miss Grant, or, you, Trace, but I was afraid you'd think I was crazy."

Schuyler was sympathetic. "I was about to confess that I've felt exactly the same way on several occasions." Her mind reviewed the bizarre events of the previous evening when she'd spotted the face in the window, not the face of a woman, as it turned out, but of Teddy Frick.

"How did you happen to be in the woods last night?" Trace was obviously interested in learning the full story.

Adam Coffin's expression was unusually animated as he related his tale. "On rare occasions I still suffer from insomnia. When I can't sleep, I like to take a long walk in the woods." Here he paused and gently reached into the pocket of his jacket. "Moose always insists on coming along with me, naturally." He cleared his throat. "Anyway, last night was one of those nights."

"I have a wonderful all-natural herbal tea concoction to be drunk at bedtime that cures insomnia," interjected Mrs. Danvers. "I'd be happy to make up a recipe for you, Mr. Coffin."

"Thank you, Mrs. Danvers." He smiled across the table at the housekeeper. "If it wouldn't be too much trouble."

"It wouldn't be too much trouble at all for the gentleman who single-handedly saved the day and our Miss Grant and Mr. Ballinger," the woman declared, two round spots of bright red appearing on her cheeks.

"Please go on with your story, Mr. Coffin," Schuyler urged, setting her coffee cup down. "You were about to tell us that you took a walk last night. . . ."

Trace leaned forward in his chair and added his encouragement. "Yes, go on, Adam."

Their next-door neighbor raised his eyes. "I'd seen lights in the forest between Grantwood and The Elms before. It took me a while to pinpoint the precise location. After all, it was a very long time ago and I was just a boy when that part of Cora's garden was closed off."

Schuyler began to see the light. "After the tragedy?"

Tension was visible on the man's already gaunt features. "Then you know about the tragedy?"

"Only that something terribly sad occurred."

"Didn't Cora ever tell you?"

"No."

"Nor Geoffrey Barker?"

Schuyler was truthful, but diplomatic. "Mr. Barker's mind has a tendency to wander."

Adam Coffin reserved judgment. "I suppose we may all slip back and forth in time when we're Geoffrey Barker's age. Time is a funny thing."

Schuyler reflected on the long and seemingly interminable hours she'd spent in the claustrophobic corridor and pitch-black room behind Cora's closet. Time had become distorted for her, and she was more than fifty years younger than the retired head gardener.

"Yes," she said thoughtfully, agreeing with Adam Coffin, "time is a funny thing."

Their neighbor picked up his story where he'd left off. "I believe I can put the pieces of the puzzle together for you, at least after a fashion. Perhaps, on one of his particularly lucid days, Mr. Barker can clarify the remainder."

"Another cup of coffee before you go on, Mr. Coffin?" inquired the housekeeper.

"Thank you, Mrs. Danvers. But this time no brandy for me," he said, smiling up at the middle-aged woman.

"It was the summer of Cora's thirtieth birthday," Schuyler prompted.

Adam nodded his nearly bald head. "Her husband had a wonderful surprise in store for his wife's birthday. Herbert Grant shamelessly indulged Cora. And why not? Herbert had a great deal of money and he loved his wife above everything and everyone else." Here Adam Coffin paused and tempered his statement. "With the possible exception of their son."

"Now I understand why the subject of the past was always taboo with Cora—she was absolutely adamant in her refusal to talk about it—but I'd always wondered if she had ever had children," Schuyler murmured.

"Their son was about my age at the time: seven or eight years old. We played together. Although he was much braver and much more daring than I was."

"We all march to a different drummer, Adam," Trace spoke up, looking at the gentleman over the rim of his coffee cup.

"Anyway, it was the end of the summer and Cora's thirtieth birthday bash was to be *the* social event of the season. Herbert had decided to fulfill her fondest dream by having a wishing well constructed in the center of her private garden. The rest of the story I learned bit by bit from my parents and from overhearing the servants gossip about it later."

"Never listen to gossip, myself," declared Elvira Danvers, who had been all ears during the conversation.

"An admirable trait, I'm sure," Adam Coffin remarked with a perfectly straight face. He went on. "It seems Richie—"

Schuyler, Trace and Elvira Danvers repeated together in unison, "Richie?"

Adam was startled. "Yes, Richie."

Trace spoke for all of them. "Who was Richie?"

The gentleman appeared taken aback by their response. "Richie was Cora and Herbert's son."

"Well, that solves one mystery," Schuyler declared with a degree of genuine satisfaction.

"Richie Grant made his mother a special gift for her birthday," Adam related. "It was a kind of hat."

"Mrs. Grant loved hats," Elvira Danvers volunteered as she stood, crossed the kitchen and returned with a plate of homemade cookies: peanut butter with chocolate chips.

Schuyler helped herself to a cookie and took a bite. "Delicious," she stated. Then she went on to add, for everyone's edification, "I can attest to Cora's love of hats. There must be several hundred hat boxes stacked in her closet."

Like any attorney worth his salt, Trace gently guided the witness back to the primary point. "What did Richie make his mother for her birthday?"

"A homemade tiara concocted from bits of wire, silver tin foil and pieces of colored glass."

"The tiara we found at the bottom of the wishing well last night," Schuyler realized.

A bald head was nodded. "Since Cora's birthday celebration was to be a gala affair for grown-ups only held later that night, Herbert Grant took Richie and me into the garden during the afternoon to show us the wishing well."

Suddenly Schuyler had difficulty catching her breath. "What happened?"

Adam swallowed hard. Tears formed in the corner of his eyes and his voice broke as he whispered, "It was such a tragedy. Such a senseless waste."

*   *   *

Trace patted the older man on the shoulder and reassured him, "It's all right, Adam. We realize it's been a long and difficult night. You can tell us another time."

Golden, intent eyes found his across the kitchen table. "Yes, another time, perhaps."

Adam wiped the back of a hand across his cheek. "No. I want to finish telling you. I need to," he said huskily.

"Take your time," advised Mrs. Danvers kindly.

"Mr. Grant gave each of us a coin to toss into the wishing well as we made our wish. Richie went first. He wanted to wish for something special for his mother's birthday, you see." The gentleman paused and tried to breathe deeply several times. "That's when it happened." His voice sunk to a mere whisper and his face crumpled.

There was dead silence in the kitchen.

The only sounds were the clock ticking on the wall, the hum of the refrigerator in the corner and the soft snoring of Buddy under the kitchen table.

No one said a word.

No one urged Adam to go on.

He would continue in his own good time.

When Adam Coffin next spoke, his voice was stretched painfully thin and nearly to the breaking point. In fact, it didn't sound like him at all. "I remember yet. Richie was laughing with delight—he was such a handsome boy—as he leaned over to toss his coin into the wishing well. That's when the tiara slipped out of his other hand and tumbled down into the water."

Trace realized that no one at the table was breathing. They were all waiting for Adam to tell them what they already knew in their hearts.

Adam sat, unmoving, as if he were carved from stone. "Richie grabbed for the tiara. But he leaned over too far. Before Mr. Grant or I could do anything to stop him, Richie had fallen into the wishing well. He hit his head on the rocks at the bottom and lay there, still as death, his leg twisted under his body, the tiara just out of his reach and a spot of blood swirling around in the water encircling his golden-red hair."

Mrs. Danvers was the first to move. She reached into the pocket of her apron and mopped at her eyes with a handkerchief. "Poor, poor Mrs. Grant."

With the floodgates open, Adam went on in a rush. "In the frenzy to help their son, the tiara was forgotten, of course. Richie died that same night of a severe trauma to the head. Mr. Grant ordered the wishing well filled in the very next day and the garden was closed. Herbert Grant died the following year and Cora was left all alone."

"Be careful what you wish for . . ." whispered Schuyler.

Adam straightened and cleared his throat. "Cora never blamed her husband for what happened, or anyone else, for that matter."

"Just herself," Trace hazarded a guess.

"I blamed myself for a long time, until Cora took me under her wing and made it clear there wasn't anything I could have done. I never replaced Richie, of course. No more than Cora took the place of my parents after they passed on. But over the years I think we brought a certain companionship, a certain friendship, a certain comfort to each other."

"You were a good friend to her, Adam," Trace stated. "And in her own way, and to the best of her abilities, I believe Cora loved you like a son."

"Thank you, Trace," the older man said. "That means more to me than you know."

"You look plumb worn out, all three of you," declared Elvira Danvers as she pushed her chair back and got to her feet. "It's time you were in bed."

"I am tired," Adam Coffin confessed.

Mrs. Danvers took command of the situation, like a general addressing her troops. "There's no reason for you to go all the way back to The Elms, Mr. Coffin. We have a guest room ready that you will be most comfortable in. There are fresh towels in the adjoining bathroom and a cozy afghan for Moose."

"Thank you," he said simply.

She looked at the three of them. "I'll wake everyone in time for dinner."

Trace Ballinger lay stretched out on the king-size bed in his room and stared at the ceiling. Despite Mrs. Danvers's explicit orders, he had no intention of falling asleep.

For one thing, he was wide awake.

For another, he had a problem.

How did a man tell a woman that he loved her?

Trace took a deep breath and absently reached out and scratched the golden retriever behind one ear. "I don't suppose you have any ideas on the subject, Buddy."

When had he first realized that he was falling in love with Schuyler?

"Honestly, it wasn't that night in the rain," he informed his canine companion. "Although I will admit that I liked her legs right from the start."

Buddy lifted his head and stared at his owner.

"I know. I know. Great legs do not a great relationship make. But every relationship has to start somewhere," he proposed. "Look at ours."

How did a man tell a woman that he loved her?

He could bring her flowers and gifts. He could kiss her, caress her, whisper sweet nothings in her ear.

He could make love to her.

Often. Very often. Passionately. With his body, with his heart, with his soul.

And he could, Trace Ballinger realized with a sigh, simply tell her so.

Chapter Thirty-Two

She stood at the river's edge.

The evening was warm, almost balmy. The sky was clear. The full moon was on the rise.

"You asked me to lay the ghosts to rest, Cora, and I believe I have." Schuyler stopped and swallowed the lump in her throat. "Your ghosts and my own. I understand now why you sent me away all those years ago. You were a frightened old woman. You were afraid that anyone you allowed yourself to love would be taken from you." There was sadness and acceptance in her voice. "I admit I was headed down that same path, but you've saved me from that lonely fate, and for that I will always be grateful." She took in a deep breath and then exhaled. "I will not be afraid to love."

Schuyler felt the wind stir the wisps of hair around her face, and she experienced a sense of peace and contentment such as she had never known before. "The ghosts are laid to rest, Cora. May you be at peace. May they all be at peace."

With that she took a small envelope from the pocket of her jacket. "You said it was more precious than priceless gems, and the love of your son was, indeed, that. I've decided what should be done with the ashes of his last gift to you. I hope you approve."

Then Schuyler opened the envelope and watched as the ashes of the tiara were picked up and carried away by the wind, up and up, higher and higher, until they reached the heavens themselves.

She blinked away the tears. Then she turned and looked back at the house; it seemed to have taken on a warm, golden hue. There was no fear in her heart, only a sense of belonging. And she realized that maybe, just maybe, she had come home at last.

That only left Trace.

What was she going to do about Trace?

Schuyler was in love with Trace Ballinger. He was surely the best man she had ever known: in his heart, in his mind, in his soul. He was everything a woman could want in a man, in a friend, in a lover.

She heard herself laughing softly, and she realized that the happiest moments of her life, the moments of unequaled joy, of greatest freedom, of truest serenity and contentment, of genuine passion and the desires of a woman's heart, had taken place here at Grantwood with Trace.

She would carry those moments in her heart always. They would give her joy when she needed joy. They would provide her with solace on those days when she sorrowed for what might have been and wasn't to be. They would give her memories to cherish when she was lonely, until many years down the road, perhaps, when her heart would beat for the last time and she would think of Trace in that final moment.

He knew he would find her by the river's edge.

Buddy reached her first, of course. Trace watched as she leaned over and hugged the golden retriever and then looked up, straightened, searching expectantly for him.

By the time he reached her side, she was leaning over the railing of Lucy's Lookout, gazing at the Hudson River, the moonlight leaving its trail across the dark waters.

"Moonglade."

Schuyler turned and looked up at him. "What?"

"Moonglade is the path the moonlight makes across the water," he explained.

"I didn't know that," she admitted.

More words came from him almost unconsciously. "The river has treacherous currents. They say it can take a man or woman down before they know they're in danger."

She didn't argue with him. "There's danger everywhere."

"Yes. There's danger all around." Trace realized he was in a strangely philosophical mood as he went on to say, "Life is like a river."

"I suppose it is."

He buried his hands in the pockets of his jeans and moved his head back and forth. He'd thought that his career, his work, was his life. Work had certainly been his salvation in the past. But now he wanted—dammit, he deserved—more. He deserved a life.

A man was damned if he did and he was certainly damned if he didn't.

She gave him a sideways glanced up and said, "Have you come to say good-bye?"

"Good-bye?" His brow wrinkled.

"I thought you'd be anxious to get back to New York, you and Buddy."

"Nope." It was another minute before he asked, "Are you leaving soon?"

"Leaving?"

"For Paris." Trace realized that was the last thing he wanted her to do. He drew himself up to his full height beside her and blurted out, "Schuyler, you can't leave."

"Why not?"

"Because I said so."

"That's no reason," she countered, laughing lightly.

He stood his ground. "Your place is here."

"Is it?" She turned and began to walk along the pathway that followed the river.

His mind went blank. It was several minutes and several paces farther along the riverway before he caught up with her. "Yes, it is."

Her answer took him by surprise. "Then we agree."

"We do?" Trace realized that his heart was pounding so loudly—in fact, it was thunderous in his chest—that she must surely hear it as clearly and distinctly as he did.

Schuyler stopped dead in her tracks. "I'll admit I've been afraid."

He had to know. "Afraid of what?"

Huge, golden eyes stared into his. "Afraid of the past. Afraid of Grantwood. Even afraid to love. After all, everyone I've ever loved has died. That's what Cora and I thought we had in common, that's why we were both afraid to let anyone near us."

"You're not afraid anymore."

"I'm not afraid anymore."

It was his turn to confess. "I told myself I was alone, but I wasn't lonely."

"And now?"

"And now I realize that without you I will be damned lonely. I don't want to end up like Adam Coffin, building my life around my dog." He reached down and ruffled Buddy's fur. "I love you, Buddy, but I need her. I want her."

Schuyler swallowed hard.

"Somehow, in some way that I don't understand, Schuyler Grant, you have become more necessary to me than breathing, more necessary than living. Without you in my life, I could have all the success in the world and still be unsuccessful." He took a sustaining breath and went on. "We have something important to discuss."

She moistened her lips. "Do we?"

Trace nodded. "We've never discussed the future. Our future." He never took his eyes from her.

"No, we haven't."

He found himself gesturing with both hands. He finally stuffed one of them back in the pocket of his jeans. "I'm no bargain. There's a lot about me that you don't know."

"There's a lot about me that you don't know."

"It takes time to learn about a woman."

"Or a man."

Trace heaved a sigh as they strolled in the general direction of the house. "I have a confession to make," he told her.

With the setting of the sun, the evening had turned surprisingly cool. Schuyler shivered and he put his arm around her. "What's your confession?" she asked.

Trace stared straight ahead. "I wasn't kidding when I said I grew up on the streets, believing that it was sometimes kill or be killed."

"Then you're just the man I'd want with me on a night like last night. Who knows what Teddy Frick would have done if you hadn't been there to stop him?"

Trace made light of his part in the night's events. "I couldn't have managed without Adam and Moose and Buddy." He reached down and playfully ruffled the dog's fur again.

There was silence.

It was broken by Trace. "We were talking about the future."

"Were we?"

"I'm not an articulate man," he said for starters.

Schuyler couldn't seem to help herself. She hooted. "Are you kidding me?"

He shook his head. "No."

"You're the youngest partner in the history of Dutton, Dutton, McQuade & Martin. You didn't get there because you're inarticulate, Trace. It was with your own two hands, your brains, your hard work and determination and your incredible ability to talk people into doing whatever you want them to do, and you stand there and claim that you aren't an articulate man."

"It's one on one with a woman that I get into trouble," he explained. "It wasn't until last night when Teddy was about to shoot us that I realized there was so much I wanted to say to you, needed to say to you, that I hadn't said."

"I know. I felt the same way."

He took in a deep breath and slowly released it. He was about to take not a step, but a leap of faith. "I never thought I was the marrying kind."

"I never thought I was, either."

"You didn't?"

"I didn't."

He scowled. "Why not?"

"I carry—*carried*—so many ghosts around with me." Then she whispered, " 'Lay the ghosts to rest.' "

After clearing his throat, Trace said, "I have a few ghosts to lay to rest, as well."

She couldn't seem to prevent the wistful sigh that slipped out from between her lips. "I know."

He was earnest. "I'm working on it."

"I know you are."

Trace stopped and gazed down into her face. He took in a sustaining breath. "I love you, Schuyler. I haven't said that in so long to anyone that I wasn't sure I could ever say the words out loud."

Her eyes welled with tears. "I don't know what to say."

"Tell me that you love me."

Her heart came to a standstill. "I love you, Trace Ballinger."

Dark, intent blue eyes found hers. "And I love you, Schuyler Grant."

"There's so much to see to," she began to fret some time later, a long time later. It was almost daybreak and they had been making love all night long.

"What needs to be seen to?"

"Well, for one thing, a great deal of work needs to be done to the house and the gardens."

"House and gardens," Trace repeated as if he were making a mental note of it. He added, "I hope you didn't fire the architect and the construction crew."

"I never had time."

"Good. We're going to need them."

"What for?"

"For starters, I'll need an office here at home. I even thought we might consider creating a separate apartment for Adam Coffin and Moose."

"What an excellent idea, Mr. Ballinger."

"How do you feel about setting up a foundation with Cora's money and using it for scholarships?"

She seemed intrigued by the possibility. "To get kids back in school who have dropped out."

"Exactly."

Schuyler's happiness was almost a tangible thing he could reach out and touch. "I was thinking the rose arbor would be the perfect setting for a wedding."

Trace paused, and it was some time before he could speak. "I must have done something right."

"What makes you say that?"

"You're the woman of my dreams and you are my dream come true," he said, as he dropped a kiss on her bare shoulder and began to settle himself again between her thighs. "I wish . . ."

"They say be careful what you wish for; you may just get it," Schuyler whispered as he came to her.

He laughed in the back of his throat. "In that case, I'm the luckiest man in the whole damned world."

Author's Note

I remember moonlight on water.

I'm a child standing at the window of a rustic log cabin, peering out at a midnight-blue lake. Waves lap at the wooden dock. Boats tug at their moorings. Moonlight ripples across the water's silvery surface. I dream of horses—I was reading Walter Farley's *Black Stallion* that summer—and of being shipwrecked on a far-distant and deserted island.

I remember moonlight on water.

I'm a girl and my family has recently moved from a small Iowa town to metropolitan New York. I stand and stare at the mysterious Hudson River and imagine I can see ghost ships slipping through the fog. I dream of becoming a world-class concert pianist or a famous Broadway musical star, of writing my first book, of being, of doing . . . something . . . anything.

I remember moonlight on water.

I'm a young woman. I'm halfway around the world. I part the curtains on the window in my hotel room and watch as a blazing sun descends in the sky and disappears beneath the brown waters of Manila Bay. I wonder how I came to be so far from home. And it's home that I dream of.

I remember moonlight on water.

That long-ago lake in Minnesota.

The ever-mysterious Hudson River.

Faraway Manila Bay.

Mighty Lake Michigan.

The Thames.

The Seine. (Ah, yes, strolling along the Seine and savoring my first moonlit night in Paris.)

I've just finished another book. (My thirty-eighth, or perhaps it's my thirty-ninth; I seem to have lost count.) This time the story is set against the backdrop of a great hulk of a Gothic mansion I once glimpsed along the Hudson River.

Moonlight on water.

I'm leaning against the railing of our deck back home in Indiana and gazing out at the moonlight as it slips across the tranquil surface of our pond, and I dream my dreams: dreams of what has been and dreams of what may yet be. . . .

Bestselling author Suzanne Simmons
introduces you to a man you'll never forget...

No Ordinary Man

Suzanne Simmons

From a magnificent American mansion to a crumbling castle off the coast of Scotland, the bestselling author of *The Paradise Man* sweeps readers away in a sizzling contemporary romance about a privileged heiress who meets her match in a handsome and stormy Scotsman who is anything but ordinary.

NOM 11/00

Haywood Smith

"Haywood Smith delivers intelligent, sensitive historical romance for readers who expect more from the genre."
—*Publishers Weekly*

SHADOWS IN VELVET

Orphan Anne Marie must enter the gilded decadence of the French court as the bride of a mysterious nobleman, only to be shattered by a secret from his past that could embroil them both in a treacherous uprising...

SECRETS IN SATIN

Amid the turmoil of a dying monarch, newly widowed Elizabeth, Countess of Ravenwold, is forced by royal command to marry a man she has hardened her heart to—and is drawn into a dangerous game of intrigue and a passionate contest of wills.

AVAILABLE WHEREVER BOOKS ARE SOLD
FROM ST. MARTIN'S PAPERBACKS

ANTOINETTE STOCKENBERG

"In a league of her own."
— *Romantic Times*

A CHARMED PLACE

In a charming town on Cape Cod, professor Maddie Regan and correspondent Dan Hawke team up to solve the mystery of Maddie's father's death. And what they discover are old secrets, long-buried lies—and an intense, altogether unexpected passion.

DREAM A LITTLE DREAM

Years ago, an eccentric millionaire decided to transport an old English castle—stone by stone—to America. Today his lovely heiress Elinor lives there—and so do the mansion's ghosts, intent on reclaiming their ancestral home. Now Elinor must battle a force stronger than herself—and, when a handsome nobleman enters the picture, the power of her own heart.

BEYOND MIDNIGHT

Ghosts and witches are a thing of the past for modern day Salem, Massachusetts—but Helen Evett, single mother, is beginning to wonder if this is entirely true. A strange power surrounds the man with whom she is falling in love—is it the ghost of his dead wife trying to tell her something?

STOCK 9/98

KATHLEEN KANE

"[HAS] REMARKABLE TALENT FOR UNUSUAL,
POIGNANT PLOTS AND CAPTIVATING
CHARACTERS."
—*Publishers Weekly*

The Soul Collector

A spirit whose job it was to usher souls into the afterlife, Zach
had angered the powers that be. Sent to Earth to live as a
human for a month, Zach never expected the beautiful
Rebecca to ignite in him such earthly emotions.

This Time for Keeps

After eight disastrous lives, Tracy Hill is determined to get it
right. But Heaven's "Resettlement Committee" has other
plans—to send her to a 19th century cattle ranch, where a
rugged cowboy makes her wonder if the ninth time is finally
the charm.

Still Close to Heaven

No man stood a ghost of a chance in Rachel Morgan's heart,
for the man she loved was an angel who she hadn't seen in
fifteen years. Jackson Tate has one more chance at heaven—if
he finds a good husband for Rachel ... and makes her forget a
love that he himself still holds dear.

KANE 9/98